Julie,

Thank you! Take care,

# FOR
# THE
# LOVE
## OF
# RADIO

A NOVEL

xo,

# FOR THE LOVE OF RADIO

## A NOVEL

The hapless adventure of a media-crazed, sex-obsessed moron.

## ED MANN

bookhouse
PUBLISHING

Book House Publishing
2950 Newmarket St., Suite 101-358
Bellingham, WA 98226
Ph: 206.226.3588
www.bookhouserules.com

10 9 8 7 6 5 4 3 2 1

Printed in the United States of America

Library of Congress Control Number: 2020913333

ISBN: 978-1-952483-07-3 (Paperback)
ISBN: 978-1-952483-08-0 (eBook)

*Editor: Larry Coffman and Pat McEnulty, Winthrop University*
*Cover design: Chris Grasha and Ed Mann*
*Interior design and production:*
*Scott Book & Melissa Vail Coffman*

*To Mindy, Ethan, and Harrison Mann, with love*

# PROLOGUE

I HADN'T WALKED 50 FEET ON THE blazing-hot sands of Manhattan Beach, and in my bare feet, when the plan came to life. Walking there calmed me, but that afternoon I was in deep thought. No. Deep shit. A wave had just broken, a mist formed, a continuous onslaught to the shore but with each, a surfer finds the slot and takes it in. The next was especially loud, breaking fast, the surfer losing the track. I squinted into the sun, now reflecting off the whitecaps as it does later in the day; piercing that glint, a surfboard flew up in the air. This was their day, every day, wave after wave, and each unique, special, offering a chance at redemption from the last. It reminded me of being on the air; I was only three minutes from the next shot at perfection, or disaster.

What was I thinking? How many laws would I be breaking? How many statutes? There are a *ton* of statutes. I might as well sit for an orange jumpsuit fitting right now. This wasn't me, but perhaps it was. I had my partner loading my pants with rocks, taking me for a plunge to depths from which I might not return. I stroked my chin, staring at the sand, tiny particles of quartz shimmering in the heat. I inhaled deeply. I had to be careful. If I were going in to do this, it would have to be at night. Non-reflective clothing. No one around. I *had* to get confirmation.

While I had access to Stu's office during the day, there were just too many needle-nosey radio geeks around: DJ's, sales hounds, groupies, engineer nerds, slouching assistants, pencil pushers. But they all had eyes, and I was one of their fearless leaders, looking to pin the leader of the pack to the mat.

Was this doable? What in my background gave me the cajones to think that I could pull off a "caper?" Who the fuck did I think I was? I was a disc jockey disguised in a suit. I was fearless at nothing. I chickened out on skydiving, twice. I fell off a horse and never *once* got back on. I was stung by bees at age two, and the sight of one now makes me run like a princess. Courage? You get a big dose of that when you're a kid and use it up in small doses, and then you're a chicken for the rest of your life. I was used up at 35, a soppy, wet beachcomber with ties to no one and nothing but my back seat career. Webster's had my picture under "wimp."

But if I didn't follow through with this, I'm a schmoe forever. And the girl of my dreams, mist. I would sink or swim with this moment. And if I'm caught, I'll be hanging out at the Federal Correctional Institution in Pleasanton with Michael Milken watching General Hospital every day while Stu cavorts around in his Bentley, smoking a stogie, laughing it up with the driver on my fucking dime.

*This* was the day.

"And you may find yourself in a beautiful house, with a beautiful wife
And you may ask yourself, well, how did I get here?"

—*Talking Heads, the '80s*

# CHAPTER 1

The Saratoga High School swim season ran throughout the dead of winter, for no apparent reason. I wandered out to the pool with the rest of my young friends at 6:30 a.m. to greet the low temperature of the day, standing at the edge of a 25-yard-long pool, steaming from its 82-degree water meeting the 38-degree air. The Santa Clara swim meet was a week from yesterday, so I dove in like I was racing, my 17-year-old body gliding through the lane like a carp. My coach was screaming along the sidelines, urging us on, even though we couldn't hear a fucking word with our ears underwater.

After the first 500 yards, he gave us a break to catch our breath and reduce our heart rates. I was heaving, steam pouring from my mouth, mingling with the chlorinated mist hovering above the pool; the outdoor klieg lights highlighting it all like the set of an Ed Wood film—*Plan 9 from Outer Space!* Man, I loved that movie. I watched it over and over, marveling at the 18-inch waist on the Elvira-like character. A high school buddy renamed the movie *Plan 9 from Outer Waist!* That was eternally funny to us.

I never breezed through a workout. It never was without monumental cardiovascular effort; I always was heaving. Perhaps it was the bucket of marijuana I smoked through the little bong I hid in my locker before diving in every day. And I never seemed to reach the end of the pool before anyone else, no matter how little I smoked; no athletic scholarship for this Jew. *"Did that even exist?"*

Before he blew the whistle for the next gut-tensing set, Coach Demontopari walked over to my lane. "Hey, Mann. What are you doing this weekend?" he yelled.

I yanked off my goggles—chlorine steam rising from my hair—shrugged and replied, "Nothing." Actually, I was planning another beer bust with the neighbors. They had this huge plot of undeveloped land surrounded by apricot orchards, and during the dull winter months we invited ourselves to a stiff brain-cell burn through the wee morning hours. Last July, our swim team hosted a late-night apricot fight there, yanking over-ripe fruit from the trees and pummeling the baseball team into a sugary mess. We'd had enough of being called, "swim fags" from the adjoining baseball diamond. The local sheriff's department never noticed us, winter or summer—no streetlights allowed in our perfect little party town.

"My brother has a diving meet at Awalt High. Do you want to announce it?" coach asked.

I was stunned. Awalt was a school down the way from Saratoga. The Awalt meet was huge, the biggest in the district. Coach's brother was the diving coach there, and he was recommending me for the job of PA announcer. What I'd done to deserve this honor was a mystery to me. My voice? It was loud enough to find me in detention at least once a month.

"Sure," I replied, gasping. *"Party? What party?"*

Coach gave me the time and place, and I went straight home to brag to my parents. Mom was thrilled. Dad—I could only guess.

The day of the meet arrived, so I got busy preparing in my bedroom.

"And now, a one-and-a-half pike from diver number three. *Please—* silence in the arena. Yes! A beautiful pike dive! Judges—scores please. Five-and-a-half, six, four-and-a-half, five. Thank you, judges."

I was practicing in front of an old Shure ribbon mic I found in my dad's closet. I worked hard to keep my voice low. At my age, it sounded like a squawk, but compared with my classmates, I was Vin Scully.

What my coach and my parents didn't know is that I longed to sound like a sports announcer. I listened to LA Dodger games on KFI, heard even in Northern California, and imagined how much fun it would be to have my voice admired like Scully's: rich, elastic, full. It was one of those private dreams kids have in towns like 'toga, where the boom of a big city can only be heard over the radio, so when Coach Demontopari approached me that day at the pool, it was as if my dream was slowing unfolding, gaining momentum, and coming true.

My parents dropped me off at Awalt at the appointed time. I brought only my voice. That astounded me. And I wouldn't have to expend one ounce of energy flailing my arms about in an under-heated pool, so over-chlorinated that my hair crackled when I touched it. Nope, I'd be dry, warm. I marched to the announcer's booth—more like a card table with a blue cloth over it—and sat down in front of a large public-address mic. It resembled the one on Johnny Carson's desk on the Tonight Show, swiveling up toward my mouth, prompting me to speak into its narrow, shiny silvery strips encircling dark wiring, strung tighter than cat gut. My big moment was approaching. A star is born!

Excited parents and students filled the arena. It was sunny and bright that day with a smattering of clouds, permitting the divers a reflection of something besides the tips of their toes as they stared down into the otherwise clear abyss of deep, blue water. The crowd hushed as each diver approached, knowing how critical it was to permit them perfect concentration on their task. There were no fist bumps or high fives up there on the board, only solitary deliberations. They were diving monks. Nothing else matters but the dive.

I figured that my announcing had to reflect that, and there were a number of ways of handling it. I could have gone with "brash, loud basketball-arena guy," or "mumbling football color-commentator dude," but decided on "hushed golf announcer." Then I could let loose with major volume to mention the crucial judges' scores as the assembled throngs applauded wildly, admiring my thundering voice box. My imagination careened.

The first diver approached, my heart pounding through my shirt. I was far less prepared for this than the diver, who seemed cool and relaxed under the pressure. He got to practice for weeks. I got to practice not at all. I tentatively announced, "Diver number one will perform an inside one-and-a-half pike, degree of difficulty, two."

Well, that went well. My voice echoed back to me like Lou Gehrig's at Yankee Stadium, saying his final goodbye. I couldn't help but smile. I wondered how many in attendance thought I sounded as cool as I thought I sounded. The delusion of echo.

The chiseled diver approached and executed his dive without a hitch; he sliced into the water like a butter knife and left but a hint of a splash where he had entered. Thunderous applause. "Judge's scores: Five, five-and-a-half, five, five-and-a-half." All good scores. I glanced over at Coach Demontopari and his brother. No reaction, just crossed arms. They were waiting for this to be over so they could leave and drink.

The next diver approached. "Diver number two will attempt a backwards one-and-a-half tuck. Degree of difficulty, three-point-five. Silence please." I got cocky and left the mic on in anticipation of the announcement of the final scores. "*Why should I flip the switch on and off constantly?*" The diver, no older than I and thinner than a cigarette, approached the three-meter board deliberately and stopped about three paces from the end. This particular board bounces up and down on springs as compared with the higher five-and 10-meter boards that are nothing more than slabs of cement jutting over the pool. These monstrosities are reserved for divers far more graceful than cigarette boy, who had to walk toward the end, jump up, land on the end of the springboard, spin backwards and flip slowly while tucking his knobby knees toward his chest, his oversized puppy-dog feet flailing, his forward momentum carrying him past the board, then extending hands and fingers to slice cleanly into the water. No errors. That was his plan.

Diver number two stood at attention, stuck his arms out in dual "Heil Hitler" fashion, lowered them, locked his elbows, and marched slowly to the end of the board. He made his jump, but his back was too arched, his momentum halted. As gravity often insures, he descended, began his backward flip, and banged the back of his head flat on the board with a *twack.*

I had the mic near my mouth and yelped, *"Oh, SSSHHHIIITTT!"*

The sound reverberated for an hour. Little children in the stands were crying. Coach Demontopari sauntered over, arms still crossed, leaned down to my level and whispered in my ear, "Stop fucking with the goddamn mic!" Needless to say, there were more judges' scores to announce, but I got a zero.

The next day, I felt less for my misadventure than for the poor diver. But after the Fog of Gore passed, I became the designated announcer at my high school, the most important job on campus. Well, at least to me. I could preach to the students, and they could admire me. I was announcing the lunch menu, the next student assembly, the color of my pants. I was the focal point for doing nothing but talking. I had their attention without butting into a conversation in the quad, or sliding into a key seat in the cafeteria, or joining the football team, where I could get seriously injured. *"Oh, really. What about diving!"* I just flipped the mic on, and everyone knew my name.

AFTER MY GRADUATION IN 1975, I took my local fame and headed south to Los Angeles, home of Mr. Scully, show business, movie stars. LA, of course, was a media hub, and I wanted to learn all about it. I enrolled at UCLA, arriving at the peak of the smog season. I climbed out of the car fully expecting to choke to death on sulfur and ozone, but instead I got a nose full of my mother's well-scrubbed kitchen floor. I grinned and said to myself, "*Pine Sol.*" Pine needles were strewn all about, and the old growth of evergreen trees gave the campus the air of a country home in the foothills of the Sierras. Of course, it was set in the foothills of Bel Air, neighboring the homes of Charles Bronson, Bob Newhart and other country dwellers. We were planted in a semi-suburban golden ghetto, and it felt like the real world of hard knocks and grizzled urban life was worlds away. It was actually just down Wilshire Blvd.

The legendary smog kicked in 48 hours after my arrival. The sky was filthy brown for days at a time. Catalytic converters were on maybe five cars. The snow-capped mountains I'd seen in postcards were invisible. My eyes stung, my nose burned, my breath was short, my workload kicked in, but I was ebullient and giddy at the prospect of being surrounded by show business while dead pine needles crunched underfoot. I felt like I could be a part of it all. And I found the campus radio station without directions. I knew just where I was going. I could even see it through the thick, brown air, but I had to get my bearings.

I often took drives around the surrounding Hollywood Hills and once ran into a movie shoot on a lonely street, so naturally, I pulled over to get a closer view. I approached a big-bellied, uber-serious cop, who was guarding the phalanx of trailers and boom mics.

"What's up? What are they shooting?" I asked.

His eyes narrowed as if a fly was approaching his nose. He replied, "It's called *Shampoo.*"

"Shampoo? They're shooting shampoo? What is it then, a commercial—the pitch of my voice rising higher with each word.

The cop's face reddened, he took a long breath, and sighed. "No, kid. The picture's called *Shampoo*. It stars Warren Beatty and Julie Christie. Now get moving before you find yourself in the shot." I inched back slowly but was bouncing around inside myself. And he called it a "picture," like it was from my camera.

Some guy, must have been one of the director's assistants, announced, "Okay, let's get another one in while we've got the light. This is take four." Then another guy yelled, "Speed!" at the top of his lungs, and then I heard, "Action!" Then, nothing, for like 10 seconds. Suddenly, here comes Beatty roaring from my right on a motorcycle, and off around a sharp corner until the engine could be heard no longer. I could see his hair for miles. Then, "And scene! Cut, and print!" Dozens of crew were moving equipment around at lightening speed.

The cop, getting redder by the second, motioned for me to leave, so I turned tail and jumped back into my little car, dreaming all the way home—not of the movie star on the bike, but of the announcer who yelled at the crew—every one of whom listened as if Moses were speaking to them from Mt. Sinai.

I SPENT EVERY SPARE MOMENT AWAY FROM my studies at the campus radio station, a shack carved out of the back of the student union. It smelled from the dust of a thousand record sleeves, of ash from cigarettes, and was less glamorous than my imagination forecast. I wanted to learn all about control boards, and mixing, and recording, and radio waves. I already knew all about the artists, like Pablo Cruise, Aerosmith, Led Zeppelin, Yes, Devo, Earth, Wind and Fire.

For each airshift, I tucked myself into the cubbyhole of a studio and sat down in front of an old mic hanging precariously from a metal contraption clipped to the front of a control board. I played what I wanted and talked about what I wished. A dog-eared sign on the wall said, "Free Speech!" written in bold, black ink, with a rusting peace sign in the corner. They hadn't washed the hippies out of the building yet. Hiking back to the dorms from the studio, I was a hero. Fellow students clapped me on the back, saying, "Good show, Ed," as they passed by. In my cramped dorm room with the door swung open, I leaned back on my bed, my listeners greeting me as they wound their way down the hall like a reception line at a wedding.

I was exhausted after one late-night shift, trekked back to the dorms, and couldn't wait to plop onto the bed—the door open, as always. Some student I'd never seen parked himself in the doorway unannounced, wearing a tie-dye T-shirt, carrying a beer—his imma-ture facial hair straggling from his chin like a pre-pubescent beatnik.

"Hey, Mann, what was that shit on the radio about the Dead Kennedys? You a fascist or something?"

"First off, who are you, and what are you talking about?" My mind raced back to my on-air rap. I couldn't remember.

"You said, "Screw the Dead Kennedys and their dead babies." Was that supposed to be funny?" We were 12 years out since the assassina-tion of JFK, but this guy thought it was yesterday. And I wasn't talk-ing about the real "dead Kennedys," but the punk band that rocked underground hits like *California, Uber Alles*. I thought they were great, and on the air I had said, "My own sister wants to screw the Dead Kennedys and have their dead babies." It was cruel and bizarre, but that was the non-PC climate of the times.

"No man, I was saying that my sister should screw them. Not you."

Clearly stoned or drunk, he persisted. "Why would I screw a Dead Kennedy, man? Are you demented or some kind of Republican?"

"Well, I'm not a Republican."

He chugged the rest of his beverage and said, "Cool then. Check you later, man."

I spent the rest of the night rolling tape in my head of everything I said on the radio that day and how crazy it must have sounded. Not everyone was going to dig me.

STUDENTS RAN OUR LITTLE CAMPUS RADIO station, some more experienced than others. The next day, I went to the head of the station to discuss the dorm complaint. He was a big-time senior and practically lived there. He smelled worse than the old record sleeves.

"Lanny, how far can I go with my material at the station? I think people might react wrong, you know, get the wrong message."

"Well, stop talking so much. This isn't stand-up. What are you, an egomaniac?"

I was shocked at his matter-of-fact solution. "I'm just diggin' the music and playing songs for friends. That's all I ever thought of this gig."

"You gotta talk the walk. You have talent, Ed, and you may want to consider the morning show." The morning show was the most listened to "daypart" at the station, at any station. My chest rose up an inch with the boost, but I still had an issue with his bullshit review.

"But you said I was an egomaniac."

"Of course you are. It's about *you*. You can't worry about what other people are going to say about your act. Are you interested?"

"Hell, yes!" I screamed.

"See?"

And with that, I was the new morning man. Same show, insane time of day. Working in the morning was anathema to college life; the show began at 6 a.m. each day and ran till 8 a.m., so I could get to class. Six fucking *a.m.*! In my desire to spread my humor and good-natured personality to the associated students of the University of California at Los Angeles, I felt the genuine need to split my time as a responsible broadcaster and as an irresponsible fraternity member, sworn to drink beer, smoke dope, and study whenever I stumbled into the library.

"Jesus, Ed. What are you doing in the john so long?" asked one of my frat pals as he entered the hallway bathroom, which hadn't been cleaned since the Watts riots.

"What does it sound like, moron? I'm throwing up."

"Are you nervous before your show?" It was 5:30 in the morning and I had to be at the station in 30 minutes. My Bud Lights were filling the toilet fast.

"Yeah, and this calms my nerves asshole." I was on all fours, cursing my decision to do this fucking radio show every day.

I cleaned my face and ran down to the station.

Suddenly sober as a clam, I announced, "Good morning, UCLA! We're looking at a high of 75 this Thursday and here's the deal. Get up, go to class, forget everything you learned, and start all over again. Here's to you." I then played a sound effect of a beer can popping open while I slugged it down, with the *This Bud's for You* theme song in the background. This almost made me hurl again. My news guy, Pete, shook his head in disappointment. He was my straight foil and kept the show in line. But I was the host and was going to do what I wanted until Lanny or the chancellor came barging into the room to stop me. Free speech, baby!

One day I was on a tirade. I came out of a Yes record, *Roundabout*, and started in.

"The school has got to improve. There are cracks all over Bruin Walk and some skateboarder's gonna get killed. Here comes one now!" Then I hit a sound effect of a screeching car slamming into a tree, metal bending, bones crunching, sirens blaring. The visual pictures were far more stunning than any motion picture.

"Shit, it's the chancellor!" I cried. "He's crashed into a pack of students and there are bodies strewn everywhere! Fucking Christ! Pete, are you on the scene? Can you get an interview?" Pete's jaw dropped to his lap and he turned white.

"Never mind, Pete. I'll do it. Hey, Chance, what the hell was that." In a drunken voice, I (he) replied,

"Hey man, what a buzz. That was killer weed. Hey, what are all these kids doing here?"

"Good work, chancellor. We're behind you all the way." Then I hit AC/DC's *Highway to Hell*.

Five minutes later, the phone rang. It was Lanny.

"Get the hell off! *Now!* Give Pete the mic and get off. You're finished."

Dumbstruck, I called Pete in to finish the show. Some show. He read the news for three hours.

And no one, not a soul, missed me on the air, not a single gesture of regret, not one sarcastic remark from my frat mates, zip. It was as if I had never entertained them before. I was a part of their lives every morning. I made them laugh, every day and gave them a reason to get up early and shave their wisps of facial hair, but they had moved on from the radio DJ guy that lived down the hall who goofed on the chancellor. My little cousin, Julie, from Beverly Hills called to console me, but I discounted that. She was enamored of anyone who rose to even the lowest level of celebrity. I figured this would be the last I heard from her, unless I got an actual gig.

Julie hung out at haunts like the Daisy, a tony little restaurant on Rodeo Drive in Beverly Hills, with pals like Tatum O'Neal, sweeping up little bits of celebrity dust. She once wanted me to talk to Tatum on the phone and pretend I was on the air doing a show. I was never curt or nasty to Julie, but that really pissed me off.

"Tell Tatum her paper moon has set!" and I hung up. Not terribly clever, but I was in no mood. Plus, she was only 13.

MY BEGINNINGS FORESHADOWED NONE OF THIS. I was a lanky, six-foot two-inch Jewish kid from small-town NorCal. My driver's license said, "Eyes, blue," but they were more hazel, with specks of gold near the pupil. I didn't wear glasses, but I squinted half the time, which gave me headaches. My hair was so thick that I had trouble taking off my headphones without pulling out chunky tufts. And I had these big, thick lips that my elementary school music teacher insisted would get in my way of playing the trumpet, which I loved. Fuck her, I thought. I was first-chair trumpet in the school honor bands thereafter. I dug music, which also drew me closer to radio.

I had a happy childhood but never thought of myself as particularly funny or talented. As a nine-year old, I sat cross-legged on the shag carpet of our suburban single-level ranch house, my dad's headphones clamped to my ears, listening to the tapes I made of local stations and the jingles that they'd play: "Music sweep at 45 on K-L-I-V," and I'd play them over and over. My imagination reeled. I hosted record parties for my friends in my bedroom, playing singles from Paul Revere and the Raiders, Three Dog Night, and of course, the Beatles, announcing each song like I was a DJ.

My parents would stand in the doorway with their eyebrows pinched, wondering what to make of it. Music for them was Beverly Sills, Dixieland, Swan Lake. Radio was Arthur Godfrey, Bob Hope. What was *this* kid talking about?

The echo off of the hard walls and floors of our bathroom enhanced the sound of my voice—low and soulful. I had the old 30-pound Ampex reel-to-reel plugged into the socket next to the sink, hooked up to headphones while visualizing myself as a DJ cuing up records and announcing the quick rap of the day.

"Hey, babies, it's Bobby Ocean slammin' em at ya, with another BIG sweep comin' on in seconds at K-F-R-C." I taped myself saying this stuff, putting my mind in their studio on Bush Street in San Francisco in 1968.

"Eddie, what are you doing in there?" my mother once screamed after I'd spent an hour in the bathroom.

"Um, playing with the machine, um, you know, the tape machine."

"Well, get out. Your father needs to use the toilet." I could hear her giggle down the hall. Clearly, she figured "machine" was a metaphor.

My fantasy life was giving me every reason to listen to the radio for hours on end, driving my family crazy by tying up the phone while requesting songs that played once an hour anyway. I was obsessed, sleeping with my little, square AM transistor radio, hearing Blood, Sweat, and Tears pound out *Spinning Wheel* as if for the first time every time.

Yet, only after leaving the campus radio station did I grasp the magic of it, the power of it; if I could hear a song repeatedly and enjoy it as I did when I was nine, I could play one repeatedly and get that same response from a radio audience, and I could do that anywhere I wished. I didn't need this little dustbowl, carve-out of a radio station to play songs for my friends. There were 10,000 of them in this country. As I spent time away from it, I missed it. My experience of hosting a radio program resonated in me, and I had to find a way to return to it. That I could be famous for this fun gig hadn't really sunk in yet, but I knew I had to get my ass back on the radio.

# CHAPTER 2

AFTER GREAT SCHOLASTIC EFFORT AND AN obligatory bout of mono-
nucleosis, I graduated, with a degree that had little to do with either
music or radio—philosophy. I'd promised my mom that I'd choose a
major that stimulated my cerebral cortex non-orgasmically. Mom and
orgasm. Bad pairing.

I left UCLA an artificially happy and orgasmic young man, with
a few fans, none of whom were university faculty. I was in cap and
gown—literally. That was it. No shirt, no pants, and the chancellor,
who undoubtedly had heard of my verbal exploits on the campus
radio station, announced our names under cloudy skies.

"Alice Manerly," he intoned, with pomp.

He took one look at my degree . . . "Edward Mann," and his voice
trailed off as if describing a bad dream. I was being sent off into the world
with a whimper, but my friends sitting in their grad robes, and apparently
some clothing underneath, had some great coke, and that set me straight.

One week after leaving the upsetting world of college, I entered
the discouraging world of work.

My dad had introduced it to me years before when I was in high
school, lounging on the couch at four in the afternoon with my bare

feet up watching Merv Griffin interview Totie Fields again, when he rumbled, "Hey Ed, what do you want to do?"

I said, "Watch this show and make a steak."

"No, I mean *do*. Like work, do." I furrowed my brow, but it couldn't match the deep furrow my dad had going. He was a worker bee from day zero. I always imagined his dad had him in a forced child-labor camp, cleaning out tobacco-stained handkerchiefs from the top drawer of his dresser, or degreasing the Brylcream from his hair, scrubbing and scouring as he dreamed of playing stickball like all the other kids in Brooklyn.

"I don't know, maybe play music." I might as well have said, "Fuck the dog."

"Where are you going to do that?"

Of course, I had no idea. I was 16. Next thing I knew, I had an apron around my waist washing dishes at the nearby steak house.

It was as if he thought, "*You want a steak, work for it, you little douche bag.*"

A COUPLE OF DAYS AFTER COLLEGE GRADUATION, I was eating alone at a Mexican restaurant and glanced at the TV over the bar. There was an odd man going on and on about Jesus and how he could save me.

"I'll be on the radio this weekend. Just listen to AM 1470 and follow the teachings of the Lord Jesus." A number flashed below for donations. I tried to ignore him as I gulped down my cheesy enchilada, but he was compelling as hell. I gave him a suspicious look as if he were there, speaking to me. I don't know what possessed me, but I wrote down the number on the screen and went home to dial it.

"1470, K-W-R-M, may I help you?" I pulled the phone away from my ear and stared at it, like I had no idea how this plastic object got in my hand and spoke into my ear.

The receptionist repeated the greeting.

Then I blurted, in my best evangelist impersonation, "*Save me! I need a job!*"

She paused for a moment—and then burst out laughing.

"What's so damn funny?" I asked.

"It's just that we get calls from people wanting to give us money, donate their estates. I've *never* gotten a call asking for anything, and certainly not sounding like my boss!" She began laughing again, louder than ever.

I thought to myself, "*Doesn't anybody want to work there on the air?*"—then said, "Well, now you've heard it all. I'm a DJ. Do you guys need help?"

"You know, I think they might. Come on down and we'll talk. You're funny."

She made me an appointment with the reverend himself and gave me directions to Corona; I had a vague memory of it from a trip to Palm Springs during school. It was a little cowtown that whipped by faster than me over a line of blow. One exit, one main drag, one radio station, one smelly town.

I drove out the next day to meet with the owner, the Reverend Cumpepper. KWRM—The "Worm"—as I termed it, was about 75 miles from my little apartment in West LA, but I had no intention of moving. I desperately needed to keep one foot in civilization, even if it meant popped rods and blown gaskets in the cramped Datsun B-210 that I stuffed myself into for more than 25,000 miles per year.

I pulled off the freeway onto a dusty road leading to a shack, literally an oversized tool shed. It was late in the afternoon. I parked and opened the car door. Then the stench hit me. It was like a hundred heifers had taken a dump and left it to simmer in front of my car. But I saw no manure pile. I was simply in cow country. In the twilight hours of every afternoon, the stench in Corona rose up like a shit phoenix, leaving every fiber of my shirt, every nose hair, every drop of sweat reeking of dung. Corona gave new meaning to the lyric "Top of the heap."

I entered the building through a screen door leading to a lobby the size of a small desk. There was no receptionist to greet me. That disappointed me—she had sounded cute. I was early, so I poked around the "grand" lobby. There were two small tables to the left that had a pile of cheap, glossy brochures with typestyles right out of a '60s graphic-arts book. I began thumbing through them and stared in horror at what they said.

"And the chosen will go to heaven to be with the Lord Jesus Christ, and those that have not accepted the Lord as their savior will go to hell. There can be no option but to accept Jesus into your life." All I saw was. "Go to Hell."

Wow. This guy was serious. I could feel my vital signs plummeting. He was certainly an evangelist, but the radio thing was his little secular hobby. I heard Emerson, Lake and Palmer, Todd Rundgren, Eddie Rabbitt piped into the internal speakers in the lobby, or I should say "speaker"—one was on the fritz. I thought, *No funny shtick for me.* In fact, no shtick, no bagels, no cream cheese, no blintzes, no matzo, no eight nights of Hanukah. If I was going to work for this guy, I might have to lighten up my rap.

Cumpepper entered the lobby to greet me, and what a sight he was: plaid jacket, mismatched pants, major-bouffant hair, crystal-blue eyes and a smile from ear to ear, though the smile was independent of the eyes—those laser blues bore through me like a powerful drill, drilling for Jews. I hoped he couldn't see the Star of David floating between my shirt and my chest hair.

"Good to meet you, son. Welcome to my little broadcast home."

He walked me to his upstairs office overlooking the radio towers, a perch with a view of his kingdom. The office was tiny and lined with plywood. And it was filled with tons of stuff that made no sense: a bronze likeness of Caesar on a long table facing his chair, a crucifix right behind the desk, a plaque from the Christian Coalition, a pants rack; apparently he liked to change in the office after working up a sweat rehearsing his evangelist routine for the TV show.

"May I get you coffee?"

I thought I might say, *"No thanks, I'm kosher,"* but thought again. "No thanks. I'm excited to be here," I said.

He grinned slightly, as if he had a fresh recruit in front on him. "I want to show you around, but first a few questions."

I froze as I sat before him. My chair was so low that my head poked up like a toddler at the dinner table.

"What did you study in school?"

"Broadcasting and philosophy."

"Very good." He nodded as he checked his little checklist.

"Do you enjoy popular music?"

"Of course. I studied music in school as well as other subjects and I . . ."

Cumpepper clearly had stopped listening as he peered around the room, completely distracted.

"Do you smell anything?" he asked.

"Pretty sure it's the cowshit."

He cranked his head and scowled at me. "What kind of language is that, young man? Is this what I can expect to hear on my radio station?"

I was feeling like I should just pick up and leave, but I needed a job, and this *was* a radio station, and he *had* been checking his checklist, but I didn't need a lecture from a bible-belting, blow-dried blowhard dressed like a picnic table.

"I apologize. I just thought that you might have been referring to the, um, fragrant odor I encountered as I drove in. Uh, tell me about the Caesar thing over there," I said, feigning interest in his interior decorating, although I did wonder what a Roman Emperor's bust was doing on the credenza of an evangelist's office.

His face became less contorted and he seemed to relax. "Please wait downstairs and I'll be right with you."

He gave me that ridiculous smile again, and I trundled down the little stairs to the icebox-sized lobby. I stared at a poster hung on the opposite wall featuring Cumpepper with his hand raised over a crowd, as if healing it. Oh brother. Moments later, he re-entered, smiling and proud, and paraded me around the station like I was Price Charles. He needed me, regardless of my choice words. After the tour, he took me aside.

"Ed, I like you," he lied, "and I think you've got a future in this business. But you could use a little seasoning, so I'd like to have you start out on the Sunday morning shift."

I smiled, thinking, "*Wow, daytime.*"

"It starts at 5 a.m., and you'll announce the call letters, KWRM, at the top of every hour as the FCC requires." He stood before me with the largest pregnant pause in history. I felt like we were having a staring contest—if I lost, I was converted.

"I don't speak but once an hour? What happens between songs?"

"Just play the tape and say the call letters every hour. Oh, and there's a script."

A script? We shook hands and I hit highway 71 for the long drive home. Along the way, my mind took off on 20 different tangents. What kind of show was this? I hadn't thought to look at the schedule and see what normally was on tap at the Worm. But I was now a professional broadcaster, with a radio station to call home and a paycheck—if only for one day a week.

The weekend arrived, my alarm clock rang at the proper moment, and I made pre-dawn tracks to Corona for my first shift. Man, that smell lingered all night. It appeared to ameliorate after daybreak, but until then, it was a horse trailer. As I pulled up to the station, I suddenly realized I'd forgotten to bring headphones. Shaking my head, I buzzed the door and the engineer, Ben, came out to greet me. He looked like a cast member from *Green Acres*.

"Hey, young feller. First shift?"

"Yep. I'm all ready, but I forgot my headphones. Can I borrow your cans?"

"Oh, you won't need 'em for this shift." What kind of radio host doesn't need headphones? How do you hear what you're doing? When I turn on the mic, the speakers shut off so there's no feedback. I didn't get it. I sat at the control board Cumpepper had shown me during the tour. Nothing special. Just like the one at UCLA. Ben got the programming lined up for me.

"Okay then. Here're your tapes. They're hour long reel-to-reels. You familiar?"

"Sure," still totally perplexed. "*No records?*"

"Now, sit right here," he continued, "and when the tape ends, just open the mic and say, "This is KWRM, Corona." That's our legal ID. And you have to read a line or two from this script. Just listen for the cue." His enthusiasm was out of line with the circumstances, which called for me to turn around and go home.

I sat down, and as Ben's last song wound down, *Hotel California* by the Eagles, with lyrics like:

> "*Her mind is Tiffany-twisted, she got a lot of pretty,*
> *pretty boys, that she calls friends . . .*"

I hit the button for the reel. Out of the speakers blared organ music, like a big Wurlitzer in a church. And then that voice filled the room.

"Good day and God speed. This is the Reverend Ralph Cumpepper, and today you will be saved! For the next four hours, I will bring you and yours salvation and free you from temptation. As you reflect on your life, a life strewn with the blasphemy of rock 'n' roll music, of scantily dressed women, of drinking and drugs, I—the Reverend Cumpepper—will be your guide."

It was Cumpepper doing his TV routine on the radio! He put me on the "God Squad" to teach me some demented lesson for my use of the word "shit," a word I dearly loved, the only word to describe this place. I became the tool of the evangelist. I was the Jew in charge of Christian programming. And he was decrying the music on his own radio station! What a fucking nut. Still dumbfounded, it was time for my line.

"Sinners repent! Find yourself in the Lord. Give yourself a chance before the second coming." I turned off the mic and sat there frozen in the studio, unable to believe my predicament.

The program went on for four goddamn hours—the ranting Christian and his dummy. And I did this every Sunday for about a month, until I gathered the courage to go to Cumpepper's office and address the issue. I caught him zipping up his pants after another costume change.

"Reverend, I know how important this program is to you, but I'm ready to host a regular music program. It's what I've trained to do. I want it badly and want to stay here."

"Have you repented?"

"Huh?" I should've heard that coming.

"Have you given up your heathen, anti-Christian ways and taken Jesus into your heart?" I was staggered by his nonchalant candor, as if he were asking me if I wanted a candy bar.

"I'm Jewish, reverend, and even so, I've been hosting a Christian evangelical program that you profit from. Every day you're playing music like *Funkytown* and *Magic* by Olivia Newton John. I heard Cat Stevens the other day, and he's now Yosuf Islam! I'm the one standing by with tapes of you in hand, cranking out verse after verse of a Testament that I know nothing about. So how different are we, you and I?"

The reverend stood there, unblinking, like his Caesar bust.

"Well, uh, I've got an afternoon music shift. How does that work?"

"Fine. See you on Monday."


THE NEXT WEEK, I BEGAN MY daily shift, my first *secular* full-time radio gig. The station's signal was weak, but that didn't stop my delusions of grandeur. I hopped on the air every day thinking Johnny Carson was tuning me in on his way to Palm Springs to hang out with Sinatra and Hope.

*"Hey guys, did you hear what Ed said today at the Worm on my way in? Now THIS guy's got talent. I need to get him on The Tonight Show soon. So, Frank, how're the broads?"*

How I ever concentrated on my show, I'll never know.

Engineer Ben visited me regularly. He was older, say 50 to my 22, but we got along. Deejaying is a pretty lonely job, and any personal contact, even from a chalky engineer who knows more about transistors than any person should, is welcome company. His look would never go down in West LA—Oshkosh overalls with suspenders, dusty brown work boots, a five-dollar haircut, and large ears with enormous ear canals. I felt like I could see his brain. But I lived in LA, and he kept me up to date on what went on in Corona, which was helpful, since 99 percent of the listeners were in Corona, shoveling shit out of their driveways. But this day, he had extraordinary news that played right in my hands.

He sat himself down, took a long sip of coffee, threw his head back and as casual as he could said, "By the way, Ed, I've heard word from on high that we'll be getting a little lift soon."

I narrowed my eyes and asked, "What the hell does that mean?"

"We've been approved by the FCC for a sizable power increase. Should boost the signal to something akin to a major LA station."

My head flew around that idea for a minute. The Worm could barely be heard past the slow lane of the freeway next to the station.

"So, are we going to crank this up to LA or just yell louder in the mic?"

"Oh, this is no joke, my friend. This is big time. The FCC's gonna let us go hog wild and talk to the metro," meaning we could be heard in Hollywood.

I think I almost fainted.

"Well, see you tomorrow, Ed," and he strolled off. This was news from a real source. One of our own. Our fucking engineer! What more confirmation did I need? I immediately cracked the mic.

"Now hear this! The Worm, I mean, KWRM will be heard from here in Corona to Calabasas. Our new power increase will bring you—me, louder than ever, all the way to Hollyweird! We're going for a major boost, so watch out LA! Now, here's Steely Dan."

I popped off the headphones, sat back, puffed out my chest, and dreamed of the job and movie offers coming my way.

The very next day, I bounced the Datsun up the dirt road to the station at 2 o'clock; a good three hours before the shit stank of twilight hit my olfactories. Cumpepper was standing at the front door to greet me.

"Hey Rev. What's up?"

"We have to talk." He took me by the arm like an angry husband escorting his wife out of a busy restaurant. We got to his office, and he slammed the door.

"What in God's green earth are you doing, young man?" I was blown away, truly had no idea what he was talking about.

"Well, I'm just here to work?" I said with little conviction.

"You said to all within earshot that our little hometown radio station was going to be heard up in Los Angeles. Did you not say that?" he boomed.

"Well, sure. Ben said that . . ."

"Ben?"

"Uh, yeah. Ben told me that we were getting approved for it."

Steam was pouring from his nostrils. His sky blues were bursting from their sockets, red everywhere—but for the blue. "Go home! I'll call you."

On the drive home, it became quite clear to me that I was not famous. I was barely employed. Ben clearly had fucked up, or lied, or was completely delusional. I shook my head all the way home, and as I got closer and closer to my apartment lo those many miles away, the station's signal faded more and more in the distance. What was I doing? I could barely sleep that night.

I awoke with more clarity and got on the phone to apologize to Cumpepper, explaining that I was simply taking Ben at his word.

"I understand. Come in at two and we'll talk more."

I felt like I might have a chance to hold on my job, even if it was at Shithole, California. I got to the Worm and Cumpepper cornered me.

"Look. I just fired Ben. But I'm not going to fire you. Ben confessed to making the whole thing up. But I can't afford another screw up. Spring is here and I'd like to begin fresh with you. My little station will be carrying Dodger games, and I want you to handle the commercial inserts, legal ID, that sort of thing. No show, just commercial breaks and button pushing. Can you do that?"

Every cell in my body was disappointed. I was going backward after having announced Ben's little lie. I went from famous to notorious in seconds.

"Of course, Reverend."

"Good. You start this weekend. It's a day game. Get here early, and check the station log for the spot schedule. All you have to do is plug the commercials into the right slots. Just listen for Vin Scully to wrap up the inning, and hit the button. Don't mess this up, Ed"

"Got it. Thanks for keeping me on."

"Right," he grumbled, and I shambled back to my car for the drive home.

I was pissed. It was one fucking comment. Now poor Ben was out of work, and I was back to hitting buttons on a board.

MY FIRST WEEKEND DOING THE GAMES arrived under sunny skies, and I couldn't imagine sitting inside, waiting on ol' Vinny to give me the cue. So, I found a shabby old lounge chair and parked it outside within earshot of the studio door, facing the blazing sun. I cranked up the speakers in the control room so I could hear the game, laid my ass down, slathered on my baby oil, and got to work on improving my tan.

This wasn't so bad. All I had to do was listen for him to say, "So at the end of 7, it's Dodgers 4, the Mets 3," run back to the studio, play two minutes of commercials for the local Worm audience, and head back out to my beach chair for more bronzing.

I began to get a rhythm going, where I could anticipate the end of an inning, dash into the studio in the nick of time, hit the commercials, prepare more iced tea, and get back to the chair. My tan was gorgeous—and it was only April.

About three weeks later, on a very warm Corona afternoon, I found an old Waring blender in the kitchen, and my cockiness rose to levels beyond my own historical standards. Instead of letting the phone lines ring unanswered, I began culling young ladies to join me for a margarita party on the sun porch. One friend told another, then another, and by the end of the third inning, there were 13 chicks between the ages of 18 and 25 sloshing down whatever I could mix for them. When we ran out of margarita mix, I began pouring straight tequila shots and making toasts. All the while, I kept an ear open for the end of the inning so I could run in and hit the commercials without getting dreaded dead air. One girl, who had to be around 19 or so, began peppering me with questions.

"Do you get to go to premieres in Hollywood?"

"Uh, actually . . ."

"How 'bout movie stars? I'll bet you know a ton."

"Well, I saw Warren Beatty ride a bike once."

"Really? You know Warren Beatty? What's he like?" She began touching my thigh while asking the question, and I hated to break her spirit by blasting out the truth.

"He's great. One of the best. You know he likes to drink Coke all day. He's like a freak for soda." I'm not sure why I said that at all. Lying was Ben's forte, not mine.

She appeared genuinely disappointed with that tepid story and her hand disappeared from my leg just as quickly as it had arrived. But no loss. She was replaced by another just as cute, just as shallow and easy to electrify, and just as easy to dismiss. And as I stood there drinking myself to a near stupor, I improved my womanizing with every conversation as they craned their necks for a moment with me—the weekend button-punching moron—to share the amazing fame I was experiencing, their slice of fantasy on the red carpet, in full view of a herd of cattle. The irony was tantalizing, arousing—a seminal moment in my awareness of fan reaction—despite the most isolated of media exposures, and I collected more phone numbers of adorable and impressionable young women than at any time in my past.

The afternoon progressed brilliantly: I mixed drinks, told egregious lies, and Vin pronounced the end of another inning as I rushed in the studio and hit my marks. I was gaining confidence that this might be the best gig in the radio industry.

By the eighth inning, the girls had departed, and I was a candidate for Alcohol-Poisoning Poster Boy. I slumped back in the lounge chair, with 95 degrees of sunshine filtering through invisible cow farts, and I got sleepy. Scully went to commercial quickly,

"So that's the eighth, with your LA Dodgers up next." I had to hit the first spot for this segment and was 40 feet away from the button, snoring. The silence actually awakened me. I jumped out of the chair, knocked over the blender, smashing it into pieces all over the porch, stumbled on the metal threshold where the carpet meets the outside door—slicing open my big toe—and raced to the control board, but I had missed my cue. Best I could figure, there was at least 20 seconds of dead air, where nothing happens on a radio station, except the sounds of snoring, and a phone call. It was the station hotline, and Cumpepper blasted away at me.

"Ed, you're fired. Pack up and go. I'll have someone there to finish the shift in 10 minutes. Thanks for nothing."

My toe was bleeding all over the floor. Fuck him. He and his Nazi crew could clean up my blood and his blender.

# CHAPTER 3

M Y LIVELIHOOD WAS SUDDENLY IN QUESTION, and I was lost one day while driving around stoned in Orange County, California, admiring the open space. Back in the '80s, the extensive parcels of real estate south of Los Angeles were a haven for "urban flight," where newly minted suburban folks got their own look-alike neighborhoods. They looked so comparable that I lost my bearings and thought I was on one side of town, when I was on quite another.

Frankly, I didn't care. I was gazing through the green haze of my marijuana joint blazing away in my ashtray. Where I went mattered less than how my synapses were firing, and a series of congruent neighborhoods, viewed through green-colored glasses, was strangely comforting and appropriate. I took another long drag and careened from boulevard to boulevard, violating seven or eight California traffic laws while munching on my fifth Ding-Dong of the afternoon.

I pulled onto a side-street from one of the oversized main drags— Beach Blvd. or Harbor—and spotted a line of people standing in front of a house, as if concert tickets were on sale. All were young, some grungier than others, holding papers and pencils.

"Hey, what's going on in there? Someone selling Rod Stewart seats?" I yelled out of the car window.

"No, man," replied one grungy young fellow. "It's a broadcast school. We're applying to be students here."

I was awestruck at the coincidence. Although I was well-schooled in the how-tos of the DJ life, they might need staffing. I was talented as hell: I could simultaneously open a mic and drink with both hands cuffed. This crowd could dig that. I snuffed out the joint in the ashtray, parked, and poked my head in. There at the front door, seated behind a foldout table piled with loose papers, was the cutest girl. She had a four-foot tall, three-foot-wide perm, wavy, jet-black hair, with bows and trinkets stuck to it like refrigerator magnets. Her lips were a thick paste of pink lip-gloss.

"Hi, there. I'm . . ."

"You weren't in line," she interrupted, and then fixed her eyes on mine. "Are you high?"

"No, no," I charmed, lying through my teeth. "I'm just inquiring if you folks need a little help. Turns out I was on the air nearby, a DJ in Corona and went to UCLA and . . ."

"UCLA?!" Her eyes widened and her pupils dilated. She began hyperventilating and I thought she might pass out. "So you must know Vince!"

"Uh, sure," I lied. "Is he here, now?" She slammed her pencil down, stood up, and ran to the back of the house at full speed, forgetting to ask my name. The kids in the line were glaring at me, perceiving that I had cut in line to gain favor from Perm Girl, who now was butter in my hands. I scooted inside the house and poked my head around.

Sure enough, it was a broadcasting school, complete with fake studios and control boards everywhere. I figured kids would have to go somewhere besides college to get in the fame game.

Moments later, a young man no older than I and about three inches taller—I don't look up from six-foot-two very often—came to the door.

"Hi, I'm Vince. Vince Steele," he announced, and he shook my hand so hard I thought it was crushed. He seemed very happy to meet me. Vince had thick, curly, dark hair that made his head look twice as large as it was, and he was impossibly thin.

"And you're the fellow from UCLA," he noted, with the most mellifluous voice I'd ever heard. "Welcome to the Workshop." I massaged my pulverized hand as we walked to his office, reincarnated from a master bedroom. There was a distressed dressing mirror—not just fake distressed, *really* distressed—and a brown chest of drawers centered below the mirror. I imagined it was filled was boxer shorts and knee socks. Opposite the dresser was a large desk. Tacked to the wall above it was an oversized UCLA pennant, like the ones cheerleaders carry around. Instead of taking his seat behind the desk, he followed me to a large sofa to the left of his desk, which I found discomfiting.

"I'm amazed to have run into you here," I said, "literally was just driving around Orange County, trying to avoid the monotony of my life and finding, well, monotony." He let out a loud, uproarious laugh that reminded me of the fake Steve Martin laugh from his old stand-up routine—head thrown back, showing off his crescent-shaped upper teeth. And then, in sudden contrast, he stopped and frowned.

"Now, Ed," he said condescendingly, "the Workshop is essentially a school, and we work for a fee. In other words, prospective students apply to the school, take an exam, perform an audition, and our staff evaluates them and decides whether to place them in the schoooooool."

What a voice on this guy. The words fell out of his mouth like syrup off a stack of pancakes. "The schooooooooool." He sounded like the HAL computer in *2001, A Space Odyssey*. Calming yet demanding.

"Vince, I have to ask you. Your voice is remarkable. Are you working on the air now?" His lips thinned to two near invisible lines. Couldn't tell if he was flattered or bothered.

"Well, yeah. I'm on KUTE 102 in LA, the disco station."

"Did you attend a school like this to get into the business?"

"Actually, no. I knew the program director. It's a long story, but I knew someone and they helped me get on after I'd worked at this terrible station in Corona, if you know it. 1470 KWRM."

Jesus! He was a fellow Wormer. "I believe we may have things in common," I said, thinking if a friend of his could get him on in LA, he could get me on, too. We stood and he led me on a tour.

The "Workshop" as he termed it was a broadcast school devoted to the training and the placement of disc jockeys. There was training in all aspects of our business: working the control board, proper elocution, syndication, preparing your program, how to deal with program directors, how to edit tape, how to deal with stardom.

We walked into an elementary studio: a cart machine for playing the 8-track tapes that contain music and commercials, two turntables, a small control board to keep track of volume and balance, and a simple microphone. It was fresh and clean and surrounded by glass Windexed to a sheen; I could see the entire operation from about anywhere in the house. I felt comfortable in these surroundings.

"I was mentioning to your large-haired girl at the front that I might be able to help out here." Sweat was forming on my upper lip; I still was incredulous at finding this place and this guy in this cookie-cutter neighborhood on a drive going nowhere.

"Okay. How'd you like a job?" I was frozen for a moment, happy but unconvinced that he was serious.

"Doing what?" I asked.

"Sales. I need someone on the phones to contact leads, see if they're interested in getting in the school. Here, look." He swiveled his chair around, grabbed the phone, and started in as if he were answering a call. "Hello, Workshop . . . yes, this is the broadcast school . . . Oh, you want to learn how to get on the air? . . . Fine. Please come by with $1,500 and we'll discuss it."

I gulped, but got only air, so I burped. Vince laughed out loud.

"Did you say $1,500? Is that what you charge kids to get in here?"

"Yep! Isn't that incredible? And they line up outside the house all day long."

I peered into the studio window and about a dozen students were working studiously on their lessons, others stuffed in studios editing their tapes. They were all around my age and many of them ladies.

I thought, *"Here's a good chance to find some chicks,"* and *"How the hell are these young girls gonna get a job at a radio station?"* There weren't but a few women on the air in 1980. What kind of hoodwinking horseshit got them to give Vince hard cash in exchange for this? What a racket.

Vince sat me down and gave me the basic rap, which seemed on the up and up. The Workshop considered hundreds of prospects but brought in only dozens each year, due to limited space. Pretty damn cool; lots of energized kids around, lots of fun—perhaps more than I considered. This guy was solid ground, more so than an evangelist in Shittown, USA.

I grimaced as we shook on it. No employment contract. He just told me to come in the next Monday and begin. I brought home volumes of material: their entire curriculum, tape after tape of edited airchecks of real DJ's, PD contacts, station ratings—an enormous cache of stuff.

That evening, I thumbed through it all and found the contact info for KUTE 102, Vince's station. Perhaps he was dropping a hint. The program director was Lucky Sinclair, a radio legend. I kept that in a special place, in case Vince ever disappeared on me.

My first day of work arrived, and I got there early, cold sober. I had my own workspace to call home for eight hours a day. It was a small cubicle next to two other out-of-work DJ's who Vince had hired on a small salary like mine, with an incentive to close leads that came from ads the Workshop aired on local LA radio stations. My job was to call on these applicants, most of whom had no knowledge of how to deal with other human beings. The calls to the guys often sounded like this:

"Hi, this is Ed from the Workshop, and I understand that you are interested in getting into radio."

*"Yeah, man. Sounds cool. Where do I sign? (belch)"*

*"Well, there are a few bases to cover here. Where did you go to school?"*

*"When?"*

*"How 'bout college?"*

*(Laughter) "You kiddin', man?"*

*"Well, uh, maybe high school?"*

*"What do you think, I'm an idiot? Of course, I went to school. Duh."*

*"Fine. What is it that attracts you to radio?"*

*"The chicks, dude. There must be tons of chicks."* I hadn't even come close to getting to the money yet.

*"Well, I'm happy to report that there are chicks, but you'll have to qualify."*

*"I've got a huge dick."*

*"Well, that should do it. Come on in and we'll see if you measure up. While you're at it, I'd like to personally measure your girth. That's even more important than length in getting you on the air. Without the girth, you're nowhere. So what's your girth?"*

*"Uh, thanks." (Click)*

Then there were the rejects . . . .

The girls were a piece of cake. The mere thought of radio fame brought them there within minutes.

Every Wednesday, the Workshop staff scheduled auditions, where a couple of dozen hopefuls sat like oversized children in elementary-school classroom chairs. Vince set up comfy leather easy chairs for the staff behind a long desk. The prospects entered, sweaty with nerves and announced the prepared scripts—with cleft palates, with mush mouths, with flinty, cracking, sing-songy, uninspired, monotone voices, all waiting like hounds on their haunches, hoping for a cracker. And we took their money, without apologies, with no compunctions whatsoever. And we knew that after they were done with us, most exited the front door to go nowhere but to their parents to cry and dream another dream all over again. Dreams cost money, and we graciously accepted it—cash, check, or money order.

But I shared the same dream and had a lot in common with them. For the most part, they were bursting with hope and nervous energy, and we couldn't have kept them out with mace.

I often roamed the halls, peeking into studios. In one booth was a student who I thought had an honest chance . . . very pretty and animated, editing copy for an ad she wanted to read. She was real blonde, like Nordic blonde, with a face that might have been carved out of ivory. I had noticed her at an audition—no cleft palate. No mush mouth.

"Hi, may I help you?"

"Oh, thanks," she replied, apparently quite relieved that someone was taking the time to assist.

"My instructor is swamped, and I'm having trouble with this copy." She had a classic voice, upper-crust Philly, like Grace Kelly, but approachable. I sat in the chair next to her, where the instructor normally sat, and she scrunched her chair close, leaning into me as she outlined her bit for me to review. She smelled as if she had just come out of the shower, like freshly picked strawberries.

I gave her copy a little touching up and caught her looking at me as I worked—I sensed that she was attracted, but who knew?

I slid the revisions over to her. "Here. This should work. Name's Ed, by the way."

"I know. Martha." We shook hands, and she held her grip for that extra millisecond, indicating that she wanted me to hang around for a while. So, I did.

"What's your story, Martha?" I noticed a sizable wedding ring on her left finger.

"I'm looking for a new career. My husband, Alan, plays for the New York Jets, and you know, bored sports wife looking for new activities. I heard the ad and here I am."

Christ, she was married, and to a fucking fullback. The flirting had to end. My eyes darted as I considered an exit strategy.

"Well, I'm not really an instructor, you know. I'm working sales for Vince." She offered up the warmest look. I extended my arm to shake hands.

"Nice to me you, Martha. See you around the house." Again, she was the last to let go.

I met another student before getting back to the phones, and he appeared to know me, and damn well. Vince's office was just down the hall, so I asked him.

"What's the deal with the students? What do they know about me?"

"Ed, you've *been* on the radio. They want to *be* on the radio. So you've got something that they want, experience on the air in *radio*." So condescending. It was Vince's one quality that I detested.

"How do they know I've been on the radio? They couldn't all be from Cowshitsville."

"I told them. Makes us look good, you know. Gives us a little credibility."

So, I was famous, but only inside the house.

I thought, "*Let's spend less time in the cubicle and get to know the students.*" Every week there was a blitzkrieg of new beauties looking to break into the business, with their leg-warmers and their enormous curly hairdos, and their pastel-colored hair bands, and their padded shoulders, and their lip-gloss. They were paid up—and yearning for knowledge, wisdom, and me!

I surveyed the studios and handpicked a few choice lovelies. I related stories of untold riches beyond their dreams, of jobs aching for talented kids like them, of stardom and Benzes. Stories about me, a living, breathing radio personality, almost living that dream. I didn't tell them that the manure smell at the Worm's studio was so overpowering that my clothes had to be shredded and burned. They learned nothing of my enormous salary, hovering near minimum wage; I had to leave a little plating on the armor.

A few months into my gig, I found an envelope on my desk addressed to me. I tore it open. My eyes froze and widened. It read:

### WhY HaVen'T yOu CALLed mE? I KnoW ThAT yOu weRe FrEe LaSt niTe.

It looked like one of those extortion notes, where someone cuts and pastes individual letters from a magazine article and leaves it in plain sight so they can see your heart pounding through your shirt. I didn't know whether to call the cops or my mommy. My eyes danced all around the place, wondering who it might have been. Why leave such an insane note? And who knew my schedule? I was getting a little panicky. Then, a tap on my shoulder.

"I didn't want to freak you out." It was Martha. She smiled at the letter, clearly digging her handiwork.

"Well, what did you *want* to do?" I asked, relieved. She was so adorable, my anger evaporated in a heartbeat. She closed in on my ear and blew into it.

"Where are we going here?" I asked.

She handed me another note, written in normal handwriting with her address in Newport Beach.

It was a good trek, and I suspected she wanted to discover if I would drive 50 miles to see her. The fact was I was as horny as Jimmy Caan in the Playboy mansion. The "extortion" note bugged me, but perhaps it was just her way—her scary, married lady, psychopathic way of leading me to the edge of a river and into a pair of perfectly fitted cement shoes. But it had been weeks since I'd been teased to the brink of orgasm at the Worm, so per usual, libido trumps psycho-bitch with scissors and glue.

I drove to her place, but got apprehensive as I parked. Who was going to be there to meet me, Mean Joe Greene? This was stupid. Her condo was only a block from the beach—I heard the waves breaking as I hopped up the short staircase to her little pied-à-terre. She answered two seconds after I knocked.

"Welcome, Ed. What do you drink?" I smelled that shower scent again. Her whole condo was filled with it, and with no defensive end answering the door, I instantly decompressed. I way preferred visiting a lady's place, as opposed to having them enter my trashy, spaghetti-stained, beer-smelling apartment. Regardless, she asked, and I came.

"Vodka tonic, if you got it."

"Sure." She slinked to the bar in a silk evening gown and poured me a strong one. She had a large easy chair, a small breakfast table with two upright chairs. I chose the easy chair. She grabbed her Armagnac and, without hesitation, sat on my lap.

"Are you uncomfortable?" she asked.

"I was before you sat down," and she tore into me after my first sip. She worked her way down my torso like a pro, hitting every nerve ending. Within a minute, my pants were down, and her hand was in my tighty-whities, fumbling around. I stroked her blonde hair while she continued to march down my chest, then to my waist, her dress hiking up as she went farther south. My mind wandered—words like "ring" and "fullback" rang in my head like fire alarms. She wasted no time making sure I knew that she wanted to please me. My breath was steam-stoked and rapid, my heart pounding. Then, a bang on the door.

"Fuck," she said as she stood up.

*"Fuck,"* I said to myself.

"Who the hell is that?" I whispered, trying to zip up fast without scissoring my junk in two. She didn't answer me and scampered to the door, opening it a crack.

"Sam," she half-screamed. "What the fuck?" Our guest lowered his shoulder and pushed the door open, the inside handle smashing the drywall. Martha tumbled to the floor and in rushed a belly, followed by a person. Sam had to be pushing 260 and clearly enjoyed beer.

"What the fuck is this shit, Martha?" he bellowed.

*"Sam? Wasn't her husband's name Alan?"*

"Look," I stuttered, "I don't want to get in between anything weird here." I went for my shoes as Sam reached down, grabbed me by the shoulders, and began moving me around the room randomly, violently. I was a five-year-old being shaken by a bad nanny.

"This is my time, and I want it back. I paid $150! You gonna give it to me? Huh, motherfucker?" As my head bounced from wall to wall, I could've sworn I saw her shrug. My only thought, aside from fear of broken bones and shaken organs, was that I was getting a blowjob from a fucking prostitute. Sam dropped me to the ground, square on my ass.

"Too weird, too weird," I mumbled as I darted for the door, stumbling over my untied shoelaces. I didn't dare look back. I couldn't imagine what drove Martha to drag me there. It wasn't like I had $150 lying around, but I wanted no more of her.

The very next day, I was at the Workshop, and there she was. I spied her in a studio, sitting in the lap of one of the instructors. I squinted to be sure it was Martha. Oh, it was her, bouncing on this guy's knee like an infant.

Later, Vince called all of us in for a meeting. I entered his office, the former master bedroom and took a seat near the bathroom while the others filed in. As the room filled, the temperature rose; the place didn't have central air. Although it was morning, my forehead was getting glossy, and my anti-perspirant was wearing thin.

"Guys, we're doing quite well. Our profit margin is up, our students are happy, and we're finding them places to work." He broke out in a wide smile. I thought, *"What about me? I'm off the air."*

"We're considering relocating to a larger facility, and want to pick up the pace around here—get a few more hungry wannabes in the program. Are you up for it?" We nodded in feeble acknowledgement.

"I'll be getting more leads, and I'm looking for bigger results. Thanks, and let's get to work." He stood, then we stood, as if he were wearing a black robe.

"Ed, hang in here with me for a minute." Vince stopped smiling. I wiped my brow with a handkerchief, less from the heat than from the tension. He closed the door after the last staffer left, and we both stood in front of his desk.

"Ed, I think you're doing great. Just fine. But without you on the radio, I have to believe that the number of students interested in our school is less than it would be." So much for me having *been* on the radio. Other staffers at the Workshop were getting on-air gigs, as were a few of the students. I was so busy working there that I had little time to shop my tape; it had months-old music on it. I was antiquing quickly.

"I'm over at KUTE in LA," he continued. "Would you like to step up to the big time?" I must have looked like a big dog salivating over a meaty bone.

"Can you make that happen?"

"Come down to the station Saturday morning and meet me at the studio. I'll be on for five hours. Anytime is fine." I felt like a lottery winner and stepped back to my cubicle to daydream for a while.

THAT NEXT SATURDAY MORNING, I MADE the drive to the KUTE studios in Glendale, a Los Angeles suburb east of Burbank. I arrived at a three-story office building, surrounded on either side by giant, old palm trees, the ones with the six-foot-thick trunks and unkempt leafy tops, dead fronds spread on all sides of the trees. I feared that they were just looking for a landscaper. I squinted into the hot California sun and rubbed my eyes; the smog was thick that day, and I never got used to it. I took the elevator, one of those slow-rising, hydraulic jobs that takes 60 seconds to go one floor. Arriving on the third floor, I expected the luxury afforded a media company in the second-largest market in the country.

What I saw was a studio about the size of the bedroom I had when I was six, squeezed next to another square room no larger than a shoe closet for the phone operator. It smelled of pizza and cigarette ashes. There were no busy sales offices, no lavish management suites, only a studio and a short hallway linking small offices overlooking aging apartment buildings and a fish restaurant that reeked of raw snapper. Where was the glamour? Where were the chicks? Vince was there to greet me in front of the mic.

"Ed, thanks for coming up." Again, that insane handshake. I hoped for an ice bucket.

"Well, what do you think?"

"Frankly, not much. Looks a lot like the Worm. What's up with that?" He began laughing hysterically.

"The studio is miles away from the offices—actually 3,000 miles, in New York. It's owned by one of the few African-American run media companies in the country. All of the suits stay there, and they let us do our thing. They're making money, selling ads and avoiding our beat-up studio. It's like a pirate station, no one but us idiot DJs."

It was refreshing to hear Vince talk this way, so candidly, with a childlike inflection to his voice; we were on par, sort of.

"Here, listen to a break." He popped on his headphones, turned on the mic, and that voice of his announced the next record. "KUTE 102! Good Saturday morning to you. Here's a new artist with a great new sound. Madonna, on K-U-T-E." His larynx rumbled like a 12-cylinder Ferrari, bouncing off the walls. A God-given box like his was rare, and I could see why he continued on the air. Plus, he was having the time of life—a smile plastered on his face.

"Sounds great, Vince. Are you the only one here?"

"Just me and the mic. Lucky will be in shortly." Program director Lucky Sinclair was the man in charge of the DJs and totally responsible for the music, the promotions—everything that came out of the speakers was on his agenda. Nervously, I paced the room, trying to get a flavor of working there on a daily basis.

"Sit down. Take it easy," Vince commanded. "He just wants to meet you. He heard the tape and is very interested." It was the early '80s, and I was all of 25, about to meet a radio legend who could give me the job of my life. Lucky was an old line DJ and had been on the air in LA since the dawn of Rock 'n' Roll. I grabbed a cup of coffee and continued pacing. Suddenly, the door opened, and in walked a breath of fresh air.

"Lucky Sinclair!" Vince announced, like the president had entered.

"Good mooooorrrrnning, Vince," said Lucky, with his trademark sing-songy French accent. His voice was as familiar to me as my mother's. He stood no higher than my neck level, had blushed red cheeks, and a shock of thick, gray hair that gave him a distinguished air. His smile was broad and genuine. He could have been a great television game-show host.

"And who is this young consort?" he asked Vince.

"Ed Mann, the young man I told you about. He works with me at the Workshop."

"Oh, are you a student?" Vince had apparently told him little about me.

"No," I interjected loudly. Lucky's head trimmed back an inch, and his smile dimmed. I tried to calm down. "Uh, no, I do sales with Vince. I'd been on the air at the Worm, uh, I mean KWRM, down in Corona."

The smile returned. "Ah, yes. So you worked for Cumpepper. A pleasure to be sure!"

"Well, I wouldn't say that."

Lucky laughed.

"You remember the tape of his work I left for you, Luck?" asked Vince.

"Of course, of course. Let's get out of the studio and let Vince do his job." He escorted me by the arm to his office down the hall, housing a desk stacked with tapes, vinyl singles in and out of their sleeves, and gold records hanging slightly askew on the wall. I felt a palpable sense of size and scope in relation to where I had worked; it was the office of a busy Los Angeles radio professional, and we were there to talk—about me. We both sat, he behind the desk, eye to eye—no seat lower than the other. I felt comfortable.

"Ed, let me play you something." He grabbed a cassette from his desk and turned to his credenza piled high with dusty tapes and audio equipment. After slipping it into the cassette player, he popped the "play" button and then faced me as we waited for the tape to cue up. What followed was *my* tape, the one Vince had brought to him, pumped up so loud I thought the whole world could hear it.

Lucky's face went blank as I announced the new record from Toto, then he continued to stare at me, expressionless as I announced the weather forecast. I felt beads of sweat inching down my forehead, dripping like tears. Two, three minutes went by and Lucky never blinked. The warm, provincial face imported from a poor Parisian neighborhood morphed into a stern, focused *visage*. The volume increased with each passing break. After four minutes it sounded as if he'd plugged my tape into a Marshall amp. Finally, I heard my last bit, and then a ringing in my ears during a half-minute silence, when Lucky yanked the tape from the machine and resumed looking at me, now with a more quizzical expression.

"What do you make of this, Ed? Is this your grade-A material?" I was covered in flop sweat and feared raising my arms, lest he see the large ovals of moisture darkening my shirt underarms. It took everything I had to regain my composure.

"Well, it's about a year old, but I sound like I sound. My voice is my voice, and I stand by it. I didn't submit it to you because I wasn't proud of it." I felt my throat tighten slightly as I spoke, but the words flowed without hesitation.

Lucky sat silent, considering. I thought I'd better speak, or he might ask me to step outside into the smoggy afternoon and clean up the palm fronds—when he said, "How about next weekend? I'd like you to get in with Vince for few hours, learn the clock, the routine here. Sound good?"

My eyes bulged from their sockets. "What was that all about? The playback. The staring?" I asked.

"I needed to hear how your voice sounds under stress, how it might change. You see, Ed, this is Los Angeles, and the pressure to perform properly is great. I think you'll make a fine addition, a fine addition," he said, grinning.

Suddenly I wasn't that kid locked in the bathroom, playing tapes to an audience of one anymore.

# CHAPTER 4

AFTER MY ORIENTATION, I DROVE HOME and pinched myself 'til I bruised. I had two jobs in Los Angeles radio, both might get me recognition, fame, money, ladies—all the things that were important to me. I daydreamed 'til my car almost careened off the Ventura Freeway.

I took a deep breath of the sulfur-tinged, ozone-infused air as I pulled into the garage at my apartment, which I shared with three other college buddies, decorated with Italian sauce and beer stains. A large shoe hung from a hook above the couch. We didn't remember how it got there. The door was open, per usual, and I bounced to the couch next to a plate of spaghetti balancing on the armrest, right under the shoe. I desperately needed to pee, but the toilet was stuffed. I could hold it. I had news. Most every evening, we assembled around the community bong to review our day. Steve, my closest friend, had already packed the bowl. I lit a match and took a long hit.

"Well, I got it," as I exhaled a green plume. My brain stalled while the THC gripped my brainstem. "It's pretty choice. I'm back on the air, and now you guys can hear me right here in town."

"What makes you think we want to hear you?" remarked Steve, looking up from the bong. He leaned over to the cabinet and slapped a Sinatra LP on the record player. "Now *this* is music." Frank went on about flying to the moon and getting someone under his skin. I shrugged and checked the fridge for beers. Out.

"Hey, I'm running out for be-bos. You want to come with?" I asked.

"Nope. Gotta go over my sales reports."

"Suit yourself."

I got back to my car and drove to the nearby food store. Ironically, I didn't walk it for fear of weaving from side to side and drawing the attention of the authorities, but I could sure drive straight. After two minutes of me driving straight while blasted, I parked and then weaved my way into the store. As the automatic doors slid open, my back went ramrod at the exquisite vision standing before me. It had to be Cindy Crawford, the model. She was at the checkout counter paying for some sort of feminine product. It wasn't unusual to see celebrities in LA, but I couldn't get over my reaction. I was completely starstruck. I got a little closer, but she had turned away from me. There were few people in the store, so I ran to get the beer in the back and sprinted to the front checkout, where she was just finishing up.

I got right behind her, again looking at the back of her head. Finally, she presented her credit card—no ring on the appropriate finger—and I craned my neck to read the card: Alex Grossinger. Hmm. Well, another celebrity look-alike. I wondered how many people had asked for her autograph. She turned and I did a single hello-nod. She was absolutely stunning.

Our eyes fixed, and I noticed a little gold Chai chain swaying gently around her neck. She took a whiff of the aroma coming from me and asked, "Is that Columbian or sensimilla?" One was my favorite strains of marijuana. I went to great lengths to find good "sens."

"You're very perceptive," I slurred. "Sensimilla, of course."

She walked past me, glanced back and said, "Nice voice," and slunk out. I was left standing at the cashier with my mouth hanging open.

*"What the hell was that?"* If Cindy Crawford were Jewish, and clever, this would be her. I paid up and staggered back to the car—and then it hit me. My foggy brain cleared for a second and determined that this feminine product buyer, and weed expert, may be the daughter of Vegas comedy legend Danny Grossinger, and she was a dead ringer for a supermodel.

I looked behind me, but she apparently had driven off the lot and out of my life. I started the car and daydreamed of the two of us dining at Chasen's, ensconced in an oversized red booth, polishing off their patented chili, licking the remnants off of each other's fingers. I drove back to the apartment to find Steve sleeping on the couch and the Sinatra record skipping over and over the same line, *"Don't you know, you fool, you never can win."*

Saturday morning found me in front of a microphone, intimately connected to a rapt Los Angeles audience, waiting for the next morsel to drip from their speakers. I had been tempted to inhale a bong hit to calm my nerves before hitting the air, but didn't think that a Bordeaux-swilling French guy named Lucky would appreciate a young, stoned DJ on his first shift at his radio station. I broke in after a song and kept it simple:

"Good morning, LA. Name's Ed, and I hope we get to know each other much better here at KUTE radio. I've got one for you from Hall and Oates, *Did It in a Minute.*"

Hey, that was easy. Like falling off a cloud. What an incredible way to make a living—it was a giant leap from waiter's wages at the Worm to a union gig with benefits. I was pretty overwhelmed. Just then, the hot line rang: a blinking red light shining right in my face.

"Hello, Ed. It's Vince. Enjoying yourself?"

"Immensely. It's amazing the energy I feel just being in a place as large as this, doing something I love."

"I've got a group of students here at the school, and we're checking you out. Make us proud."

My next call came from Cousin Julie, who was always convinced of my budding celebrity. I had tipped her off when I was on.

"Hey, Jules. Any new celebrity friends?" I thought of mentioning Miss Grossinger, just to play her usual game of "who do you know?" but who knew who she really was? Perhaps the young, beautiful heiress of the Rhode Island Grossingers. Or just another cute broad with a famous name dropping into a market to buy Kotex.

"Uh, yeah. You! Mr. Mann, KUTE-FM. Mr. Mann, KUTE-FM." I kind of liked the sound of that—but for the borderline catatonic tone. I began shuffling through the dozens of music and commercial carts, sorting them in order for the next few breaks. I struggled with organization, particularly *that* morning—my first LA airshift! My nervous-energy level was in hyperdrive.

"When can I come see you up there?" she asked.

"Oh, how 'bout a thousand years? Jeez Louise, I just got here, Julie!" She fell silent for a moment. I felt bad. I had no reason to raise my voice to my only fan. "Come on down next weekend, and I'll show you around."

"*Wow!* That's great, Cuz! Can I bring a camera? Mr. Mann, KUTE-FM." Then she began talking to her cat. "Hey, Misty. Do you hear Mr. Mann on the radio? Meow, Meow, Misty. Meow, Meow."

"*Christ almighty.*"

Two hours into the shift, the phone op came in with a message. It read, "Tom St. John on line four." I was incredulous. The great St. John? Tom was a radio veteran, currently on-air at the station's competition, THE BIG Z-FM, the city's leading radio station. He was a guy I admired deeply, and he was on the line—for me.

"Hello, this is Ed."

"Ed, Tom St. John. I've been listening to your first shift. Not bad."

"I haven't done anything yet."

"You arguing with a compliment?" Tom asked.

"No, no. Not at all. I'm a bit overwhelmed. What can I possibly do for *you*?"

"Just wanted to wish you the best. Lucky is a good man. You'll learn a lot. By the way, you drink?"

"Hell, yes."

"What say you and I meet and discuss things."

What the hell was going on? One hour into LA radio and I'm tipping drinks with legends. Perhaps radio celebrities did this all the time. After all, we were in the media center of the universe, so let's get smashed! I never even shared a sandwich with the DJs in Corona. This had to be interesting. After my shift, I hung up my headphones, drove home, and spent the afternoon considering which shirt I should wear. It felt like a date.

I suggested that we meet in Hollywood at a little place I know called the Tiki Tai. It'd been there for years and pours frou-frou drinks—Mai Tais and Pina Coladas—that sort of thing. I arrived first and ordered my 151-proof Long Island iced tea from a table a few feet from the bar. The walls and ceiling were adorned with Polynesian hula skirts, postcards, seaweed samples, surfboards, t-shirts, photos of drunken patrons wearing their drinks, lifesaver floatees, pirate skulls and crossbones emblazoned on flags, empty bottles of Bacardi, and tropical tchotchkes collected since the place had opened.

The speakers blared Don Ho records and Jamaican Muzak. Legend had it that a local sailor of the South Pacific had lost everything, came home to LA, and opened a bar to reflect on his glory days terrorizing tortoises and hooking marlin. An enormous blue one was hanging precariously above the bartender—the actual owner—hoping to make a living on dry land serving sweet rum drinks. He and his son ran the place. The Tiki was dark, overdone, and often mocked by the clientele glued to their chairs at the bar for their obligatory six-drink minimums.

"Hey Mack," slurred one older fellow, sucking down rum shots like Blackbeard. "My coaster's soggy. Get me one from the ceiling there, the one with the pretty girl with the lei."

"You're here for a lei?" replied the owner.

"Yep. Grab me the coaster and a condom, and I'll be on my way."

That got a good laugh from the dais. Only a minute later, a broad-shouldered man with a Beatle haircut, wearing a green Lacoste pullover shirt, entered and saw me looking at him.

"Ed?"

"Tom?"

He grabbed my hand like we'd known each other for months. His eyes virtually vanished behind corrective coke-bottle thick lenses. "Good we could meet under these circumstances," he began, his smile pasted onto a broad, pale Irish face that made me instantly comfortable.

"Drinking as a circumstance . . . I always thought of it as a means to an end."

He laughed. *Out loud.* Wow. He thought I was funny. This was cool.

"What are you drinking, by the way?"

"L.I. iced tea."

"That won't do at all." He waved the waiter down.

"Sir, get us two Jack Daniels and Miller Lite chasers."

The waiter froze and gave him a smirk. "We don't serve that." He'd been through this drill. I sobered up quick, realizing that I had picked the wrong bar.

"Which?" Tom demanded.

"Either."

"You don't serve *either*?" He stared at the waiter and then glared at me like it was my fault. He went for his pocket, whipped out a five to pay for my drink, and leaned into me.

"We're leaving," he said. I was in no position to argue as he led us out the door to his car.

"Hop in. We'll get your car later." I obeyed, and he drove at an absurd rate of speed down Sunset Blvd to Cahuenga, screeching over the pass alongside the Hollywood Freeway and into Reuben's, a slick bar that served his drinks of preference and large, heaping deli sandwiches. It looked like an Irish pub that crashed into chrome plating. Tom had a place.

We spent the evening laughing and drinking. Into our fourth hour of inebriation, he asked me if I'd like to submit an aircheck to his program director at THE BIG Z-FM. I was flabbergasted and told him that I wasn't nearly ready and he should continue drinking 'til he sobered up. Clearly, sobriety wouldn't find me until morning, so I grabbed a cab home and returned to the Tiki for my car the next day.

Tom listened to my work regularly and gave me honest critiques. We began meeting often at Reuben's. It became "our" place. He continued to ply me with drinks as if he were conducting alcoholic experiments on Jews.

One evening, while testing the outer limits of our livers, he threw one out to me.

"Have you ever worked for a union shop?"

"Nope. Well, the closest I came was the dishwasher union at a restaurant when I was in high school."

"What were the benefits, sponges?" We both laughed at that one. Then he got frank.

"You're going to find yourself between a rock and hard place."

"What are you talking about?"

"Well," he gulped down yet another shot of Jack and huffed out a long, flammable breath. "On one side, management hired you, brought you in. On the other hand, the union protects you from them.

Gives you security. You should know this shit." He then changed the subject to his favorite pubs in Chicago, but I thought I'd look into it the next day.

Indeed, KUTE was a union gig, covered by the American Federation of Television and Radio Artists, AFTRA, so everything from the paycheck to the medical plan was affected, and much to my fiscal favor. Management had gotten me here, yet I was tied to a union sworn to shake them upside down until their pennies fell into our hands. I saw a notice posted on the studio bulletin board just a week after Tom and I had our discussion. A meeting was scheduled and, on the notice, in bold type was printed the words: *No Management Allowed*. I began to sense the price I might pay.

My first union meeting was more like a jock meeting: pizza, beer, joking around, and they held it at the station, in a small conference room across the hall from Lucky's office. We didn't get down to business for more than 30 minutes, until the union dude hit the gavel and shut us up.

"Hear ye, hear ye. *"Who was this, Paul Revere?"* We are convened to open a meeting of AFTRA members working for KUTE radio. All present say, "yea.""

"Yea," said we. We were present. There we were.

"We are open for discussion on item one—working for non-union signatories." Needless to say, no one spoke, everyone wracked with fear. I leaned over and, under my breath, asked one of the jocks seated next to me what the tension was about.

He whispered back, "You're not—under any circumstances—allowed to work in the industry on a non-union job while you're a member of the AFTRA union, or you can kiss your card and then your job bye-bye."

My mind whirled. Was this guy paranoid, or did he know what he was talking about? What about the Workshop? It was "in the industry?"

It was certainly non-union. I was working there; I needed the money. How did Vince do it while Lucky knew? Did the union know? Did anyone give a shit? If I questioned it, the union dude would follow through with a memo, which would float upstairs to some Jimmy Hoffa-type ready to size me for a pine box. My mind floated to scenes from *On the Waterfront*. Now, I was the paranoid one.

Then, Vince opened his mouth. "Excuse me, sir. If one of us owns a business in the industry that isn't a union signatory, where does the union stand on that?"

I was getting a thyroid condition from hearing it all. The rep drew a long, tired breath, jerked forward and focused his energy on Vince, unsmiling.

"It is my understanding, from the union's perspective, that hiring union employees as a non-signatory is strictly *verboten*." Verboten? Who was this dude, a Nazi war criminal? Vince stared at him, glanced at me, a sweaty mess in the corner, and Colonel Klink moved on.

"Any other questions on this?"

The news girl broke in frantically. "Can I get mental-health coverage?"

"Sally, take these," I said, and bounced aspirin across the table in her direction. Big laughs, but I was sure I was getting tossed from either the station or the Workshop.

After a silent ride down the pneumatic elevator, I waved Vince over to my car.

"What do I have to worry about here? What did you get me into?"

"Don't sweat it, Ed. You're okay. The union doesn't give a shit about anything but concessions. It's a scare tactic. I won't report you, but don't fuck with Lucky."

"Why would I do that?"

"Just don't cross him, like talking with other radio people at Reuben's about working at other stations."

"How the hell do you know who I'm talking to?"

"I saw you the other night. Reuben's isn't exactly a private club, and I'm not, ever, going to make my Workshop a union house. You can count on that." I felt like a hostage. He gave me a searing look, a warning for sure. Vince got me these jobs, and he could get me out of both with a wave of his hand.

Back at my apartment, I loaded up an XL bong hit and sucked it down with gusto. It was close to midnight, and my thoughts careened into paranoid swirls of green. I could quit the Workshop, but Vince might go nuts on Lucky and I'd find myself on the street. I may have to get to Tom and think seriously about working THE BIG Z, but Jesus H, I was only two years out of school, and it was one of the top stations in the country. If that little plan didn't work out, I had nothing, and Tom would disappear in a poof. I slept fitfully that night, my mind whirling.

# CHAPTER 5

Vince greeted me at the Workshop the next day like nothing had happened. I smiled grimly and took my seat at the long table. It was judgment day for the hopefuls lined up for their auditions. The group of us sat with our notepads and coffee. The nervous applicants took their little kindergarten desk-chairs, and we stared at each other until they all arrived. Many looked distracted and one actually broke open a *People* magazine, thumbing through it like he was at the dentist.

Without warning, our eyes moved toward the door as a vision entered the room. She was right out of the pages of *Vogue*: about five-foot-10, fabulous rail-thin legs, blondish hair, irresistible green eyes, brilliant white teeth that shone like polished ivory, even under our shitty fluorescent lights. She sat down like a leaf landing in the grass, with her little butt scooting in between the desk and the chair, her legs swinging in behind. After she situated herself, she looked directly at me, grinning. She was a human jumper cable.

I smiled, cocking one eyebrow, like John Belushi.

"All right, folks," announced Vince. "Welcome to the Workshop and the beginning of your careers on the air. In front of you are our staff members. Most work on the air in LA radio now. You may be next. I'll be pairing you with a Workshop staffer, and they'll have you perform a series of tests, vocal and written. Are you ready?"

They nodded anxiously. The girl and I locked eyes. We didn't nod. We were two dogs, sniffing each other from afar.

Vince paired me with a young guy from the Valley and, as luck had it, the girl. Her name was Lori. She lived in Orange County and grew up dreaming to be on the radio. Sounded familiar. I ran her though the paces, completely ignoring the guy. He mysteriously failed to qualify; we unconsciously kept the ratios weighted toward the applicants that sustained our lascivious appetites. OK. Consciously.

I retired to a chamber in the back for a minute to make her sweat. Then I burst through the door.

"Lori, you made it! Congratulations." She gave me a sweet hug and wrote me a check right there. She couldn't have been more than 21 and apparently had 1,500 bucks sitting in her account. Impressive performance. Then, a little wink before turning and leaving. I was smitten and prayed silently that she wasn't a prostitute or an evangelist.

Lori quickly became my project. Her voice tumbled out of her mouth like a gentle stream. There was no doubting her talent; she was nearly ready to work as is. On her first day of instruction, I bumped into her at the entrance. We exchanged glances, then stares, and I made a bold move. I asked her to dinner and, to my great delight, she agreed.

I chose a casual restaurant a few miles from the Workshop, and we decided to arrive separately, in case someone I knew was there. Dining with students was not explicitly prohibited in the clauses of the school's accreditation with the Board of Education, but it wasn't promoted either. I didn't give a shit. She was fabulous.

She came on time. We took seats in the back, hardly romantic or suggestive, simply private. She wore a loose-fitting sundress, the low-slung décolletage that showed off her long, elegant neck. As she sat, her little tush went in first and the gazelle legs followed. Breathtaking.

"Where are you from?" I began.

"The Midwest. My family's from Detroit. Dad's a pastor at our church, and mom stayed home to raise us." She tugged at her dress while I shifted uncomfortably. "I've been kind of rebel by trying to get into the radio game. One of my sisters is a nun, and the other spends her time looking for a husband."

The group of women I got along with best, besides the women of the tribe, were Catholics. Their repression was delectable. "What are you looking for?" I asked, as I sipped the house red, the tannic acid making my mouth pucker.

"A life. A career I can love. Maybe someone to come along for the ride." So charming, like Grace Kelly: refined and elegant, yet fresh and sweet as a peach. I could barely concentrate on what she was saying; the green eyes were all I saw. "Lori, it's clear that you'll do very well. Who do you like on the air? Who do you admire?"

"Besides you?"

I practically melted. "You've heard my show at KUTE?" I asked, my eyes wide as dinner plates.

"It's the kind of broadcast I'd like to do. Funny, musical, happy."

*Booiiinnngg*!

This was no ordinary ingénue. As we stared into each other's eyes, sipping our wine, giggling, I felt she was more than a fan looking to prop me up and provide me a shallow sense of pride. My confidence was soaring to dizzying heights. She spent the evening listening, taking me in, and I had little doubt that she could recount virtually every word I said; her baby greens vibrating as she absorbed every morsel. I wanted her mouth.

We departed as we arrived—separately—but found ourselves standing together at the valet. I took her ticket with mine, waved down the attendant, she leaning into me gently as we waited in the cool breeze. I slowly draped my arm around her to warm her, wanting to protect her. She was already toasty. As her car pulled up, she gave me a gentle kiss and gazed again into my eyes, and I knew at that moment that I didn't dare disappoint her.

# CHAPTER 6

VINCE TOOK PRIDE IN MY GROWING stature as a radio personality in LA, and he allowed me to coach students at the Workshop. It gave me sweet alone time with Lori without having to spring for dinner every night. She was a rapt listener and learned the tricks of the trade quickly: how to edit audiotape, use the mic, work the board. She demonstrated a passion that I recognized. And she was clever, often popping off punch lines for my little set-ups during our sessions. Vince walked by, looking in on the studios where we worked, lifting an eyebrow as if taking mental notes. I wasn't alarmed, and she was oblivious.

After weeks of daily exposure to one another, I was anxious to move our budding friendship to a more intimate space. We agreed to meet up at a motel, about one grade up from "semi-seedy," and figured on departing the Workshop at staggered times to avoid drawing attention to ourselves.

I arrived first and laid down a credit card at the front desk. It wasn't fancy, but money was short, and I guessed that she didn't care if we were ducking into the Hotel Ritz or the Motel 6.

My overnight bag and I arrived at the room, a first-floor job just off the parking lot, steaming in the afternoon sun. I cracked the door and was pleased to see a well-appointed space for the rate: a queen-sized bed, full bath, clean carpet, and I threw in champagne on ice—nice touch, I thought. She would arrive in about 20 minutes, so I got out of my stinky clothes, cranked the shower knob on Hot, and slid under the stream. Every muscle decompressed in a start and I smiled.

I went for the soap; it was still in that fucking box that motels put it in. I ripped the cardboard and found the soap shrink-wrapped inside. I was struggling with it when I heard a voice.

"I'll get that." It was Lori, and I was wet and naked. I opened the shower door, seeing that she had already disrobed. She climbed in and kissed me hard, the water rolling off our skin. I loved kissing her; we were about the same height, and there was no need for me to hunch down; just a little bend in the neck, and we were locked in.

"You're early," I remarked.

Her eyes ventured south, and she grinned widely. "And you're ready."

We tore into each other, she soaping up my backside as we faced each other. Then I turned her around and got to work on her perfect breasts from behind. She was so aroused I almost believed she was faking it—"*oooohhh, aaaahhhiiiiiyy, ohhh, jeeeeezzzeussss!*" Wild.

Unbeknownst to her, I caught her reflection in the shaving mirror hanging at face level—her eyes rolled up in her head, eyelids fluttering. This was no act; she was happy. I rolled my eyes up to the heavens and thanked God, or whoever was up there.

She climaxed first, and I followed shortly thereafter; I expected to see a porno director leaning forward in the chair near the sink saying, "And *cut. Print* it!" We dried off, each of us working on the other's hair. I bent down and caressed her legs, she mine. It was quite lovely, almost as I imagined a honeymoon, two people preening each other. I led her to the bedroom, where we tucked ourselves under the covers, turned off the lights, and within five seconds began laughing—howling out loud. Then came a sunset session in bed. It was tender, exciting, exhausting. I fell asleep with her arms draped over me.

Morning broke and we didn't speak. The champagne high expired. Each of us now clearly awkward: turning away from each other in modesty, dressing quietly. While I put my socks on, my thoughts coursed up, down, and around avenues I had hardly considered; my experience in long-term relationships was nil, and this seemed to be moving in that direction. I didn't know what love was, but this sort of felt like what I thought it was.

*"Go with the flow"* was a phrase that stuck in my head. Hell, I flowed with most every moment flung at me throughout my young life. I didn't engineer meeting Lucky, or Vince, or Tom. I didn't ask my swimming coach to put me in front of a microphone at the big diving meet. I didn't ask for the morning show at UCLA, and I didn't sit in Reverend Cumpepper's office, pining for a job I didn't know existed. They all waltzed into my life. There was no blueprint.

A thought struck me: who was I to discount the idea that maybe these people had a design to meet *me*? Simply being on the radio had a way of bringing people to my circle that might not otherwise appear, like a king holding court. I shrugged while fumbling with my belt, she with her bra. *"Kings didn't fumble with their belts."*

And this applied to Lori and me. I wasn't a big believer in fate, yet there we were, pretty goddamn happy together. We were clean and rested, each wondering what was written in the next chapter. I pulled my shirt out of the overnight bag, cinched my belt, and looked at her for the first time since waking. She was smiling—but giving away little.

BACK AT KUTE, I WAS THAT kid in the bathroom at my parent's house playing with the mic and tape recorder. I had a job at a big-time radio station playing music I loved—a rarity. I was developing a way of mixing music, segueing songs like *Funkytown* and *Let's Groove* as if they were playing at a club. I matched the beat of one song as I started the next, and the listeners had no sense that I had changed songs until the lyrics were sung. Phone calls to the station were up, and I had a good slice of the audience calling me for requests, even before I arrived, and I arrived every weekend, sometimes sick, always sober. Never missed a shift; I didn't want to offer up any reason for insubordination.

Lucky and I had been getting along well. He encouraged me, showed me proper mic technique, how to imagine that I was speaking to one person—a trick of the trade. I admired his familial style, his lack of autocratic thunder. We appreciated one another. One particular Saturday he invited me to a meeting in his dusty, record-strewn office before my shift; he broached a subject that I found uncomfortable.

"Ed, have you met with the union?"

"Well, uh, yeah," I replied.

"Did they ask you not to speak about it with me? I shifted in my seat, looked to one side, then to the other, as if there were an early exit to this discussion.

"They mentioned that, yes." Lucky leaned into me closer. I could smell brie on his breath.

"You know, Ed, you can come to me with any concerns. Anything at all, certainly if it involves the station. You may feel at liberty to open up to me. After all, I hired you."

He smiled, but his eyes were totally focused, no laissez-faire, laugh it up Lucky. He wanted information, and I remembered my conversation with Vince outside the union meeting: all the union brass wanted was concessions from management; they didn't care about them, or about us. I was betting that they were pressing Lucky on some issue, probably money, and he wanted inside dope from me—the big dope.

"Lucky, I really, um, I really don't know much about this. You hired me, but the union was pretty firm with me about keeping their agenda private. I'm sorry, but could we go over my show? I had some ideas."

He stood up immediately, thrust his hand out, and dismissed me summarily, unaffected by my declaration.

"That's about that. We'll talk more later, I'm sure," he bellowed.

I shook his hand in the typically loose, up and down twice routine that French guys do when they shake hands, and I left carrying a bucket of disillusion. He was privy to something—something that the union didn't even discuss with us.

Vince was home when I called around 10 o'clock after my shift on Saturday night. "What in the world is going on with the union and KUTE, Vince. You appear to have a handle on this."

I heard this slurping sound over the phone. "Can't be sure, but there's something up." I heard him swallow and exhale with a loud sigh. "Jesus. Brain freeze."

*"Milk shake."*

I waited patiently until he gathered himself.

"You know, Ed, there's really nothing you can do about it. Remember, the union doesn't care about you."

Well, that was comforting, and condescending as usual. We hung up, and I sulked around the apartment before drifting off.

Monday came around quickly, and I had called Lori zero times since our last episode the week before. I wasn't much on form in my 20s. I drove down to the Workshop and assisted in preparations for the move to the larger building. I felt the excitement of boxes being packed while students were busy hosting their fake shows in their little studios throughout the house. But I didn't see Lori. There was, however, a brunette in Vince's office, chatting away. I approached to say hello.

"Ed, come in and meet Audrey."

Audrey stood up, all five-foot-11 inches of her, and I reared back. Her auburn hair hung down to her hips. Her neck defied the laws of physics, longer than my hand from wrist to fingertips. It was an

Eiffel Tower neck. And she was brickhouse-stacked above a 23-inch waist. Her back was ramrod straight as she greeted me. Barbie was in the building.

"Nice to meet you, Ed. I've heard a lot about you from Lori."

My eyes quickly popped out of their sockets. She stood with a pole up her ass, her smile fixed, getting a huge kick out of my reaction. "She's my sister."

Holy Christ! A bionic version of Lori. I couldn't get over how many gorgeous women were attracted to radio, and they were bringing their sisters.

"Audrey will be our new receptionist and an assistant to me," Vince continued. I tried to calm down.

"So, you're clearly not the nun," I joked. She laughed, but Vince stared at me unsmiling: this conversation was over.

"Well, nice to meet you, Audrey. Where's Lori today?"

"Oh, out sick. I'm sure that she'll be back soon. She just goes on and on how much she loves it at the Workshop, and I couldn't miss out on the chance to see it. Next thing I know, here I am, working for Vince."

She turned her head, keeping her eyes fixed on me. I felt heat from my pelvis but tried to ignore it. Vince turned his head toward the door—three's a crowd. I offered my hand and she gripped it softly. It felt like Lori: sweet, affectionate. I was waiting for her to mention Lori and me, as in—"*So, you and Lori are fucking, eh?*" Sisters do that shit. I turned to leave, but Vince interrupted me.

"Ed, pack up your stuff. We're moving in two days."

I gave Audrey another quick glance—she was still looking at me—and I meandered through the large corrugated boxes stacked throughout the house and toward my desk.

My extension rang as my hand was engulfed in white-foam packing material. I pulled it out of the box, and my fingers were covered in little dots of Styrofoam, clinging to each pore. I swore while I picked up the phone.

"Well that's a fine greeting." It was Lori.

"Sorry," I replied, my eyes bulging. "I-I-I was just packing."

"Are you quitting?"

"Oh no, Jesus, no. We're moving, you know. The Workshop, to that larger . . ." She interrupted me by laughing.

"I know, silly. I'm at home, sick, but you probably know that." So, she knows I met her sister. What the fuck did she say? Did I shake her hand too long? Did my out-of-control dick rise up when I met her? *"Shhhheeeeeiiiittt!"*

"Yeah, I knew. Your sister told me."

"Isn't that great?" she continued, her voice rising to new heights. "Vince had a position for her. She has no desire to be on the air or even be in the business. She's an administrative assistant and very efficient. You know Vince. He loves organization." At least the sisters weren't at odds.

"I'm sorry I haven't called. There's no excuse, really. I'm just an ass, you know."

"Yes, I know." Cute, but I seemed to be off the hook.

"Can I see you soon? Outside of here," I asked.

She paused, and I felt sweat forming on my forehead.

"I need a little time. Just a little." Another pause. "I need to understand how I feel."

"*A familiar song.*" "I get it. I understand," I said. "I'll see you in the new building."

"Great, Ed. Thanks." She seemed relieved.

I continued packing while thinking that if she needed some time, then I should have some time. But she knew that I didn't need it, or maybe she did, and I was taking time away from her anyway for some despicable reason . . . *Ugh*, I was thinking *way* too hard! I needed to get air.

The house had plenty of windows facing the street, but there was no substitute for the outdoors, and it was a gorgeous day. I stepped out for a Coke, took in the sunshine, and gulped down a deep breath of pristine California air just as a big-ass diesel truck passed by, spewing out several pounds of thick, grey, choking fumes. I doubled over in pain, hacking out the exhaust particulates from my lungs. The truck left a trail of carcinogens hanging in the air for about a minute while I recovered and stared off into the distance. I didn't have a pleasant escape from anything, anywhere. I turned back to go inside, far worse for wear, and continued packing, thrusting my hands back into the foam.

The next day, I gathered up a pile of the smaller items in an office that still featured the original decorating; decals and posters of Scooby Doo and Batman were stuck on the paneling; clearly some kid's bedroom in another life. I went to pee in the bathroom; it had a child-protection latch on the toilet. I looked down and groaned. It pained me each time I entered. Some moron always re-latched the seat cover as if four-year-olds were still living there. I unlatched the cover, raised the seat up, did my duty, reached down at childhood level to flush, put the seat back down and, like an idiot, I re-latched the seat—if I had to go through that routine, so should everyone else.

I was sitting cross-legged on the floor, stacking loose paperclips into small cardboard boxes when Audrey poked her head and that giraffe neck into the room. My head jerked up.

"Hi, were you looking for something?" I asked. She straightened her back, giving me the impression that her head might broach the ceiling. I began to smile.

"Yes, actually. You." She walked slowly toward me, closing the door behind her. I was far from alarmed, but she wasn't slowing down. I noticed that she had shed the conservative clothes she wore during our first meeting, in favor of a cleavage-revealing V-neck sweater that gave her neck even more length, and I had the impression that she was hiding grapefruits in her bra. She was statuesque.

"What can I do for you?" I asked.

"I wanted to say that it was nice meeting you yesterday." Her voice warmed, echoing her sister as she inched inexorably closer. I was getting uncomfortable sitting only three feet from her while she towered over me, so I stood. I leaned over to brush my pants straight, and when I faced her, she kissed me, hard. I was too shocked to comprehend what the hell she was doing, shocked into submission. After about 15 seconds, I pulled back, but unintentionally displayed my arousal.

"What do you think you're doing?" I demanded, my dick halfway down my thigh. She leered like a vulture eating her prey.

"I'm doing what I want. And I wanted to kiss you from the moment I saw you."

"You are aware that I'm with your sister, and that . . ."

She grabbed me mid-sentence and pushed me into the wall, banging my head against the Batman poster, almost stunning me, giving her another shot at lip-locking my mouth. I was forgetting all the implications and let her have at me. She worked feverishly, rubbing her pelvis against my leg, pulling her top down at the collar, exposing her breasts—the roundest, biggest, firmest things I've ever seen. Nothing in Playboy compared. An architect could have used them to draw perfect circles. I massaged them, her nipples extending. My thoughts were clouded, unformed, misshapen. I wasn't considering consequences, only impulses. I was a base animal, uncontrollable. I felt like eating red meat.

She was really whaling on me now, trying to work my pants off, when I suddenly went cold. This wasn't me. I wasn't a heel. I pushed her off me onto her back, and leaned over her. She moved closer, unsure if I was preparing to pounce or end these shenanigans entirely. I wasn't sure, either, but I stopped and rolled over onto my back next to her. She was breathing like a cross-country skier, her monumental chest heaving. I was between embarrassed and unrelieved, each breath taken in huge gulps.

"We can't do this," I said between breaths. "This is wrong."

"It's right for me. Do you think I do this all the time?" she asked. I leaned over her once again, my hands propping me up on either side of her, her breasts spilling over my hands.

"I don't know you from Eve." I raised my voice louder than I had intended. "And you come in here, knowing full well that I'm fucking your sister, and that gives you the ticket to pull off your top and slide your way in? You don't find that slightly creepy, just a little invasive?" My libido had subsided and I became irritated, more with myself for giving in to her advances.

"Look," she replied. "You slept with Lori once. One time. And you didn't call her for days. She was ready to walk right out of here . . ."

"And now you're here to take her place?" I interrupted. "Fuck you."

I turned back over to see Vince standing by the door.

"Get in my office, Ed. Now," he demanded, like a stern daddy. Audrey cupped her exposed breasts and dashed to the kid's bathroom. I gave her a stare of overwhelming anger and walked down to Vince's office, my shirttail untucked and hanging out at the back. I closed the door behind me and sat down.

"Well, that was clever," he started. "And wonderful timing. You'll never know who just left my office while you were getting hard in the other room." He stood over me, tapping his foot at the pace of a Punk Rock song. I imagined *Submission* by the Sex Pistols:

> *I'm on a submarine mission for you baby*
> *I feel the way you were going*

*I picked you up on my TV screen*
*I feel your undercurrent flowing*
*Submission going down, down*
*dragging me down"*

"I give up. Who?" I was still yelling.

"The Workshop's rep from the Board of Education. So, not only do they hear that one of our instructors is screwing one of the students, he's also fucking one of the employees, who turns out to be the student's sister."

"Vince, she attacked me in the other room. I was the one that stopped everything . . ." The long, hollow pause was louder than me.

"Yeah, as loudly as you fucking could," he screamed. He began pacing, clearly in deep thought. He was now in some sort of hot water with the Board but he was hesitating.

"Are we done, you and me?"

He didn't answer, didn't change his pacing pattern, kept moving. *Submission, going down, down* . . . He didn't want me to go. Finally, he stopped, but he picked a spot on the wall to the right of me as he spoke. Indirect speakers get on my nerves, but this wasn't Vince's usual way. "Ed, you're the most popular guy on the staff. I'm not going to just dismiss you." He paused, still fixated on the wall. "What if you present a letter of resignation to me, I pass it along to the Board, and we leave it at that. You stay, keep your gig, but they think you're gone."

Holy Shit. I had hand! I was on the air in Los Angeles and that carried weight.

"If you can guarantee me a raise, I'll do it." Man, that was balls. Vince considered it, rubbing his lower lip.

Vince finally looked at me. "Another five bucks an hour. *Then* will you do it?"

"Done." I extended my hand, and he returned a loose, wet palm. So much for his trademark vice grip. "But you've got to keep your mouth shut to Lucky. What do you care if I talk with Tom St. John and end up at THE BIG Z? It's a much bigger radio station and only gives you more credibility."

He hung his head. "Not a fucking word," he replied.

On my way down the hall, I thought how implausible all this was. I could sleep with the students, hump one of their sisters, do it in front of the Board of Education, and get a raise.

I passed the kid's bathroom and she still was there, putting the finishing touches on her makeup. I knocked gently on the open door.

"Hey there, Audrey," I began softly. "We should talk." She was facing the mirror, applying her lip-gloss, then stopped abruptly and faced me down.

"Fuck you? Is that what you said to me? Fuck you? What do you want me to say after that?" she began, still steaming, her voice cracking. I kept my voice down, this time.

"You're right, completely right. That was wrong. I was impulsive, and as I vividly recall, so were you. But I'm really very sorry for saying that." I gave that all I had, hoping it was enough to prevent her from going to her sister with the whole tale. Blood is thicker than water, and Lori and I were pretty watery.

"I put my heart out there, Ed." She teared up, gave me a firm hug, and stalked out of the room. I don't like to reduce women to their body parts—but she had *parts*. I was beginning to appreciate the whole, too.

# CHAPTER 7

I WAS ON THE AIR SATURDAY NIGHT when my intern entered the studio after my break. He pulled out two of the music tape carts from the rack in the control room, then walked to the production studio, where he began rubbing the carts on the tape eraser. I was floored. He waltzed back in like nothing happened, reslotted the carts, and waltzed out.

I announced another record, closed the mic, and he reentered— this time taking more than 20 carts with him. Again, he headed to the other studio, erased them, and returned them to their slots. I asked him what he was up to, and he continued as if I wasn't there. I was losing track of the carts that he had erased. Sweat was dripping from my nose onto the board.

I plugged in the cart that for the next song on the list and had no clue whether it was a blank. It was musical Russian Roulette. I hit the button—and sure enough—nothing. I rushed to find another song, plugged it in, static. Minutes of dead air were accumulating, and the station sounded as if it had shut down.

The intern continued to erase everything in sight when the phone op barged in saying that disgruntled hordes of listeners were calling, screaming that they couldn't hear any songs. I was panicking, on the verge of tears. Nearly all of my carts had been wiped clean, and I had nothing to play. I opened my mouth to speak, and nothing came out. I took a deep breath to scream, and there was only silence. My eyes bulged as my mic fell to the ground. *Aaarrrrrrggggghhhhhh!!!!!!!*

I awoke with a start. Another bad radio dream. I was getting them regularly, this one worse than others, vivid, and in color—rare for me. I wiped my brow and stumbled to the bathroom to splash my face with cool water. I didn't dare go back to sleep until I could clear my head. I walked quietly past my roommates' bedrooms to our filthy living room and flipped on the TV to watch "Cal Worthington and his dog Spot" sell used cars at two in the morning.

Sound sleep found me again on the couch. My mouth hung open, drooling on a cushion until my pal, Steve, stumbled in half asleep, looking for Milano cookies. He dropped a plate, and I was shocked into consciousness as it smashed to the hard kitchen floor. I yelped, screaming in pain. I had opened my eyes too quickly, pulling loose, dry cells from my corneas. Tears were pouring from my eyes, my hands locked over my closed eyelids, my face now wet with the tears.

"Fucking Christ, Steve! Goddammit, that hurts." It felt like iron filings were poured into my eyeballs and being stirred by a blender. I'd had episodes before and an eye doctor diagnosed it—RCE, Recurrent Corneal Erosion he called it—nothing life-threatening, and it rarely bothered me, but I had to put this cream in my eyes before going to bed to prevent it.

After my nightmare, I should have reapplied. Now, this—this pain-in-the-ass roommate brings me back to hell. Jesus, what if this ever happened with a girl around! I finally got my eyes to settle to where I could open them without that sting, but they were still tender and sensitive to light.

"What *is* your problem?" asked Steve, like I was disturbing him.

"It's nothing, man. Nothing." The TV was playing an infomercial for those old Dean Martin roasts. And there was Danny Grossinger, dishing insults from the dais, screaming how good looking Dean was and asking why Governor Reagan hadn't lowered *his* taxes.

"What are you doing out here anyway?" Steve mumbled.

"Couldn't sleep. Had some crazy damn dream about an intern erasing all my music in the studio while I was on the air. Fucking radio dreams."

Steve was cleaning up the cookie crumbs and the slivers of china from the broken dish.

"Maybe you need a psychiatrist," he suggested.

I turned to face him, my eyes still watering. "I need a shrink because I have dreams?"

"I'll bet they mean something. Usually a problem buried deep in your subconscious that can only get out in a dream." He began eating the crumbs he'd picked up from the dirty floor. I couldn't look at the guy, much less listen to his bullshit.

"I don't believe that crap. A dream is a dream," I replied, yawning.

"Suit yourself," and he slunk back to his room.

I sat back, pensive, wondering if I was psychotic. I thumbed through my address book, found Tom's number, and was going for the phone—the clock read 4:45 a.m. Better wait a few hours.

I dozed off, with the cream in my eyes, and had an innocuous dream about surfing. I awoke fresh as could be expected after spending hours sleeping on a couch that hadn't seen a vacuum in weeks, then walked a few steps to the kitchen in the morning twilight, stepping on more Milano cookie crumbs. Damn Steve. I was always cleaning up his mess. I reached down to wipe Milano crumbs off the soles of my feet and scoured the floor with a wet hand towel.

I boiled some water and spooned in the instant coffee, took a long sip, and listened to the traffic building on Wilshire, just a block from the apartment. The caffeine hit the spot quickly, swabbing the decks of my jumbled brain—polluted with precision by my full-of-shit room-mate. In the light of day, I thought that these dreams were foreshad-owing; that it might be time to make a move. Fuck, who knows . . . it was still too early to approach Tom, so I dressed, grabbed my keys, and headed out for breakfast.

I arrived at the carport below, and thanks to the wonders of tan-dem parking, I was blocked in by Steve's car. I swore as I climbed back up the stairs.

"Steve," I yelled as I knocked on his door. "Get up and move your car. You're blocking me."

"Why?" he replied, as if I were asking him for money.

"Because, I'm hungry!"

"I have more Milanos in the cabinet." I got a whiff of the sweet scent of marijuana; he was lighting up. Bile was building fast.

"Steve," I screamed, "drop your joint and move your fucking car!"

He bolted from his room in a cloud of green, reeking as he shuf-fled through the debris on the coffee table.

"Here." He flipped his keys to me. "Move it yourself."

What a dick. I felt like biting his nose off. Just as I was getting some traction at work, my lifestyle was still entrenched in college horseshit, living with a stoned intellectual in a disgusting, cramped space, filled to the brim with sickly sweet smoke.

I spent the morning looking for a new place, a new life. As I drove off, I forgot about food, took the Santa Monica Freeway to the beach to begin the search.

What I found was glorious. There were three places to choose from: a small single apartment about a block from the ocean, another smaller, brand-new one, and a double, where the present tenant needed a roommate. And no tandem parking with any of them. I put in applications for all three, with deposits, and found a diner where I devoured five large pancakes, celebrating my bold move.

# CHAPTER 8

I N THE MIDST OF THE CHAOS, I blew off calling Tom; things were relatively quiet again and my confidence level was rising. I had trepida-
tions about calling Lori, though. There was no doubting that her sister
had spoken with her about our fling thing. And I still had the bump
on the back of my head from that push against the wall poster by a
giraffe with huge breasts. I wasn't clear how to handle it; I wasn't even
sure I wanted to handle it. Lori and I were becoming a memory, and
I was busy making a move of my own. I let the weekend pass without
doing a thing.

Monday arrived, and the Workshop was scheduled to open in the
new building, large enough for double the students we had crammed
into the house. I always felt that we were bursting at the seams there,
but I loved our deceptively quiet setting, punctuated by a truck blast
every hour or two. The house was on the way to the new building, and
I wanted to check on any little items that may have been left behind by
the movers on Saturday.

I drove over early in the morning and pulled into the side driveway where I could access the service entrance. The lights were off, and
it was dead quiet. No one there. It was disturbing to walk in and find

such silence in a normally vibrant setting. A moment after opening the door, I was struck by what I saw. The boxes were stacked high, neat as a pin—no moving company had come. I went to switch on the lights—and zip. No electricity. I shrugged and thought that I'd messed up, got the date wrong. They'd be there later on, I thought.

I headed to the kid's room, where I'd made such a scene with Audrey, and scoured around for anything loose I might have left in there, when I heard a hammering on the front door. Then the sound of metal on metal, a clamping noise followed by a click. I walked to the door to see what was up, turned the handle, and pushed, but it only opened a crack—not enough for me to see what was blocking my exit.

I felt panicked and went for the back door, which opened onto a small yard. I jumped the locked metal fence along the side of the house opposite the driveway, trampled through the overgrown weeds in the narrow side yard, and climbed a wooden fence leading to the front of the house. From the top of the fence, I leaped to a concrete landing, where my eyes caught a bright reflection of the morning sun off of the front door. There was a large metal door lock, preventing entry to the house from the front, like one of those clamps that real estate agents use to give private access to homes for sale. Above it was a note, perfectly centered on the door and held there by a giant nail, as if it was a roof shingle. Clear as day, it read: *Closed By The Board Of Education.*

"*They know about me.*" I read on, and it became clear to me— Vince was running a business out of a private family residence, with no authorization from the state of California. My bedroom adventure had been a sideshow for the Board rep while he contemplated how the place might look with a giant padlock on the door.

I walked to the car with my knees locked and my jaw hanging open. I sat in my car, drooling, staring straight at the blazing sun. Ten minutes passed and I finally cranked the ignition and drove to the new building in silence; I couldn't bear to hear even the radio.

When I got there, I peered into the window next to the locked door and found empty space. Everything, the new build-outs, the new carpets, even the long construction tables that had the architectural plans sprawled out before me just days ago, had been moved out, likely overnight. I shook my head, disbelieving during the long drive home.

I checked my messages upon arriving. Only one.

It was Lucky. "Ed, I know there's a union meeting again today. I urge you to vote no and to consider the consequences of what the union is asking."

Well, fuck me. No one said shit about a union vote. Christ, I had three—*three*—deposits on apartments at the beach—with one of my jobs in the hands of the authorities and another apparently in control of union thugs.

I called Vince to get answers to both of my questions. No answer. I collapsed on a chair, in fear of losing all of my income in one day. Thank God, Steve wasn't there to talk his bullshit to me. The phone rang. It was Tom. He had heard of the union vote during a staff meeting at THE BIG Z, and told me that the air-staff at KUTE was voting to strike.

"Get me a resume and a tape of your work today," he said. "I'll see what I can do."

I went to my room—and sure enough—I couldn't find my damn airchecks. I *always* had copies lying around. And the only other people who had copies were Vince and Lucky. Fucking perfect. I went to the junk drawer in my bedroom and scrounged about, deep inside, cutting a finger on the edge of a metal hinge. And then, in the far corner of the drawer, I spotted one, pulled it out, bandaged my finger, and packed the tape in an envelope. My last tape. I dropped it off at the post office, drove back to the beach, lit an old joint from the glove box, found a bluff overlooking the Pacific Ocean, and stared at glistening waves for the rest of the morning.

# CHAPTER 9

THAT AFTERNOON, I HAD THREE NEW messages waiting for me. I'd been approved as a tenant for all three apartment openings. While I wondered how I could afford a move, I turned on the television, flipped to the news, and moved closer to the screen—as if that could improve my vision of the scene unfolding before me.

The picket line of KUTE DJs was marching in a circle in front of the studio. There were seven of them sporting hand-painted signs, yelling at the cameras, "Health benefits for talent! We're not monkeys!"

Management often claimed that a monkey could do our job, and that wasn't far from the truth. We pushed buttons and said things like, "Here's *Physical,* with Olivia Newton-John!" And we were paid full-time wages for four-hour shifts. If a monkey was a lazy, egomaniacal dope who could get high, get blow jobs, read a book, finish a crossword puzzle, and still have plenty of time to complain about how tiring it was to sit in a studio for four hours listening to the same songs over and over again, then yeah, we were monkeys.

I tried Vince again, no one there. And I didn't see him on the line during the news. I thought to call Lori, but I realized consolation was out of the question: *"Sorry you went out of your way to get Audrey*

*a job with a man being investigated by the state while his associate—
me—tried to bang her in a kid's bedroom. Are you free Saturday?"* She
was gone, for sure.

I spent the evening telling my roommates how great things were
and how much I loved living with them. They thought I'd lost my mind.

Tom received the package the next day. "Your tape sounds great,
and I want to get this to the Big Girl now." I couldn't help but giggle at
a Big Girl at the BIG Z.

"Who the hell is that?"

"She's THE BIG Z station manager, calls all the shots. Pretty sure
there's a slot open and you'd be great for it. Just wanted to tell you that
you're ready and to expect a letter."

"Yeah, but when? You know I'm essentially out of a job, and . . ."

"Ed, you got THE BIG Z sound, my friend. We'll throw down a
pint together at the pub soon." My spirits rose slowly, like the bubbles
in Tom's Guinness.

# CHAPTER 10

IN 1983, THE BIG Z FM was the biggest radio station in Los Angeles. The highest ratings, the greatest visibility, the hippest thing since Studio 54—a phenomenon in its time. Throughout the '70s, it was a mediocre dance station with lousy ratings but had climbed to the top in short order during the early '80s. And for years, it stayed there, untouched by the competition. It was now the most listened to station in North America, and they were going to hire *me*.

THE BIG Z management, I was told, took extraordinary measures before making any changes in the staff. Their jocks were all radio veterans. Tom had been at the mic since the '60s, Ron Dixey, Z's famed morning man, had been doing radio programs since his college days in South Carolina, and on staff at Z, Gary Owens, one of the greatest to ever sit in front of a microphone. There wasn't a DJ I knew who wasn't influenced by Ron and Gary.

As Tom had forecast, I received a letter only a day after our conversation. It was addressed to me from the general manager of THE BIG Z, Lindi Anthony, "the Big Girl." I tore it open, and my tape fell out of the envelope. It had finger smears all over from it, presumably from everyone evaluating it. The letter said I was in consideration for a prime weekend position, and that we should meet to discuss options. I immediately thought of the Publishers Clearing House letters that everyone receives saying, *"You Won!"* Of course, those were come ons, teases—this was fucking real! I danced through the apartment like Travolta, shimmying from one room to the other, throwing my arms in the air, screaming.

I called Lindi, who couldn't have been more gracious, and she asked to see me the next day. I didn't sleep all night.

The next morning, I showered and daydreamed of my first airshift there. A limo would deliver me to the studio every weekend. I'd have best headphones, the funniest jokes, thousands of fans, giant paychecks, wall-to-wall women. I dropped the soap, bent to grab it, and banged my head on the low-slung showerhead. *"I gotta calm down."*

I hit the road for Hollywood, where so many of LA's great stations had made broadcasting history—KNX, where Bob Crane did a morning show for years, KMPC and KFWB, where Gary imprinted his name as the supreme wordsmith of radio. I developed a nervous twitch in my right eye as I was escorted into her office, an enormous affair that took me aback: A huge mahogany art-deco desk was at the center, and modern art—Kandinsky I thought—housed in metallic frames, hung on each of the four walls. To the left was a pop-out bar with fresh ice in the bucket. No Caesar's bust. No pants rack. No dusty records, but there *was* a cassette player.

I sat alone, sweating for about a minute in the cushy, black-leather, straight-back chair, placed off-center but facing her chair across the desk. The program director arrived first, grabbed my hand like a man running for office, and told me how excited they were to have me there. I smiled, and he smiled back. Then, a nervous pause. This guy wasn't much for chit-chat.

The Big Girl entered, and she was big indeed; a good 250 in her birthday suit, although pretty in a handsome sort of way—her cheeks sinking into middle age, glowing with freshly applied face oil, and a thin-lipped, ear-to-ear smile sketched on her face as if it could vanish with a snap. She dressed big, too. Her square-shouldered, pale-blue Escada business suit was accented with a silk Hermes scarf—swirl after swirl of ornate, circular patterns. I was getting hypnotized. And she carried a brown Chanel bag around like Queen Elizabeth. Her black hair was coiffed up high with perm-curls, a feeble stab at a style more fitting for girls 20 years younger. The whole package lent her an air of motherly authority, yet friendly and approachable—I could see how she got that gig when ladies didn't often crack that ceiling. My back straightened as she took a firm grip on my right hand. I could smell the Chanel Number 5.

"Thank you, Ed, for choosing to work at THE BIG Z." That stopped my eye twitch. I took a seat and responded quickly,

"Hey, it's good to choose." Now, that's hardly the funniest thing ever said, but I was George Carlin for the laughs it got. They doubled over. I was funny before I even stepped into the room, thanks to that audition tape. I was "pre-funny."

I reflected for a moment on her comment; she had the professionalism to thank *me* for contacting her. She must receive 200 to 300 tapes for every available on-air position. Astounding.

"What do you think of San Diego, Ed?"

My chin jammed into my neck and my scalped tightened, pulling my hairline forward. It must be what hyenas look like when threatened by wild boar. "Uh, it's just lovely. Why do you ask?"

"Well," she said, her head turning away from me, the smile diminishing, "we have a full-time spot open at our San Diego station and you'd be perfect for it. We'd like to have you part of our family, and this would be very high profile for you, Ed. Full time. Afternoons."

I was shocked. Pissed really. Who would be my audience, sailors and Orcas? I was used to smog, dammit, and an oily, overly coiffed, glass-ceiling-busting-bitch wasn't going to take that away from me. This was bait and switch!

"That's, um, not what I'm here for. I live here. In Los Angeles. That's where I want to stay. This is where I want to work. I hope we haven't had a misunderstanding." And with that, my legs straightened and I pushed myself from the chair to a standing position; my brain had nothing to do with it. My body was on its own. I felt my colon liquefying. I was ready to turn and leave, but then, without changing her expression, she said,

"Ed, are you ready to play ball with us?"

"Where?"

"Here, young man. Right here. Two days a week and fill-in. When can you start?"

"Would it be too forward of me to say, *Now*!?"

They laughed 'til they cried, motioned me out of the office, and showed me the premises. Through that whole exchange, the program director was silent. This lady ran the show. My brain was coming back online, followed later by my colon. I didn't feel my feet as I walked the halls and studios of THE BIG Z-FM. I never heard another word about fucking San Diego.

THE BIG Z WAS PERCHED ON the 19th Floor in the Motown building at Sunset and Vine, downtown Hollywood, one floor from the penthouse, and the studio overlooked Los Angeles to the south. Lindi and Silent PD introduced me to the midday guy, Pat. Crazy nice. The welcome mat was out.

I looked to the right of the control board to the window. It was a clear day, with a view past Catalina Island—gave me the feeling that the whole world was listening. Below was a straight-on southbound shot of Vine Street, and if you were myopic, it was Anytown, USA. I could see the Z-28 Camaros and the Jeeps that so many kids were driving then, the spiked hair, the pastel t-shirts tucked under the narrow-lapel jackets with the sleeves drawn up. Everyone thought they were on *Miami Vice*. A group of pedestrians making their way to the food court on Vine had these boom boxes held up to their ears, 30-pound earphones. I wondered if they were listening to Z at that moment.

My only disappointment was the studio itself. It was dirtier and more ancient than the Worm's in Corona. They hadn't updated the equipment since the '60s: old dirty knobs, instead of the sliding "pots" that adjusted the volume of the records and the mic, and music carts with finger smudges all over the most popular songs. Having worked in trash heaps that called themselves radio stations, I was OK with it, but it raised an eyebrow. However, there was one heady feature that caught my eye: groupies. At the left of the DJ's chair, there was an area no bigger than a few feet square, where three very young ladies were lounging about, giggling at anything he said. I was in awe. This was prime time, and I would have to live up to it.

They handed me the union contract, and promised me that their deal with AFTRA was unique from other stations in LA; it was of no concern that KUTE was on strike. The Z guys weren't striking and had no plans to. On my way out, she handed me my schedule, handshakes all around, and I left the studio with a huge load off my shoulders and gold dust sprinkled on my ass. I was the luckiest little shithead on the planet Earth. I called Tom as soon as I could.

"It's done. I'm in. What do I have to do to thank you?"

"Celebrate. Let's get drunk." So I joined him for an evening of alcoholic debauchery that landed me back home at 3 a.m. Slept like a baby.

Noon rolled around before I awoke. I stumbled into the kitchen for a glass of OJ and called Lucky. He was furious.

"*Quoi*?!" which is French for the serious form of "*what the fuck*?!"

"I've taken a position at THE BIG Z, and I want to thank you for everything you've done for me. You've taught me so much and . . ."

"I had plans for you, young man. Plans," he interrupted. "I saw you as the next morning man here. Mornings in LA. Isn't that what you wanted?"

I sighed at the thought of a full-time morning gig with him by my side. "Luck, I don't have to tell you, but the DJ's are on strike and you have scabs on the air. The janitor is doing my shift. I had a chance to leave, so I left. I had hoped that you'd send me off with a flourish, your best wishes."

All I heard was silence. His job was on the line with this strike, and he was no spring chicken in a business of spring chickens. The silence grew. "Well, then, I wish you the best, Lucky." I said unconvincingly.

"Au revoir, Ed. I'll be listening." His voice trailed off to a whisper, and I felt that I had betrayed him. The station changed format to Easy Listening Muzak only months after I left. Everyone was let go, from the jocks to the janitors. Straddling two ships that were sinking, I had jumped to a third, with treasure in the hold, and never looked back.

# CHAPTER 11

WELCOME TO THE BIG TIME! THERE was a large pizza stain—a common theme in my life—on the counter next to the control board and dog-eared memos stuck with safety pins to a bulletin board to my left. A fine mist of dust had settled on the eons-old carpet. And surrounding the board, rack after rack of scruffy music carts. Nothing was clean, but everything was perfect.

I was on air for all of 15 minutes when I noticed the phones light up. Two dozen callers knew me by name already, only a slice of the hundreds of thousands listening in pickup trucks, malls, boats, offices, Disneyland. They called from Beverly Hills, Irwindale, Compton, Watts, Studio City, Laguna Beach, Hollywood. They wanted to meet me, to dedicate a song to their dog, to say "hi" to their sister, to hear Michael Jackson's *Thriller*, to plug their company, to have me pay their rent. And, of course, I got a call from my cousin Julie, who acted as if I'd landed on the moon. "I'm *sooooooo* happy for you! I can't believe it's you. Mr. Mann, THE BIG Z FM. It's Mr. Mann, THE BIG Z FM." She said it over and over like a savant.

Each time I broke the mic for a break, the room fell silent, and 30 seconds before the end of a song, a bright-yellow light flashed above me, a warning to slow down, to listen, to concentrate. You're alone with millions of people. There was a weight to the place, an energy that flew about as the jingles screamed, "BIG Z FM!" It was lightening in a bottle floating along a river of air into half of all car radios, home stereos, walkmans, shoe stores, hotel rooms, boom boxes, and even inside the headphones of a few 10-year olds, wishing to do what I was doing right then. My ass was parked at the summit of my own dream.

I finished my shift at 10 on Saturday morning and got a slap on the back from the DJ following me, who happened to be one of my idols, Big Sam. Everyone was BIG here.

"Good show, Ed. You got it goin' on, man!" My eyes widened and I shook his hand like I'd won a thousand dollars. Sam weighed more than 300 pounds and almost knocked me over with his blessings. I hung for a few minutes to watch him work with the panache of a skilled craftsman. He had *the* most polished technique; each word rolled off his tongue like a greased toboggan sliding down a freshly combed ski slope, each sentence delivered with a clever economy of words so the message was both heard, and completely understood by the largest number of listeners.

And he was prepared—notes about the artists to the left, station liners to the front, comedic lines to the right. This was no slapdash, throw it out there radio program; Sam showed me, in one break of the mic, how to cement the intimate correspondence he developed with his listeners. I'd heard it before—the funny lines, the absurd take on events of the day that I immediately related to. But now, I was seeing it unfold live and in creative, hilarious layers—like the news he reported about finding a saber tooth at the La Brea tar pits and popping right into a live commercial for Flying Tigers Airways. Or when he intro'ed Prince's *When Doves Fly*, saying "It's so wonderful, unless you're a statue, looking up." My favorite was when he rapped about the song, *It's a Groove Thing*, adding "Look! I've got one in the glove box!" Then segueing into the traffic report without losing a beat. He was the cleverest broadcaster I knew, and I had a lot to learn.

I signed a rental agreement at the beach for the single; I was finished with roommates, and making enough money at THE BIG Z to afford the luxury. The day after my first BIG Z shift, I began sorting through my stuff and began to pack. Perhaps symbolically, I threw away everything connected to my old, bullshit lifestyle: bong pipes, a hash pipe, another hash pipe, hash, Jack Kerouac novels, ratty old t-shirts, a decaying metallic peace sign, Vince's curriculum binder. It was satisfying to carry it all out to the giant green trash bin by the carport, dust flying with each heave. Steve stood by, lording over me as if I was tossing out his father's remains.

I went to shake his hand as I left, and he gave me a quick hug.

"I'll be listening. Let's get together soon," he said, with no conviction.

"You got it," I promised with even less conviction. I poured myself into my Datsun B-210 and headed to the beach, to live. By myself. On the way, an old quote I once read from John D. Rockefeller popped into my head: *"A friendship founded on business is better than a business founded on friendship."* My business friendships had landed in me in a gallon of bong water and a couple of horny siblings. Perhaps new friends could take me somewhere more profitable. Or maybe old Rockefeller was full of shit.

Immediately, my lifestyle changed for the better. After dragging multiple loads of my crap from the U-Haul into the apartment, I took a long look out the window. It wasn't much, but it was there: a view of the Pacific Ocean. A slice of heaven, but only a thin sliver of water between two large condominium towers built in front of the apartment. They rose too high to see much, but I could see it between them. And it was the most refreshing feeling I had in years.

With each deep breath I could feel the electrolytes in the moist, smog-free sea air wash away the years of green tar collected in my lungs after a decade of smoking weed. I promised myself no more bong hits, no more green-haze-filled rooms, no half-used joints to fire up. That had to end. This was a new life. My dreams were coming true, and I had to eliminate anything that might slow me down. Thrusting my fist into the air in celebration, and then into the fridge, I reached for a beer. I wasn't ready to give up everything.

Only two weeks into the job, and I was settling in nicely. I dug the music, phone calls were lighting up, and I felt momentum building. The phone was my barometer; if I did a funny bit or said something they dug, I got a pat on the back from the listeners. It was akin to getting laughs at a comedy club, except later.

I regularly announced the phone number to the Z listeners and was blown away each time the little square lights burned, with callers struggling to reach me, sometimes waiting an hour or more. I got a sense of approval from them and found that many desired more from me than humor or music. Before phone sex was in vogue, I was getting sexual cues from any caller who cared to get a rise out of me. THE BIG Z had a deep effect on the audience. The station touched people in their glands. It wasn't long before I could tell whether they were attractive, if they were blonde, if they were blind, if they had excess flab slapped on their hips ...

I was too new to have gathered the large harems of groupies I saw drooling around other jocks at the station, but a few made the trek to Hollywood, and damn close to 99 percent of the time, I was correct in my assumptions about their game. One girl, Amy from down in Orange County, entered the control room with a huge white placard draped on her. All it said was, "I love Ed!" She was a pretty blonde, and sported enormous tits that kept the placard sticking out at a 45-degree angle from her chest. I had pegged her right down to the wide grin that exposed every molar in her mouth. She was man-sweaty with nervousness as she watched me do my thing on the air while trying desperately to show me that she was Jewish.

"Oh, Ed, you're such a *meshuganah*!" she'd exclaim after most anything I said. "Oh, that David Bowie is such a putz, I could *plotz*." I figured the body about right, but the eager-beaver sweaty-yenta routine? I hustled her out with a peck on the cheek as she bounced away—her placard bouncing ahead of her.

About two months on the job, a phone line lit up in the studio—and stayed lit. I let it blink for 15 minutes, then finally picked up.

"THE BIG Z . . . oh, it's the Playboy mansion and you're all listening to the show in the Grotto tonight? Well, isn't that intriguing? . . . what does 'intriguing' mean? Doesn't matter . . . anyway, what can I do for you ladies? . . . Miss December wants to WHAT me??! Put her on . . .

"Hi . . . yes, it's me."

"Is this you? Miss December? . . . Yeah, I can play that song. And if you don't like it, how can I call you to find out what you'd really like?"

Then she gave me her phone number.

I thought it might be bullshit, but my new instincts kicked in. I tried calling, and it actually fucking worked. It was her.

She agreed to meet me at the station in the light of day and was right on time, dressed down in gray sweats, tennis shoes, and no makeup—undoubtedly at her best in the Grotto at 1 a.m., not a fluorescent-lit office building at 11. I blanched slightly at the sight of her with no mascara or lipstick—striking nevertheless—but when she stood to greet me, her figure was unmistakable and spectacular: she was average height, quite muscular, and underneath her grey sweater top swayed a pair of phenomenal 40 DD's. She couldn't hide those behind armor. I led her to the production studio, where

I teased her ego by having her record a set of silly liners to use later on my show:

"Hi, this is Miss December, and Ed is an idiot. It's torture listening to him, but at least he plays great music." Absurd self-deprecation—it was becoming my thing. She enjoyed these teasing plays, and I suggested we get a bite to eat.

Having read her Playboy Playmate profile, I knew that she liked Thai, and there was a great place only two blocks away off of Sunset. We found a table, and she ordered like she had written the menu.

"What made you and your girlfriends call me the other night?" I asked, looking for a stroke.

"We had nothing else to do, and we were really high." She took a sip of her Thai iced tea. I was disappointed she didn't call for a more personal reason.

"What made you think about modeling for Playboy?"

"Jesus, look at these!" She pulled her shoulders back and pointed to her breasts, taking up all the air between us. Enormous, and juxtaposed against her slight waist and lean arms, it was too much. I was getting aroused.

"Yes," I gulped. "I can see why. Stupid question."

She gazed at me, tilting her head to the side slightly as if she wanted me to kiss her, then went for her fork to shove more Pad Thai noodles into her mouth. She peeked at me whenever I looked away, a very appealing schoolgirl shyness.

"Do people recognize you often?" I asked.

"Sometimes. Do they recognize you?"

"How could anyone recognize a voice?"

"I could spot yours a mile away. No one has heard you in a market or on the phone and thought it was you, the DJ from THE BIG Z?"

"Nope but I always thought it might be cool, to be recognized in public for what you do."

"And what do you think I'd be known for?" She took another long, thick noodle and attempted to suck it down her throat seductively, but the noodle slapped her cheek, staining it with peanut sauce. We both laughed out loud.

The meal ended, and I walked her to her car.

"I hope to see you again," I said softly. "Can we hook up for another meal?" She offered her hand.

"I'll call you, Ed. Thank you for reading my profile, you sly dog."

I blushed immediately. Since her appearance in the magazine, every date must have taken her for Thai. I waved as she drove off and no longer wondered how members of the semi-famous crowd hooked up. The "I'll call you" routine was familiar, and I didn't suspect she'd phone me, but only two days passed when my shiny new phone rang in my shiny new apartment. It was Miss December.

"Are you free Saturday?" she asked.

"I work weekends, you know. Every Saturday night is out. Wait, hold on." I ran to the bedroom to grab my schedule. "Let's see, I've got Tuesday or Thursday. How does that work?"

"Where do you live?"

"Manhattan Beach."

"Mind if I drive out on Tuesday."

"Tomorrow, Tuesday?" I asked.

"Too quick?"

"No!" I practically shouted at her. "That's fine." I gave her my address and spent the evening floating about the room. A playmate was driving to pick *me* up. Me. A man being picked up by a woman. And not just any woman. A clever, stacked, funny, peanut-sauce slurping, self-deprecating, sexed up Playboy model. I could barely sleep.

While driving around the next day, I turned on the station to hear: "That was Sting, *King of Pain*, and I don't know what it felt like for Ed the other day, but it certainly wasn't painful. Mr. Ed and Miss December, yes—*that* Miss December—hooked up for a special lunch. I think we can expect dinner and dancing later this week, is that right, Mr. Ed?"

Tom had decided it would be *sooooo* clever to broadcast my antics to the greater LA metropolitan area. He played a sound effect from the old Mr. Ed talking-horse TV show, "Hello, I'm Mr. Ed," followed by a sample of Miss December saying, "Ed is an idiot. It's torture listening to him, but at least he plays great music."

I sulked in the bucket seat of the car, unable to move my mouth. *"Fucking fine! What if she heard that?"*

Tuesday night arrived none too soon. I couldn't remember anticipating an evening more eagerly. I cleaned up every corner of the apartment, dusted every counter, Windexed every piece of glass. It was cloudy that evening, and I thought I'd paint in the ocean on the window to ensure the view, but quickly trashed that idea. I checked the music on the stereo, the wine in the liquor cabinet, the ice in the freezer. Everything was accounted for. We were two stars colliding and the setting had to be perfect. I called the restaurant to double check the reservation, too.

A knock on the door came as scheduled. I opened it after pausing a few seconds by the door handle, calculated casual. I flung the door open and was blown back by a Venus in a tight t-shirt that enhanced every curve, a pair of loose-fitting Levi's, and brown pumps that gave her a little added height, which I preferred. She was a bodacious hourglass.

"Please, come in," and I made a wide, sweeping, nervous gesture with my left arm, welcoming her in like Igor in *Young Frankenstein*. My eyes were popping out of their sockets, and I strained to keep them north of her breasts. She offered a half-smile and planted herself daintily on the new couch.

"What can I get you?" I rubbed my hands together as if I was cold. My behavior, which I regarded from an out-of-body state from above, was forced, unnatural. When intimidated in the least by a woman,

I gave myself scathing reviews, recounting everything I said and thought one moment after I said and thought it, like an instant-replay recorder lodged in my brain. I was distracted by my own mannerisms, speech patterns, clumsy gesticulations.

*"Oh, Christ, what a stupid thing to say. I'd better look directly in her eyes or she'll think I'm disinterested. Wait, I'm looking too long. She'll think I'm a letch. But I AM a letch! Now she knows. Shit, is that sweat forming above my lip? What about under my arms?! I'd better grab the napkin under my drink. Oh fuck! I almost spilled the drink. I'm an idiot. It's only a matter of time before she sees that."*

"A beer, if you got one."

I fetched a Heineken, opened it at the counter, and poured it into my bachelor-grade glassware.

She swigged a good third of it down and exhaled big, then looked me in the eye and said, "You gonna sit down or do I have to pull you down?" So I obeyed.

She nuzzled against me like a cat, and I put my warm hand on her left thigh, feeling her leg muscle pulse in a reaction to my touch. And I was pulsing plenty.

"I smell tuna for dinner!"

"Excuse me?" she replied, rearing her head back a couple of inches.

*"I'm such a fucking oaf."* "No, no, I made a reservation at a place up from the beach. One of the best fish houses in the South Bay."

She seemed a little embarrassed by her own overreaction to my idiocy. "I'm betting that I have enough to eat here, right now," she said with a salacious smile.

I smiled awkwardly at her direct manner, but felt my nerves relax, my eyes scanning every inch of her, taking in every nuance as if she were a finely crafted statue. She snuggled even closer, wrapping her arm around my waist, then turned me around to face her—a bold move that I did not resist in the least—and she kissed me. Our mouths opened wide like sharks, teeth clanging, tongues lashing, tasting each other.

We groped on the coach for at least five minutes, wrapped tight, feeling every corner of our bodies. My hands now had a confidence all their own, moving down from her shoulders to her breasts, undoubtedly real: soft yet firm with her youth. She was visibly aroused through her tight white cotton sleeveless shirt. And of course, I kept reviewing my skills silently as we progressed, looking for fault, trying to teach myself something. I had to be ready when I quizzed myself later.

Without warning, she said, "Thanks for a great evening."

My penis and I were incredulous. She stood and grabbed her purse.

"You're leaving? You drove out here for a kiss?" I asked, my voice going up an octave.

She stood over me, her boobs swaying a mere two inches from the top of my head. "*Tuna? I said tuna?*"

"You're wonderful, Ed. Perhaps we can do this again." She extended her hand, and I shook it limply as she headed for the door.

I was speechless and helpless as I watched her depart. She turned to look back, her eyes sweeping the room in a nostalgic gaze. It was the oddest look, and the most bizarre behavior I'd ever witnessed. I bolted from the couch and grabbed her arm.

"Where the hell are you going?" I demanded, turning her toward me, sharply. She looked down at my hand, and I eased my grip.

"I wasn't sure if this was right. You seemed distracted."

"*Oh CRAP!*" She read my mind while I was reviewing my own behavior.

"No, it's right. It's perfect. I guess I was, you know, shy about this."

"You? A BIG Z DJ. Shy?"

My confidence was perking up. "Well, yes, a bit. Please don't leave. We haven't had dinner, or even finished our drinks, or . . ."

With no warning, she grabbed my crotch and put a lip lock on me hard enough to make me lose my balance. We both tumbled to the floor and plowed into each other for more than two hours—the sweet rewards of honesty.

We lay there for another hour or so, letting the sweat dry. As I began to doze off on the floor, she picked up her purse and scooted out the door. I didn't jump up to stop her or even mumble a word of objection. She left, and I thought to myself how wonderful it all was, but how lonely I now felt.

Of course, I'd informed everyone at THE BIG Z of my plans for the evening; Tom had broadcast it to the city of Los Angeles on the highest-rated radio station in town. I didn't relish having every friend and relative of mine in Los Angeles privy to my exploits, but I had a 6000-watt mouthpiece on the FM dial, so I went on the air the day after the date and improvised a rebuttal.

"Many of you in the vast BIG Z audience must know of my alleged exploits with one Miss December from Playboy magazine. Other jocks have been blabbing on the air over the last few days. Well, I might say that we had our date, and she was larger than life. I'd love to kiss and tell, but that may be just too titillating for your young, impressionable ears to absorb in one fell swoop. So, I'm going to tell you this. She came to my place, and she left my place. You won't see any paparazzi shots of us, because we never left my place. My apologies to Frank's Fish House for skipping out on our reservation; we stayed home and ate each other. Now, here's *Frankie Goes to Hollywood* on THE BIG Z."

I closed the mic and sat back, watching the phones light up like a Christmas tree and thinking to myself, *"She's gone for good after that."*

# CHAPTER 12

"I JUST DON'T KNOW. THIS HAPPENS EVERY time. I feel like I can control these situations, you know. I'm getting approached by boatloads of chicks. As quickly as one sails away, another arrives, and I'm spending my life waiting for the right one."

"You're falling into a pattern," declared Tom. We were at Reuben's, powering down Jack and Lite Beers the day after my sexual adventure, and though he had stripped me naked in front of THE BIG Z listeners, I had just done the same to her. Not a genius move. I felt he might lend a helpful ear.

He threw his head back, gulped down a double shot of whisky, and let out his patented pinched exhale. I just sipped away at mine like it was cough syrup.

"Have you ever thought about getting more serious with one of them? Moving things along?" Tom asked.

That was an interesting concept, but beyond my experience. I hadn't even had a girlfriend in college. Women were making all the moves and I dictated no boundaries. No limitations. Everyone was welcome, and consequently, free to leave. And then I sealed the deal by blabbing about it on the air.

"Isn't your perspective a little slanted?" I asked. "You're married."

"How do think I got married? Waiting for her to ask me? Ladies need to be chased, even if they're chasing you. The big question is what do *you* want."

I licked my lips. "Well, maybe I like to be chased," I chimed.

He shrugged and looked right in my eyes.

"Trust me, Ed. You don't know what you want," and changed the subject. "You know what? You're sounding great on the air. Really good. Maybe one day, you and I do a show together. Not sure what, exactly. Something that can make us more dough, something on the side."

And on that inebriated note, we ended the evening with hugs and back slaps. Tom had a way of getting to the heart of the matter, cutting through the flotsam and jetsam, bruising the ego, but then applying salve, giving succor. I appreciated the approach and the drunken compliment, but this paperweight of radio semi-fame was getting a little heavy, and I was aimless.

On the way home, I cranked on the station and heard another one of our BIG Z jocks bragging about writhing in the mud with a girl at the Tropicana, the big lap-dance bar, where hot oil and mud wrestling were staples for losers who couldn't get dates with Playboy playmates or actresses. I suddenly felt lucky.

Once home, I ran to the kitchen, pulled out a notepad and listed every girl who had approached me, come on to me, teased me, slept with me. I tapped each name with the back end of my pen, remembering something odd and disturbing about each one with each tap. Not *one* would I go after again, consider for a partner, or attempt to make a life with. I was awestruck by my results. Even Lori, my sexy, green-eyed apprentice, had these insane sisters who enlisted in convents or chased each other's dates.

I turned to a blank page, and now tried to think of any women who had shown only cursory interest in me. I sat there, scratching my head, sweating over the paper like it was an SAT test. What kind of egomaniac *was* I? I couldn't think of one woman who didn't want me? I *am* an asshole. I threw my pen down, hard, and stomped to the bathroom.

There he was in the mirror. The face of the monster. I shook my head and washed that face hoping to wipe away the idiocy. At that moment, one name came to me—the stunning beauty I didn't even know. She was comfortable in her skin, and she happily walked away from me. Well, why wouldn't she . . . I was wasted. Yes. It was Alex Grossinger. Her name rang in my head like a bell. But really? I only saw her exiting a grocery store door. I spoke with her for one fucking moment, stoned out of my mind, looking for beer. But she had accurately guessed what dope I was smoking. *And* she dug my voice. Now that's perceptive, but who knew what she was thinking? She was buying tampons.

ONE NIGHT ON THE AIR, A fellow buzzed me at the studio door, a new DJ at THE BIG Z hired to do a part-time shift. He barreled toward me like a linebacker, point A to point B in full stride, practically goose-stepping with his arm extended.

"Hey, Ed. I'm Stu!" he announced in clipped, brash, earsplitting volume. "You Jewish? Me, too. Do you like to ski? I love it. How about we get together and do a day on the slopes? Two skiing *meshugenahs*." He was loud, presumptuous, abrasive, and yet I took a liking to him.

"Yeah," I responded gingerly. "Let's figure that out."

He turned before I could finish, waving his production log behind him, and bolted into an adjacent studio. And then it came to me. I knew that voice. That name. I began giggling. Stu Rossi. He'd hosted a radio show at another station in town and I recalled it right then. It was ludicrous. The program was called, "Pillow Talk Time," where he played love songs and announced dedications to lovers over the air.

The key was his delivery. Instead of toning down his sweet rap for the ballads, he amped it up, sounding like an electric Stratocaster regardless of what he was saying, each word getting progressively louder:

**"HERE'S YOUR LOVE SONG DEDICATION, ALICE. *ENDLESS LOVE*, BY LIONEL RITCHIE. ALICE SAYS, I LOVE YOU, BILL!!!"**

It was the most insane program I ever heard, and I laughed out loud every time I heard him.

So, Z hired Stu and apparently felt his style of announcing songs at full scream was perfect. We were a pretty loud group of DJs, and he'd fit in fine.

Only one month into the job, The Big Girl and Silent PD asked Stu and me to appear at venues across the city at "Weekend Warmups" every other Thursday. These events were rock concerts, but minus actual musicians; thousands of fans drove from miles around to see us. Just us. We had no act. We weren't comics. We only had to show up and throw out BIG Z t-shirts. We luxuriated in the elixir of fame and were agape at our fans' reaction. We were shallow shits.

For these appearances, we were each given black-satin jackets with our names stenciled next to THE BIG Z logo. We resembled security guys, minus muscles, as we exited our limo, filing past the hundreds in line waiting to see us inside. The actual security guys parted the crowd and paved the way for us to get to our cordoned-off section of the club.

My first appearance was at Acupulcos in West Covina, a suburb of Los Angeles, and inside, insanity ruled. The crowd was stacked on bleachers five deep and bracketed by long, fully stocked tables arranged for eating and drinking, and we did both in copious amounts. I marveled at the comparative loneliness of hosting the radio show, versus appearing at these wild "Warmups." Even the seasoned veterans among us were stunned by the crowd reaction.

Evidently this one was larger and more electric than anything they could compare it with in their careers.

Our job was to entertain in the most general of ways: we tossed out t-shirts and signed autographs, we danced with the girls, we shook hands like politicians. When it was my turn to the mic, I was treated like I'd won an Academy Award. I made a few marginally witty comments, then a girl dragged me from my beer for a chance to boogie down with her to Huey Lewis' *Too Hip to be Square*.

She was cute indeed—about five-foot-three, a healthy chest, auburn hair. As we danced, she moved seductively toward me, away from me, back toward me. Now, I'm a fair dancer, but a lot of my usual moves that Thursday evening were substituted to disguise what was going on in my pants—sort of a stiff-legged hop and a skip while I bent over to obscure the bulbous lump growing at record speed.

If I had straightened my back, well, things would've been plainly obvious—and there were fans all around, watching me writhe and twist. This game of hide-the-growing-salami continued until I was called to the stage to act silly again and give away treasured BIG Z t-shirts. We had to look casual, smooth, hip. Not an easy task while wearing satin jackets and skintight Jordache jeans aiding and abetting the swelling behind my zipper.

I announced that I had shirts and more shirts, drinks and more drinks, when a lady back in the crowd said in her loudest voice, "Hey, he's got a hard-on!"

I whirled around to escape, but this was a theater-in-the-round venue, and by turning, I was exhibiting myself to more and more fans.

The girl who announced my condition was none other than my five-foot-three beauty. I was now being publicly pilloried by the very instigator of the hard-on I had tried so desperately to conceal.

It was Stu's turn at the mic, and he had prepared a version of *The Dating Game* called "Dirty Dating Game." I was surprised at his level of preparation—typed flashcards and three stools fronting a psyche-delic backdrop that the security guys hauled in. He had been a night-club owner and did this routine in his clubs, back when Jim Lange was still hosting *The Dating Game* on ABC. It surprised many of our attendees, who there for the shirts and the drinks, not prurient she-nanigans. The show went like this . . .

"Hey, Everybody. I'm Stu Rossi, and welcome to the Dirty Dating Game. You, sir. Please read from this card and ask bachelorette num-ber one what her favorite tool is." Stu also put answers to the questions on the cards. The proceedings immediately went off the rails.

"Uh, what's in your toolbox?"

The girl then replied, "Huh?"

"Your toolbox. What do you like?" he asked again.

"A hammer?" The girl looked up at Stu and shrugged, unsure if she was right.

The male contestant asked, "Is that the right answer? It says thick piping on my card."

"Oh, I see it," said the girl. "Screws. I like screws!"

Stu started sweating and moved along to the next pairing. The audience was in disarray, milling about, chatting amongst them-selves and muffling the host—loud as he was. The room sounded like an airline terminal. He was bombing, so I jumped on the mic and simply said, "Okay, thanks, Stu. That was Stu Rossi, the loudest man in Hollywood, and now back to more of what you came here for: *t-shirts!!*" And the crowd went wild. Stu refused to speak with me for the rest of the evening. I didn't think he'd ever forget it. I ignored him and distracted myself by imagining every woman in the club naked.

Regardless, Stu and I were paired at many of these appearances, and we found common ground—a sense of humor and we played off each other well. We even wrote an act so we'd have something to say other than, "want my autograph?" Before a movie house packed with

BIG Z listeners, awaiting a pre-release screening of the new Richard Pryor movie, *Brewster's Millions*, Stu and I got up in front of the crowd and I began our clever, refined, vaudeville rap.

"Hey, Stu. How you do?" I began.

"Hey, Mr. Ed. What's with the long face?"

The audience went cold.

"Uh, you got a problem with my face? Let me look a little closer at yours. Let's see. I could play 'connect the dots' with your freckles and make a Monet." I pulled out a pen and began writing on his face. This drew crickets from the crowd, who came to see a movie, not two douchebags who thought they were Laurel and Hardy.

"Let's see," continued Stu, forging on like he was killing. "Your mother's from Texas and your Dad's from Brooklyn. What does that make you?"

"A Jewish cowboy." Tumbleweed. Cold sweat was pouring from my forehead and dripping onto my satin jacket. Then, from the back row, I heard a familiar voice.

"What else you got, cracker?" It was Pryor. The crowd roared at his presence, and the tension was broken.

"You sir, get a free t-shirt," I exclaimed, and threw it toward him in the crowd. Pryor had broken the ice, and the crowd eased up on us. After the film started, we sat back and laughed at a real comedian for the next two hours.

SEEING A JOCK AT WORK IN person is not the treat one thinks it is. When we speak, the monitors are off, and you can't hear what's going on over the air, except the voice in front of you—no music, just a voice. It's a pretty dull affair, but I'd never seen Stu do his radio program. Remembering his unintentionally hilarious "Pillow Talk Time" program from before he was hired at Z, I popped by the studio one day while he was on to get an in-person taste.

He'd told me he was an entrepreneur and had gotten started in something called radio syndication, where shows get sent to stations across the country: countdown shows, live concerts, interview programs, and Stu had been doing a little of this work on the side. He called it StuRadio. I was intrigued, but I didn't have to ask how he had the time to do both that and his live on-air show. It turns out that he did them at the same time, right there in the control room While a song was playing, he'd have a phone conversation with a client, segue to announce the next song on-air, and then go back to the phone, pitching like an Amway salesman, and he'd do this for an entire four-hour shift. Here's what he sounded like.

On phone: *"Hey, it's Stu from THE BIG Z, I mean, from StuRadio . . . yeah, we can do that, I can get you the program in, uh, wait."*

He puts the phone down, pops on the headphones and opens the mic. *"This is THE BIG Z, and here's David Bowie!"*

Back to the phone. *"So where were we? Oh, you want the show in two weeks? We can't do that until we cancel the other contract, oh shit. Hold on."*

He slips his headphones back on and clicks the mic. *"THE BIG Z-FM and that was Tears for Fears, Everybody Wants to Rule the World. Back after this."*

Off with the headphones and back to the telephone. *"I'll get you the contract and then you're in!"*

That was Stu's day, every day. It was a circus act, and I developed a newfound respect for him.

I later asked him about the business and he shrugged me off, changing the subject immediately. I wasn't offended. It was his deal, and I had my own problems.

My personal-appearance schedule filled rapidly and provided me with yet another forum to meet women I barely cared for. One evening, we were cordoned off at a hotel in Orange County on a raised bleacher, tossing t-shirts to the fans, when Amy showed up, carrying the same cardboard banner with my name on it that she wore up at the studio in Hollywood. She was stockier and more muscular than I remembered her—all sinewy, and taut—and after casually peaking under her placard, I could see that she sported the biggest pair ever seen on a fit woman. Somehow, though, she was completely unappealing. There was no sultry or sexy there, just pure gusto, with throbbing sweat glands.

"Could you sign this for me, handsome?" she began with a husky Lucille Ball voice, her brown, beady eyes wider than a pair of cannon muzzles. I pulled out my Sharpie and signed her sign, which was bouncing up and down against her prodigious chest as she rocked on the balls of her feet to the beat of the Thompson Twins playing in the club.

"There you go," I said with finality, but I couldn't help myself. I had to pry. I sighed silently at the sight of us: Willing Woman facing the Brainless Libido. I scratched my head, my eyes darting about as if there were an exit. Then my mouth opened and words came out.

"How've you been, Amy?" I asked. She lit up like a grease fire.

"Oh my God! Great! You're *soooo* cool, Ed, for remembering me. Wow, it's really hot in here. I'm like *schvitzing* it's so humid. How do you stay so cool in your black jacket? Wasn't it a perfect day today? I was at the beach playing Mah Jong."

Jesus, she was spouting. Every gland pulsing. She began to perspire more as we spoke, and the collar of her top displayed a dark ring of moisture growing wider by the word. It was disturbing, but Ed the moron pressed on.

"Jeez, thanks, Amy. Do you ever, uh, get to LA often? I mean, I saw you that one time. Maybe next without the placard." I was having one of my out-of-body experiences, levitating, listening to myself go on with this damp, eager young woman, who was annoying even from up there in the rafters. And there was no chance of her cutting it short after I began quizzing her. I zoomed back to my body and continued blabbing.

"I'm there when you want." She pulled out a pen, grabbed my hand and wrote her number on my palm, then drifted off, glancing back at me as she paraded with her banner at that odd 45-degree angle.

I was not of sound mind and body when I picked up the phone the very next day and set up a time and place to meet her in Redondo Beach: Stoney's, a nightclub with an adjoining hotel.

She arrived early, bouncing, her chest jiggling as she shook my hand. Under her floral halter-top, I could see a cantilever bra that resembled something longshoremen use to hoist freight. We took a seat in a remote corner of the club to talk. I couldn't remember a thing she said—I was there for one thing.

"Damn, it's noisy in here," I exclaimed, a good excuse to exit the club and mosey up to the front desk of the hotel. I gave them a credit card as she stood, wife-like, beside me. We got to the room, and she jumped me. No hesitation whatsoever. She was in charge, and right on cue began working up a sweat to alarming levels. Her bra fell away, and I heard a clang as the underwire hit the metal post of the bed. She humped up and down on top of me, bouncing like mad, the springs under the mattress straining under the sheer kinetic force, my hipbones bruising. I was concerned I might be losing my erection under this barrage but held on to finish. I felt like I should win something.

She rolled over, her enormous chest heaving. She must have worked off 10 pounds in water weight. "Is this the way you like it?" she asked, wheezing with each breath.

I thought, *"Is this the way anyone likes it?"* "Frankly, I've never been tossed around like that. It was, um, adventurous, like a thrill ride."

She froze a second at that comment and with good reason. No one wants their sexual technique to be considered an attraction at Six Flags.

"But I loved it," I said, attempting a consoling tone.

"That's what I wanted to hear, darling," she said, and then jumped to her feet on her way to the bathroom.

*"Darling?"*

I rolled over to her side of the bed, and the sheets were soaked straight through to the mattress. I was disgusted. I could've swum laps over there. My clothes were at arm's length, and I made an executive decision that a sleepover was off the program. I was half-dressed by the time she reentered the room.

"Where do you think you're going?" her voice turning flinty.

"I really have to get back, and I don't think . . ." I couldn't finish the sentence because there was a fist in my mouth. She fucking punched me. I staggered back a couple of feet, holding my lip, blood now all over my hand.

"What the hell are you doing?" I screamed.

She began breathing heavily again, cradling her offending hand in the other, in obvious pain from bashing her knuckles into my teeth.

"I chased you down. I followed you from your days at the Worm, you creep. And now you just want to run away?" She was fuming mad and hyperventilating. I was more shocked than upset and wanted desperately to calm her down.

"Look, Amy. Let's talk about this. Take it easy. There's no need for violence. That's just going to hurt both of us." Actually it already did.

"I think a call to your mother might be in order," she puffed. She was beyond consolation.

"My mother? How the hell do you know my mother?"

"Oh, I've been in touch with her. She thinks I'm fabulous. Just perfect for her boy, Eddie. Wouldn't she be pleased to learn of your violent streak?"

She clearly was out of her mind. I pushed her aside to run to the bathroom, but she tripped me, sending me sailing across the tile floor on my chin. I turned to grab her, but she reared back, out of reach.

"What kind of fucking devil are you?" I crawled on the floor toward her as she ran to the far side of the bed, in fear of retribution. Her muscled frame would be no match for me on fire.

I tried to get up but only made it to one knee, still glassy from the hits. She grabbed her monstrous bra, which I feared she'd swing at me, then zipped up her jeans and jetted out the door before I could get to my feet. I went back to the bathroom to soak my lips, returned to the room, and looked back at the bed—my soaking-wet bed—and plopped down on the dry side to get a few hours of sleep. She was playing me like an organ, her hands banging on my teeth and her feet stepping all over my family. This shit had to stop.

# CHAPTER 13

"How would you like to be THE BIG Z Millionaire?" The Big Girl had me alone in her office only a week after the Amy episode and was firing off ideas for me. I wanted off the appearance circuit for a minute, but she saw the attention I was getting around town and wanted to take full advantage of it.

"You'll have to excuse me, but are you promoting me?" I asked in pain, my jaw still smarting from the dual hits to my mouth and chin. She laughed nervously.

"Well, sort of. There's a station promotion we want to do where one of you DJs goes on the town to give away money to unsuspecting listeners, like in a mall or at McDonald's. You'd really be helping out the team." She stared at me pointblank; I obviously had no choice, and there apparently was no money for me, the "Millionaire."

"Sounds great," I fibbed." So, how does it work?"

"Well, we give you a stack of hundred-dollar bills and a tape recorder. Then you ask a bystander what their favorite station is. If they say, THE BIG Z-FM, you give them a Benji and tape their reaction. If it isn't their favorite station, tell them what their favorite station is and start again."

Hey, what's a little on-air fraud among friends? I was intrigued but concerned. Once word got out in the mall that someone was giving away money, I'd be followed by mall hoodlums coming out of Mervyn's and Macy's. *"There he is, in front of Wetzel's Pretzels. GRAB HIM!"*

"When do I start?"

She didn't respond right away, narrowing her eyes. "You look like hell, Ed. You up for this?"

"Yeah, I just took a fall in my bathroom. I'm cool. *"Isn't that the excuse beaten spouses make about their busted jaws?"* How 'bout tomorrow?" We shook on it and thought of a major positive: maybe stalkers wouldn't know my whereabouts in advance.

So, twice a week I popped out of my dented Datsun—*there's* a dead giveaway—and informed unsuspecting strangers that I was really a millionaire. I'm lucky I wasn't mugged or killed. The listeners were very sweet, and thrilled to get the money. And back in the mid '80s, a hundred bucks to most of our listeners was a good hit. Shit, I was tempted to ask myself the questions and give myself the bread.

After the first dozen suspects had been cornered, I'd given away about $600. I trekked back to the station and edited the pieces together to form a "promo," making it sound like thousands of excited fans were getting unheard of money.

*"Here's a hundred for you, and you, and YOU!!!"* "WOW, thanks, THE BIG Z Millionaire. You're the greatest millionaire ever! WOOOO HOOOO!!!"*

The station played it on the air once an hour. Our fans met the Millionaire, got money, got on the air, all because of me! I came away from this first experience very pleased to make these kids so happy.

Day two began just as successfully, and I was feeling like the Sheik that lived on the big corner lot on Sunset in Beverly Hills in that famed, monstrous mansion, surrounded by miniature nude female statues so anatomically correct that the neighbors torched the place on general principles. But he still was "the Sheik of Beverly Hills," the richest guy in town.

I was passing out the lucky bucks by the front gate of the new Beverly Center shopping mall on Beverly and La Cienega Blvds. when I saw them. It was Alex Grossinger, getting out of a limo with her dad. I squinted to be sure. Yep, and crap, they were headed straight for me. While I was taping the "millionaire winner," she glanced over, but nope. No recognition. I sighed as they passed me.

"You all right?" asked the contestant, excited by his windfall.

"Yeah, yeah," as I moved in another direction from where the Grossingers were going and continued lightening my bulging wad.

After a couple days of this nonsense, I was back at the beach place when I got a call from my cousin.

"So you're giving away money, are you? How rich do you think you are?"

"Very funny, Julie. It's the station's dough, but it's like I'm one of the not-stingy Gettys throwing money to the multitudes," I replied.

"Aren't you concerned about getting, you know, mugged?" Great. All I needed was for her to ramble on to my parents about my new gig as LA's most public rich guy while they wonder if I've completely lost my mind, passing out cash money to total strangers without security. Hell, I needed security on dates.

"Are you a lunatic?" asked my dad, who was caller number two. "You're already on the biggest station on the planet. Why are you doing this little menial shit?"

"I, uh, I thought that I might be helping them out, being a team player, you know. Getting a little extra work."

"Oh, really? What are they paying for this?" he demanded.

"Uh, well . . ." I stammered out.

"Jesus, first the Worm and now this. We didn't raise an idiot. For Chrissake Ed, you graduated from one of the top schools in the country, and you're risking your life in a mall, handing out money like an intern. If they asked you to run across the Santa Monica freeway at rush hour, I'll bet you'd do that, too." He was venting plenty now, and I'd heard enough.

"You know, I'm doing something that's truly amazing, Dad, and I work for people who appreciate me. I'm sorry I'm not a banker living in a penthouse in Beverly Hills. I'm sure that would make you happy. Your son, the real millionaire." I felt a catch in my voice. I had let him get to me. "You'll see where this leads. It's called faith," I said with finality.

"We love you. You know that."

"Yeah, I love you," and I hung up, torn to pieces like a beat-up kite jerked in the wind. His point was unsettling; I had accomplished something but was headed in the wrong direction.

My nerves were shot, so I called Tom for drinks and dinner at Martoni's, a Hollywood media hang serving every drink known to man, and old-school Italian pastas. Martoni's was known for its creamy Alfredo sauce and a wannabe Mafia maître' d dressed in a tux. He had to be six feet, 320 pounds, with a withering gaze that took me down to four feet nothing. He showed us to our booth along a wall that had a picture of Dean and Frank staring at us from the Sands Hotel, circa 1962.

"You know, it's crazy, Tom. I got to the place of my dreams, but look at me. I'm a punching bag. It feels like the end of the road and I'm almost 30. My God, women are beating me up in hotel rooms. I'm giving away cash in malls. Is this as good as it gets?"

Tom, his head buried in his plate, slurped down his cannelloni in one gulp, and said, "This shit again? Do I need to write it on a blackboard? You've got to ask yourself what you want. The universe isn't going to tell you. No one's going to give you power, or money, or prestige, or chicks, or respect—unless you know what you want and then ask for it."

He washed his food down with an Amstel and wiped his mouth, leaned forward on his elbows and glared at me, his garlic breath wafting over me in one sickening wave. "Go in and ask for a promotion. You deserve it, Ed."

He was right. I should march in, first thing in the morning and ask for more shifts, more something, anything that paid me more—and let the chips fall. I didn't know what the hell I'd do without Tom. He was my tough-love, drunken Irish angel, and he did it while stuffing ricotta cheese into his face. I popped him an Altoid on the way to the car.

The next day, I sat down with the Big Girl and laid it on the line.

"I feel that I should get more in the way of daily work by now. Some way of getting on the air more often."

She pondered for a moment, giving me no clue. "Do you like to fly?" she asked.

"Uh, yeah. Where?"

"Nowhere in particular. Well, over freeways in a helicopter. Billy needs a fill-in guy, and the work is paid like a shift. Interested?" I was taken aback with the instant results.

"I don't need to pilot the damn thing, do I?" I wondered.

She laughed. "No silly. You'll have a pilot, and all you do is announce traffic jams, accidents, that sort of thing. And you'll be paid for a full shift with each flight." She handed me Billy's number and sent me off. I was thrilled out of my pants—until I saw the actual helicopter.

Commander Billy, as he was called on the radio, was a tall, charming, mustached, swashbuckling throwback to the wartime Alaskan bush pilots, bedecked in a leather hat and a linen scarf. He resembled Errol Flynn, and just as mild-mannered. Billy invited me out to Long Beach Airport, where his tiny Hughes 269B was stored in a hangar away from the main terminal. This contraption was small, like VW

Bug small. At six foot two, I couldn't see how I could squeeze into it, although Billy was two inches taller and seemed to manage. He related his daunting routine to me: up at 5 a.m., check the aircraft, fire it up, crank up the radio and broadcast traffic reports throughout the morning for both Ron Dixey, the morning man at THE BIG Z-FM, and for the great Gary Owens on the AM band.

He wrapped up the morning shift at 10 each morning, reparked the copter he called, "Yellow Lightening" and headed home for a nap, repeating the routine at 3 and finally calling it quits at 7. He performed this meticulous task day after day, year after year. And he did it without a broadcast partner: he flew, he surveyed, he announced. He was my new hero.

My first training run was just before the 1984 Summer Olympic Games in LA. We were only two weeks before the opening ceremonies, and I was psyched to get a feel for the city from above. Refurbishing projects were everywhere: the old Coliseum that housed the '32 Olympics, LAX, UCLA—and I was going to see it all from above. Billy and I strapped in for the afternoon run, and we took off, as if on wheels, forward like an airplane, as opposed to straight up. At about 1,500 feet, we were traveling at 90 knots. My ass was vibrating from the motor, which felt like an old blender, and Billy was showing me the ropes while preparing for his first broadcast of the afternoon. All I had to do was sit there, take in the sights, and listen.

We motored up the Long Beach Freeway; I could see the Queen Mary in the distance, and moments later we were over downtown, where Billy opened the mic and began his first segment.

"We have an overturned vehicle on the number-one lane of the Harbor Freeway, jamming up the northern commute from South Central in the downtown slot, and it looks like clear sailing over the Santa Monica westbound toward West LA. This is Commander Billy on THE BIG Z."

It was like watching a man ride a bike and hammer nails at the same time. He steered the copter, watched the freeways, knew exactly where he was and what was happening, and announced the gig. Fantastic! I was enamored by his dexterity and passion for his work. He flew me over the Coliseum where so many preparations were going on. I could see the painters working on the new blue motif and the big Olympic symbol on the Peristyle, the track was being cleaned by at least 40 workers, everything looking brand new. I got a sudden rush of pride at seeing my city prepare for this worldwide event, launched under the warning of massive traffic jams, terrorism and other disabling disruptions—none of which would come to pass.

Billy handled the duties during the Olympics, and I was surprised to see Yellow Lightening on television one day doing traffic reports for Al Michaels and Jim McKay, the announcers of the Games on ABC. They grabbed the feed from Billy and put in on TV, illustrating for the world how little traffic there was in Los Angeles then; I found myself going to events in disparate suburbs of the city, only to find clear freeways and blue skies free of smog. The only terrorists were a group of male swimmers found sleeping in the female dorms at UCLA. All told, I was getting pretty anxious to get airborne, mic in hand, clearing the traffic and helping old ladies across the street.

After the Games ended, the commander deemed me ready. My first announcing shot was alongside a pilot Billy called Redondo Donny. He was this beach bum, wore Hawaiian shirts every day, and had sand all over his sandals. He rode the Hughes 269B like a motorcycle. Donny's favorite stunt was to approach the Hollywood sign on Mt. Lee at top speed, and right before he got to the giant "H," he would pull the stick back and head straight up over the hill, almost brushing the sign with the landing gear. He was nuts, but I liked him. If I needed to take a leak, he'd touch down at a park in the Santa Monica Mountains above Mandeville Canyon. I'd find a bush and leak away.

Aside from the Mt. Lee incident, the broadcast was uneventful and went without a hitch. The next time up, things went even smoother, but I noticed that the fuel gauge was a little on the low side after we touched down.

"Hey Redondo, I'm sure you know what you're doing, but how much fuel did we have left?"

"Oh, about three minutes worth." I blanched.

He landed with only three minutes to spare in an aircraft with no fucking wings.

"But we could've auto-rotated down into the San Gabriel River bed." Billy had told me about this: it's a technique used by helicopter pilots to land with no fuel in a bone-jarring, circular, controlled crash.

"What if we weren't near the river at the time we ran out of fuel?" I asked.

"Sayonara, muchacho!" My stomach turned. I climbed out and called Billy, recounting the tale, and he simply dialed up another pilot for the next shift.

"Yeah, Donny's kinda nuts. I shoulda told you."

"Uh, yeah."

Meanwhile, the recognition I got from these initial broadcasts was enormous. I received fan mail from girls all over the city. I was recognized over the phone with operators, waitresses were doing double takes while I was ordering, and all of it was less important than I'd thought it might be. I'd been burned too many times, but I was in my own dream, taking solace in the loneliness of the control room studio and the little yellow helicopter that kept me on the air and in the lives of the listeners. I was having fame my way.

My new pal, Stu, began filling in for Billy as well. His pilot was called Napalm Larry. Judging by name alone, I thought I'd lucked out. He didn't run the 'copter through obstacle courses or inches over the waves like Donny did, but he scared the living shit out of Stu: Napalm had flashbacks. He was an old Vietnam vet who got the radio gig on his Army credentials from flying troops into the Tet Offensive. Over drinks one night, Stu gave me a blow by blow of what seemed to go on in this guy's distorted head:

*"70,000 Vietcong were coming at him. It was early 1968. He had to make the napalm drop and make it right on the money. The Long Beach freeway was up ahead about five nautical miles from our present location. Wait, is this LA or Saigon? Where the hell is the air support?! The orders were clear, make the drop and beat it out of there, full throttle. There's a SigAlert on the 405 and 14 commandos are trapped inside an outhouse near the river. Is that the San Gabriel River or the Mekong Delta? Fuck it! Make the drop and auto-rotate down to the action, a car fire at the Slauson cutoff. Get Charlie Company on the com. "This is Charlie Company and we're under fire!"*

"I was hysterical. And every couple of hours, Napalm shuddered and made a grunting sound," Stu said.

"What did you do? Did he explain himself?"

"He just shrugged it off and said he was getting treatment, went on about the Viet Cong and how they chopped some guy's head off in his unit."

"We've got to put a stop to this. We can't keep going up with these maniacs. We sat in silence, ordered another beer, and then Stu had an idea.

"What kind of radio's in Yellow Lightning?" he asked.

"Got me. Looks like a typical two-way."

"How 'bout I go see if we can do these reports from the ground, using just the radio. We get Dixey and Owens to use helicopter sound effects in the control room and make like we're in the air broadcasting. We can do it in the other studio, get the reports from the CHP. Billy gets half of what he reads from those reports anyway. What do you say?"

I had to admit, it sounded like genius. Stu had strung together a solution from a likely disaster.

Stu went to the Big Girl the next day and said three words: "Jews don't fly."

She allowed us to give his idea a try, and the next time I had to fill-in for Billy, I grabbed a two-way radio from engineering and found a quiet studio. I didn't really need to *see* a fender bender to report on it. When Dixey cued me, he turned on the fake copter effects, I clicked on the two-way and I was back in the air—on the ground—20 feet from Dixey's studio. Most staffers at the station didn't even know I was grounded until they saw me through the studio window.

On my first day, I did three reports without a hitch and Dixey hit the sound effects just right. My fourth report went somewhat long. I was rapping about a stalled prison bus on the shoulder of the Golden State Freeway in the heat of the summer when the effects cart in his studio jammed. Ron brilliantly went to one of his character voices and said, "Hey, Ed, your helicopter sound effects ran out!"

I said, "Looks like I'm going down next to the convicts." Next thing I hear is bowling alley sound effects.

"Ed, what are you doing bowling?"

"Hey, that was a strike, Ron. And thank God they have air conditioning."

Suddenly, the sounds of a baseball game are ringing in my earphones. Ron's got a million of these tapes.

"I hit that one out of the park, Ron." I must have heard from a hundred friends about the incident. It was great radio.

BUT TROUBLE FOUND ME SOON ENOUGH. I was on the air for a music shift and had to perform the EBS test. This is the test where a long, irritating tone interrupts whatever's happening on the air so the public knows that they can tune in to THE BIG Z and learn where to get information in case of a national or local emergency. The pre-recorded man on the cart tape would say that this is a test of the Emergency Broadcast System, and it's only a test, and to relax, drink an iced tea, and forget everything about impending doom, for now. What's the point of that? It was like one of the old duck-and-cover drills I did in grade school to get ready for the A bomb, as if a plywood desk was a preventative measure. This tape was going to save no one's life. I hated the test with a passion; it stopped everything in its tracks. I literally could hear the listeners turning off their radios.

On this particular afternoon, I was rushed. A song by The Human League was about to end and the test was coming up fast. There were actually two EBS carts, both marked with similar labeling: one with "*something, something, EBS, something,*" and the other, "*something, EBS, something else.*" I grabbed one of them and plugged it into the cart slot, without reading it further. Hell, I'd done this dozens of times.

I announced, "We'll be right back after this earth-shattering word from our pre-recorded friend." I hit the button and I heard: "*This is not a test. This is an actual emergency. Please tune to another station and learn your fate. . .*"

Shit, it was the actual, it's-an-emergency-and-we're-all-about-to-die cart! I panicked and sat on my sweaty palms for about 15 seconds. Sweat was pouring off of my fingertips. I pulled the cart and replaced it with a song.

I imagined teaming hordes of Z listeners jumping from the Vincent Thomas Bridge in order to avoid nuclear holocaust. Jesus fucking Christ, did I kill someone?! Of course, the phone lines began ringing like crazy. I didn't dare answer them. In the distance, I saw fire engines barreling up Vine Street toward our studio.

At last, I cracked the mic and said, "Our crisis has been averted. This was a test, and only a test, of the Emergency Broadcast System. Please be advised that there is no danger. Please go about your business."

The listener must be thinking, *"My business? Okay, I was about to slit my throat after I shit my pants."* A moment later, the hot line blinked red. I picked it up.

"Orson Welles, may I help you?" Not funny. It was the Big Girl.

"Stay there, stupid. We're on our way." Five minutes later, she burst in the control room as only the Big Girl can burst, accompanied by two heavyset policemen.

I was pulled off the air and rushed like a terrorist to a darkened room at the station to determine if I harbored a nefarious motive for sending the City of Angels into a total panic. Of course, it was a mistake, but it took me nearly 30 minutes to make my case, most of which included testimony about how dumb I am. Then, they simply left me alone for about an hour. All I could think about was how disappointed my dad would be if heard a word of this.

*"I knew it!"* I could hear him say.

That hour was rougher than the questioning; heavy breathing, cold sweating, visions of my old man berating me. They filed back into the darkened room, glared at me, and said to go home and "get a clue." All this for inserting the wrong cart into the machine.

# CHAPTER 14

ARLY THE NEXT MORNING, THE BIG Girl summoned me to her office for a private meeting. I figured I should bring a box for my stuff and kiss my friends goodbye. She weighed her options to replace me—but came to the conclusion that I was a "talented moron."

Tom, my biggest, and perhaps my only fan, was very understanding and made a brilliant suggestion. He and Stu called my place from a speakerphone. Neither were on the air at that time, and I couldn't figure what they were doing in the same room.

"We're taking a road trip and you're coming," said Tom.

"Pack what you need. We'll be right over," echoed Stu. This was so out of order, but so was I.

Two hours later, I clambered into the back seat of Tom's Jeep Cherokee behind my two older buds. We jumped on the coastal route from LA, ostensibly to see one of Tom's radio buddies in San Francisco, and settled in for a long weekend away from LA in the heat of mid-summer with the clothes on our backs and little else.

Somehow, I'd remembered to bring my toothbrush. Tom forgot his, but he didn't forget the hootch. I was struck that I hadn't ever seen Tom do drugs, aside from distilled beverages, so this was an odd turn, and I'd pretty much given it up on dope, but what the hell. One more for old time's sake.

So, we lit up. *"Why are those bugs on the windshield staring at me?!"* We cranked on the radio, with THE BIG Z fading into a background as we passed Santa Barbara and found a clear FM signal from some distant market. DXing, as they called it, was a pastime of mine since I was a kid, listening to anything bouncing off the ionosphere from anywhere I wasn't and into my radio. One night at the Worm, I got call from a gaucho in Argentina. That blew my mind.

Anyway, we heard this young FM DJ, perhaps his first job on the air: "Hey, it's *Jessie's Girl,* and it's Rick Springfield from the soaps. And here *she* is!" We could hear him futzing with the mic and the cart machine, then a loud crash: the audio equipment was falling to the floor. The music finally cued up, and we heard him yell, "Jesus!" Very funny. Tom was partially deaf and turned up the volume painfully loud.

We stopped to eat about every hour and continued breaking the law as often as possible, making extra sure that we performed only victimless crimes. Speeding doesn't fall into that category, but it was mid-week with few motorists traveling in our direction, so we took a straw poll and raised our personal speed limit to about 85. The winding two-lane road was disconcerting, but my partner handled the curves—and the weed—with composure. We almost hit a pedestrian foolish enough to walk along a main highway. I nicknamed him, "Splat."

Stu kept relatively quiet during the trip north, occasionally thumbing through his company's sales reports and avoiding the marijuana. He seemed better suited these days behind a desk than a studio mic and a wild and crazy trip apparently didn't entertain him. His presence wasn't making sense, yet it was he who called me.

Upon arrival in San Fran, we stumbled out of a cloud of green smoke and greeted my new friend, Henry Conner. Tom had known him for years and gave him a huge bear hug. He was a famous DJ at an important station in the Bay Area, KFRC, one of my early dream stations—as a little kid, I imagined working there. Henry had a "cracked," wacky sensibility, and like most radio people, looked nothing like he sounded. I'd heard his brash, confident act for years and pictured him as athletic and poised, with piercing blue eyes, a blond coif flopping from one side of his head to the other. He'd be tall and gallant, with women grabbing onto his coattails, dragging along behind him, anxiously anticipating the next gem to fall from his mouth. He'd have perfect teeth.

Henry was heavy and short with the pallor of a hospice patient. His hair was long in places, short in others, and his gut overhung his belt by a foot. That belt never saw the light of day. A large pepperoni pizza was an appetizer. If Henry ever were to face the gas chamber, his last meal would be anything, as long as it was covered in ranch. I loved him immediately.

We got a quick tour of the station, and Henry even taped a segment for airing later that night, featuring the two of us. He called himself Eggs Benedict and I was Gooey Sauce. It made no sense, but that visual made for great radio. We later had an impromptu listening session with the station's music director to review the new stuff that had arrived that day. He cranked on the new one from Wham!, *Wake Me Up, Before I Go-Go*, featuring a new artist named George Michael, and we danced around the music director's office like kids in a playground.

By mid-afternoon, Tom suggested we get going. I followed like a boy scout, surprised to find more driving ahead; I had thought that this was the end of the road. Stu was preoccupied in deep thought throughout the day, staring at us with empty eyes, as if he were watching us on TV.

We climbed back into the car, Tom and Henry in the front, Stu and me in the back. After motoring west on California St. toward the Golden Gate Bridge, Tom made an announcement:

"Redwoods or Bust!" Henry pumped his fist but bumped it severely on the roof of the car, yelping like a kid. They were committed to see the Big Trees. The bigger, the better. I knew the Bay Area well, and there were some fine redwoods north of The City, just past the Golden Gate Bridge in Muir Woods.

"Here's your exit, guys," I announced. "My folks took us here all the time when were kids." Tom and Henry didn't flinch and we drove right past. I shrugged; there was another exit to take us to Muir. I poked Henry in the neck and made it clear that this was the last chance. Henry put his doobie aside, grabbed the map and shoved it in my face, his finger pointed at a town I'd never considered a destination: Eureka.

Eureka is about 250 miles north of San Francisco. So, if my calculations were correct, we'd traveled about 450 miles on winding, gut-tensing coastal roads from LA to San Francisco, and were now looking at another 250. Double that for the roundtrip back to LA. That's 1,400 miles to see—Eureka!

We stopped before nightfall and saw a real Sequoia. It was huge. With all the weed in my system, I was certain I heard the tree say, *"Touch me and you're dead."* Eyes wide with paranoia, I hopped out of the car and wandered through the forest with my friends. I noted a slight drop in temperature, but didn't give it that much thought. I hadn't packed a sweater, but how cold could it get? It was summer in California.

After about an hour of crunching leaves underfoot and tree voices echoing in my ears, we headed back for the car and tore into our stash of junk food. The weather cooled as we chewed our way north through the Cascades, between the hot, dry Sacramento Valley and the coast, then west toward our destination city. The sun was setting as we motored up the 101, and I caught an alarming sight ahead: a fog bank curling over the hills toward us. I rummaged around the backseat to find the Chronicle and checked the forecast. Inland temp, 102. Coastal temp, 54!

Jesus, and that was the high. I was wearing a short-sleeve t-shirt with THE BIG Z logo on it—not enough cotton to get me through an evening this close to the Oregon border.

Darkness fell as we barreled over the Cascades, and we were out of Ding Dongs. I proposed dinner. "We haven't eaten in 45 minutes!" I screamed. Four long minutes later, we spotted a sign off to the right of the road reading, "Samoa Cookhouse." Tom pulled up, and Henry jumped from the Jeep to check it out. Stu and I sat shivering in the back. Moments later, Henry poked his head out and said,

"It's a trough, bud!" Henry grew up in Mississippi and evidently ate from a large hole.

We got to the door to find the décor of an early twentieth-century logger feedbag: a wooded dining room, checkerboard tablecloths, and a big board detailing the menu for the evening: meatloaf. That was it, meatloaf, with a side of mashed potatoes. The boys were thrilled. I took a look around to get a feel for the clientele. To the man, they were wearing plaid shirts and sported thick beards. Their hands were more sand than skin. These were lumberjacks, and this was their spot. Only moments after we sat down, they brought us the evening's fare. To this day, I've never seen a slab of meatloaf so enormous. It was easily two inches thick and a foot long. It engulfed the plate. The mashed potatoes crowned the meat like a hat, steaming gravy spilling over everything. I licked the plate clean.

The topper was dessert. We ordered apple pie. They brought us an entire pie—*each*. The whipped cream alone had more calories than I consumed in all of 1984. We asked for a doggie bag, and our server shot back a look that could kill.

"You'll eat it here, and you'll eat it now," said the look. We stuffed our faces, burped in unison, and headed for the car.

After about 20 minutes, and shivering our timbers, we arrived in central Eureka and happened upon a Red Roof Inn. The second we opened the car door, we were overwhelmed by the smell of dead carp. I almost fell over, my olfactory glands aching. It was everywhere. A building had been torn down in front of the hotel, and a dog was barking at the pile of rubble, apparently pointing out the carp.

There was a curious line of unsmiling, bedraggled people waiting, as I later discovered, for their ration of Government Issue cheese. And with the cold mist draping the scene, it resembled a film noir set in the backcountry. Barbara Stanwyck must be around somewhere. I had a sense that we had gone back in time to the Great Depression. Stu was oblivious.

We lugged our baggage to a room with enough beds for the whole crew. With so much to do, in so little time, we lit up another doob and turned on the local radio station. *The Look of Love* by ABC was jamming. We washed down our Samoa dinner with a little Jack and a lot of beer and heard a local DJ do a break outro-ing *Dance Hall Days*.

"That was Wang Chung dancing in the hall, with more cool California hits up next." Then, dead air.

We sat up on the edge of our beds, Heineken sloshing in our mouths.

"*I said, up next!*" Finally, a commercial came on. We all spewed foamy beer on the pre-stained carpeting, howling with laughter. Another green jock. Radio was full of them far from the madding crowd of Los Angeles, where they'd be purged from the air and eviscerated in the press. It had to be his first job in radio, perhaps his first week. Tom thought it might be fun to give him a call, make a request, tell him we love him. He picked up the request line immediately.

"Hi," Tom said. "We're in town for fashion week, and we want to come over now and have you try on a few new items from our fall collection." That got the first reaction from Stu since we left LA—guffaws and tears.

There was a long pause, and the young jock replied, "I'd love to."

We burst out in hysterics. Tom told him who we were and he flipped out, telling us what a huge fan he was of THE BIG Z. I couldn't believe the reach of this radio station. He invited us over, and we embarked immediately while the idea was fresh.

The same dog was barking away at the pile of rubble across from the hotel. And the carp smell was still there, lingering like grim death as we piled back into the car. Tom lit up yet another doob. I reluctantly inhaled a deep, mind-altering toke, and immediately coughed it out like a death breath. Tom and Henry thought that was hilarious, but I was losing it. Stu just sat there. The passing trees were looking very alive.

Our young DJ friend opened the front door and escorted us past a small throng of locals who worked there, lined up on either side of a long aisle. They were grinning as if they'd never seen strangers before. I swore one was nodding and mouthing, *"Your majesties."* We had cheese waiting on paper plates, then more grinning.

"I'm Brad. I can't believe it's you guys. And Ed Mann in person! Holy shit."

Astonishing. I had groupies 1,000 miles away! I was unable to mutter out more than a groggy, "Uh, thanks, Brad," while cracker crumbs fell to the floor from my plate. Brad didn't care. He was in the presence of greatness, his hero, me.

"You guys wanna go on the air? Do a quick break?" he asked exuberantly. Tom jumped right in.

"Well, if you're such a big star up here, Ed, why don't *you* go on?" I was seriously stoned by this point and had only marginal use of my faculties. I thought if I cracked the mic, I might piss my pants. Before I could object, Brad, who had to be no older than my car, dragged me to the control booth and tossed a set of headphones to me. The guys stood there, smirking, waiting for me to screw up. A Flock of Seagulls was just ending when Brad broke in on-air.

"We're honored to be in the presence of one of Los Angeles' biggest radio stars, Ed Mann, who's up here for, uh . . . Ed, what are you doing here anyway?"

*"Good question."*

"Well hello, Jim. I mean, Brad. I'm here with my pals from THE BIG Z and God only knows what we're doing here, but we love the smell."

His eyes widened in wonder while my boys began snickering. "What do you mean, the smell?"

"Well, you know. Carp. The Carp smell. I can dig it, man. Lovin' the cheese, too." I could feel my brain go off the rails and had no idea how to bring it back.

"Anyway, is there anything you'd like to say to our audience?"

Only one thing came to mind. "Holy shit, I love Alex Grossinger!"

Nonplussed by my profanity, Brad forged ahead. "Tell me, Ed, is that a friend of yours?"

"Oh yeah, Brad. She's gonna be my wife. You'll see." The deep end was approaching fast.

"You're getting married?" he asked.

"Yep. I'll have to kill him first. Danny G.—he'll never let me marry her. I'm washed up before I got started. So someone's gonna have to clear the way!"

My friends collectively dropped their jaws while Brad sat there in silence. I whipped off my headphones and fell over the threshold of the open studio door, landing face-first on my nose. Stu grabbed me and shuttled me to a couch in the lounge down the hall. Brad popped on a Huey Lewis cut and rushed in to get me water.

"You fucking passed out, man. What kind of drugs are you guys on?"

"We'll handle it," interjected Tom. "He's a tad stoned. Your Humboldt County weed was too much for him."

Brad headed back to the studio while Tom grilled me.

"Who the fuck is Alex Grossinger, Ed?" He was slapping me lightly on the face. I indeed had passed out.

"Oh, hell, I barely know her. You see, there was this line at a grocery store and, well I can't think right now."

Meanwhile, young Brad was taking calls from listeners, star struck that Danny Grossinger's would-be son-in-law was in Eureka. "Who's invited to the wedding," one female caller asked. "Are they planning to have little Grossingers?" And an old favorite, "I hate Jews!" It was moronic.

"We've got to get out of here," stated Tom, flatly. With that, my guys dragged me to the car and off to the CarpCheese Hotel to crash, hard.

THE NEXT MORNING, I WAS FACED with an inquisition. More like an intervention. Henry had stepped out for coffee, and my BIG Z comrades cornered me.

"Ed, we have plans for you, but smoking dope and swearing on the air isn't one of them," said Tom, sternly.

"Look, man. You brought that shit up here. I only smoked it." I replied idiotically. "*Plans*?"

"Yeah, but I didn't go on the air and make a fool of myself. Some greenhorn disc-jockey can sound awful and amateurish, but you don't have that option. This is the equivalent of hitting bottom, my friend, and high-profile jocks don't get second chances screwing up anywhere. Believe me. I know. I've been canned from the best stations in the country for much less than this. And I never went on the air stoned."

Tom's tone had taken on an insulting, didactic air. Without think-ing, I leapt from the chair and took a swing at him, a roundhouse right that barely grazed his nose as he reared back. A turtle could have avoided it.

Stu grabbed me. "He's not kidding, kid. We have plans. Now sit down and think. *Think!*" He was screaming now, and this was about the first thing he'd said during the entire trip. I had little choice but to listen. My mind was a miasma of nerves, and the three of us glared at each other, contemplating a very long drive home. Then, Henry burst through the door.

"Y'all want some caffeine? Worst coffee on the planet, and they have it right here in Eureka. We some lucky sum bitches!" Henry's light tone had arrived just in time as I slurped my way to consciousness.

I began packing, which amounted to a shirt, and ambled to the car for the long drive home. After giant donuts and muted apologies, I sat motionless in the back, and the rest of the ride home was silent, until we cruised past Clear Lake.

"Ed, you realize that one more screw up like you had in Eureka and with the EBS test at THE BIG Z, you're gone—maybe finished in LA radio entirely," Tom said, completely offhand, without turning his head toward me, as if he was commenting on the weather. Stu turned to face me from the front passenger seat.

"Chief, there're only a couple of things an ex-DJ can do." Chief. Stu loved little fucking nicknames, but I was not amused. "Acting, which you've had no training in, voiceovers, which takes years of fighting guys like Casey Kasem to the announcer booth, or a business you can own, like syndication—marketing and distributing radio shows across the country. I do syndication, and you've done work in marketing. Didn't you do that at a broadcast school at one time, the Workshop?"

Stu had done his homework and had written this little pitch in his head before the trip. I'd wondered why he came with us all this way when he clearly didn't want to be there, his mind in the clouds. What was supposed to be a fun, THC-infused, male-bonding trip to the frigid North Coast, turned into an inquisition. And for reasons I didn't yet understand, he was pitching me.

"Are you asking me to join you in StuRadio, your company?" I asked.

"I'm asking if you'd like to join Tom and me in starting a new one."

Christ, Tom had already signed up. "As a host?" I asked.

He paused, eyes frozen for a moment. "Marketing, kiddo," and then dug something out of his wallet. "What do you think of this name?" Stu shoved a credit card in my face, pointing at it.

"*VISA*?" I asked.

"No, man. Down there. It's printed below the numbers. 'ROSSI.' We want to add a 'RADIO' at the end. 'RossiRadio.' Sounds cool, huh?" That sounded remarkably like his original company, "StuRadio." He *really* liked his name. I couldn't discount his enthusiasm for me, and Tom was following him, like a pod in *Invasion of the Body Snatchers*. They had poured the Kool-Aid. *"Here, take a sip!"* But why me?

"Tom, what are you planning on here?" I asked.

He hesitated, and still didn't turn. "I'm in," he monotoned as we headed inland, the temperature warming significantly. "It's time for me to do something different, and this is it."

I stared at him, checking each side of his head to see if a gun was pointed at his temples.

"It's a great plan, Ed, and you can be our marketing guru, get the stations signed up. I'll be the CEO guy, and Tom will come up with show ideas as our programming man." Stu had this all figured and kept it close to the vest. Very cool character for such a loudmouth.

"I'm flattered that you'd think of me, Stu, especially after the events of the previous day. Let me consider it for a minute. All right?" My head was spinning.

"Sure, but we're getting started soon, you know. Right now you can say that you're calling from the number-one radio station in America, and frankly, we don't know how long you're gonna be there."

An unnecessary asshole comment. Stu turned back to watch the trees fly by while I simmered in the back, flexing my brain around the plan. How many times would I have a chance to make something of myself in a business? This would hit my dad in his narrow pleasure point—becoming an owner of a company. He'd been an entrepreneur for years and was always thumping his chest, so proud of the companies he'd launched and piloted to acclaim.

There were big-ass questions to ponder: How much longer would I be on the air, famous in my fiefdom? How would this business make money? How would I? How could I trust Tom as a confidant anymore? He hadn't hinted at any of this. And Stu was one loud mystery.

We continued on down the highway with no further commentary about these "plans." We left Henry behind in San Francisco, and it was well after nightfall when Tom dropped me off at my beach pad.

"Think about it, Eddie boy." He gripped my hand firmly, no shaking.

"I will, Stu. I will," and I popped myself into bed within three minutes and stared at the ceiling for about 90 more.

# CHAPTER 15

THE NEXT MORNING, I RUMMAGED THROUGH a pile of old notes that listeners had passed along to me at a Warmup party weeks ago. I found a wrinkled Post-It with a barely visible phone number scribbled in pencil and remembered it immediately. The guy who gave it to me told me to dial it up if I wanted to get on television; try my hand at another medium. I hadn't thought him serious but kept the note in the pile with the others. I massaged it around with my fingers, working the creases out of the small, square, yellow paper. I had to give this a shot before jumping behind a fucking desk.

"CBS," said the voice on the other end of the phone. Holy shit. The number was for the television network.

"Yes, Suzy Sharmen, please." Without a response, I was put on hold.

"Y&R?"

"Who's Y&R?" I asked.

"Young and the Restless. How can I help you?" I was taken aback. This was the real deal.

"Yes, Is Suzy available?" I asked.

"This is Suzy."

"Ed Mann, Suzy, from THE BIG Z FM? I was passed this note weeks ago at a personal appearance and . . ."

"When can you come in?" she interrupted. She wanted *me*. To come *there*.

"Well, um, I suppose today or tomorrow."

"The sooner the better. I've got a small part that needs to be filled, only a few lines, but I know you can read lines, right?" I actually shrugged my shoulders as if she could see me.

"Of course. Where do I go?"

"CBS Television City on Beverly and Fairfax. Do you know it? I'll have a pass for you—Ed from THE BIG Z. You'll be great! Just come to the security gate, and we'll take good care of you." I felt like my vista had opened a crack.

"See you then." I began going through some old books, looking for acting tips. I spent the rest of the afternoon in front of the mirror, practicing lines from a David Mamet play.

I shaved my face as close as the razor could get, found a tie that actually matched my shirt, and drove to Hollywood. Heading down Fairfax, the building loomed in front of me but now took on an entirely different perspective. I made the left on Beverly Blvd., and there she stood, with that big *eye* staring at me, daring me to enter. *CB fucking S!*

TV City was a marvel, an imposing, squat, black and white structure surrounded by Technicolor street life; striking sharp edges of mid-century architecture shadowing the aging, welcoming Farmer's Market. It housed game shows, The Carol Burnett Show, which I attended years ago, and now, I was on my way to work there.

As I drove up, a commanding guard at the lot gate greeted me by ignoring me, as I supposed he did anyone he didn't know. Once I presented my esteemed credentials, he made eye contact and said, "Right this way, Mr. Mann." In that moment, I felt as if I belonged at the Columbia Broadcasting System.

I parked and walked through the glass doors into the building, almost tripping on the props and giant boards that had to be moved in and out for all the scene changes. They littered the hallways. Winding my way around the maze, I found Suzy, who welcomed me like I was Harrison Ford.

"Wow, great to meet you, Ed." She smiled 'til her face almost cracked. "Right this way to makeup." I followed behind like a doggie on a leash. "Here're your sides, you know, your lines for the day." I had only two, one in each scene.

"Well, not too much memorizing here," I said, as I flipped to my spot in the script. "So, how often do I get to ad lib?" Suzy froze, her gaze instantly transforming from adoring thankfulness to piercing abrasiveness. Furrows appeared above deep-set eyes. Jekyll and Hyde.

"You'll do nothing of the sort. The marks are placed with great care, and the other actors depend on the lines as cues. They need to be read as is, period!" She led me to the makeup area in silence, but by the time we arrived she was Happy Suzy again. "Break a leg!" she cheered.

I took a seat in front of a mirror, the counter before it filled with multi-colored makeup jars for different pigmentation.

"Your dressing room is down the hallway there. Let me know if everything fits."

I was relieved that she had cheered up so dramatically, but I didn't think that she'd allow me to get on her bad side more than once.

Getting made up was surreal. Every blemish, gone. My skin tone, perfection. After I arrived in my dressing room, I checked the wardrobe. Everything fit. My scene as the backstage photographer didn't come up on the schedule for hours, so I killed time exploring, met some of the crew, and joined them in solving a crossword puzzle. I shook hands with Jack Ford, the president's son, who had a regular part on the show. I ate like a pig at the craft service table; there was a complete Sunday-style brunch right there, and I couldn't imagine how these actors stayed so thin—until I realized I was the only guy at the table. I was in Anorexiaville.

I waited and waited. Then I waited some more. I was told that acting was more waiting than acting, but had no idea that I could finish *War and Peace*. I even snuck onto the *Price is Right* set and watched the public file in, thinking that many of them were going to make more money than I that day.

By the time my first scene was scheduled for taping, I'd been there for seven hours, antsy, yawning. Suddenly, an announcer on the set yelled, "Scene 14, photographer, journalist, and extras. 60 seconds!"

*"Crap!"*

I stepped into position, my knees shaking from the adrenaline and the sheer urgency of the moment. I had only one line in this scene. They cued me, "five, four, three, two . . . ." I stood there, staring wide-eyed at the camera. Nothing came out of my mouth. Like an idiot, I'd forgotten my one line!

"Cut!" the director yelled from the booth. Then I said something that I'm sure prevented me from acting on *The Young and the Restless* ever again.

"Fuck, that should go on Dick Clark's Bloopers show!"

The whole crew, who knew I was a numbskull DJ and could've cared less about THE BIG Z, glared at me. They had been there since seven in the morning. Who the hell was I to hold them up with some stupid comment?

I was thinking, *"What the fuck was I thinking?"* I felt like a nervous high school band trumpeter, who missed the last high note. The stage manager counted down once again, and I said my line—but it was too late. I was cooked.

Suzy came out after the scene and shook my hand. "Um, thank you," she muttered.

"That's it? I'm done?"

"Thanks for coming to CBS." She was a woman scorned.

I skulked back to the dressing room, got dressed, and found my car. I pulled over at a fast-food stand to grab a shake, and the girl at the counter gazed at me.

"Are you an actor?"

I was confused, then realized that I still had my stage makeup on.

"Not anymore."

# CHAPTER 16

LIFE AT THE BIG Z FM continued merrily along, and my EBS error moved into the bad memory department. I was even commissioned to fly to Philadelphia in the summer of '85 to cover a concert that I'd barely heard of, something called "Live Aid." I frankly didn't know what to expect but was pretty excited to get a free trip to the East Coast to hang with some big-name artists and other radio people.

I arrived to a 95-degree day, with record-high humidity. The Philly rapid transit—air conditioned so well I considered staying in the train all day—took me to JFK Stadium, the old hull of a venue I thought had been torn down. As I exited the subway, I was greeted by humidity more stifling than any I had ever experienced, and I'd been to Florida in the summer. The air adhered to me like a polyester suit with static cling. There was no respite. It was unforgiving, and not a hint of a breeze to cut the brutal heat.

As I entered the stadium, I took in a view of at least 90,000 screaming music fans. They were screaming at nothing. No performers on stage. The big screen was blank. They were clearly hyped. A couple of roadies were roaming the wings, cigarettes hanging from their lips, looking busy. And Bob Geldof was off-stage, gesticulating wildly at a group of young underlings wearing laminates. They looked terrified. *"Shit, I've got to avoid this guy."*

Geldof organized the whole event from his head; he was a visionary who had the privilege of knowing every great artist of the day and how to pull their strings. Bob could get Sting to play guitar riffs with his ass cheeks for the right cause. He was an artist in his own right but became famous for this—his charitable work to feed starving Africans. He was noble, he was talented, he was a sweating, gesturing maniac.

By any measure, Live Aid was a massive undertaking, featuring two major, simultaneous concerts—the one in Philadelphia and the other at Wembley Stadium in London. Each venue had jumbo screen views of the other, and the broadcast trucks fed the acts via satellite across the Atlantic as they played. The live television audience saw it all in record numbers.

Phil Collins began his day performing in London, jumped on the Concorde, and played drums for the Led Zeppelin revival that evening in Philly, replacing the late John Bonham. The feeling I experienced there was like no other in my memory—before or since: an intense vibration of sound, of people, of overwhelming kindness and joy, as if a sweet, giant angel was kissing me for hours.

Two large security men motioned to me, and I was shuttled with dispatch to the backstage area, catered under makeshift tents. The food wasn't spectacular—bowls of macaroni salads surrounded by flies, deli platters, carrots—but the company was extraordinary. Brian Adams, Teddy Pendergrass, who was wheelchair bound after an accident, Zep, U2, Madonna. I gathered up some nerve and greeted Madonna a few minutes before her appearance. She looked fabulous, just like her videos, resplendent in a shimmering blazer, gobs of jewelry, and tons of makeup caked on that heart-shaped face. She was shorter than I had imagined her.

"Hey, Madonna." I thrust my hand at her, "I'm Ed, a DJ from LA. I played your records as you were coming up and just wanted to wish you luck out there today."

She was quite shy and replied, "Oh, thanks so much. I love you radio guys. What station are you with?"

"THE BIG Z."

"Oh my God! You guys are *the* best! And you're all the way out here?"

"I wouldn't miss you on stage for the world." I was laying it on a little thick, but she was still that sweet Midwestern girl from Detroit, and I'm sure she loved to get stroked. Maybe she'd mention the station on stage, make me a hero. Shit, maybe she'd mention *me*!

"I just want to thank you, thank you for everything."

And what the hell did *I* do? I practically pushed her onstage, and she was wonderful, outstanding. I thought she could take over the world with her confidence. Sure enough, she did. But, alas, no mentions.

I sauntered away from the backstage area; it had no ventilation or access to the action in the crowd. I wanted to sense the concert from the stands, so I climbed over a series of bunkers and returned to the middle/upper rows, where I was overcome by an awe-inspiring sense of belonging, a palpable perception that something wonderful was happening, surely not unlike Woodstock.

This was a generation growing more caring and giving, and it was demonstrated to me right there in the sweltering Philadelphia heat. During a break in the set, the Philly fire department shot huge streams of water over the crowd, happily drenching us. I thought it was the most remarkable moment of the trip, like a perfectly timed rainstorm in the putrid heat of summer, shared by tens of thousands of my closest friends.

I sucked long and hard on a doob, passed around by my new neighbors, caught up in the love. I checked my watch. Crap! I was late for a call to the station. The Big Girl was expecting me to phone in on-air reports from the concert, providing listeners in Los Angeles a taste of the experience. By that point, I was stoned out of my mind.

I exited to find a pay phone and attempted to collect my dope-fogged thoughts, which wasn't unlike sifting through the trash for a sandwich. I had only 10 seconds to prep for my report. "*God dammit I've got to get my mind clear!*"

Big Sam in LA gave me a lead-in: ". . . THE BIG Z-FM, and we've got Ed on the line, live at Live Aid."

"Hello LA, this is Ed, and I'm at the AFK, I mean JFK stadium in Philadelphia for Live Aid. It's a fantastic time we're having. Brian Adams just performed, and he was fantastic." My brain was getting thick, and I was beginning to repeat myself. "Next on the program is Madonna, who's scheduled to perform *Holiday*, and they're watering us down right now."

I'm certain no one knew what the hell I was talking about. I lowered my voice to achieve a kind of Jerry Lewis, charity event sensitivity. "As you know, we're all here to feed *starving artists* in Africa, so give what you can."

Sam paused and said, "Right." I'm sure he started thumbing through his notes to see if Live Aid gave one shit about feeding starving artists.

I spent the rest of the day in the stands, partying with total strangers, bonding with the world, and worrying that the Big Girl might have had enough of me. By nightfall, the temperature had cooled, and the music turned to the past as Led Zeppelin performed in a reunion that was never to be repeated.

I flew back to LA on the redeye, sporting a Live Aid t-shirt and headed straight for the beach.

"Live Aid! Jesus, you were there! What was it like? Did you meet U2?" It was a golden weekend, and I felt like I owned the world.

I got back to the station on Monday morning to pats on the back and kudos all around—mostly from the secretaries—who asked if I brought back more t-shirts. Of course, I didn't. I was nothing if consistently negligent. From others I got a strange vibe. Maybe just jealousy in the air. One DJ motioned to me as I passed him in the hallway, pinching his thumb and forefinger together at his lips and inhaling. I began to worry if everyone had figured out how inebriated my reports from Philly were. Maybe they thought that I was silly from the heat and humidity of the moment.

I almost got past the Big Girl's office, but she motioned for me to come in.

"Ed, close the door behind you." She gave me that trademark Lindi look; a stare impersonating a smile. She must have practiced that for hours in front of a mirror.

"There are rumors floating about that you were not, shall I say, clean and sober during your broadcasts from Live Aid last week."

"It must have been a contact high. Everyone around me was smoking. It was a concert, you know. I don't do drugs." I lied emphatically, almost believing it myself.

"Do you want me to play the tape?" she stated flatly.

"I remember what I sound like!" I was nearly shouting. "And I knew what I was doing."

"You can't go on the air stoned. This is a multi-million-dollar facility, supported by advertisers that just don't get that. I have to protect them. They pay the bills. And you, one of my prized guys, goes out and does this?" She was getting red, and I noticed how her face matched her scarf.

"Look, I didn't get to THE BIG Z because I'm a poor broadcaster, I . . ."

"You got here because I hired you! I took a chance on you only a few years out of school. You don't think I know what I'm doing?"

Sweat was accumulating on my upper lip, and I wiped it on my sleeve.

"Clearly you know what you're doing, but it's hardly unusual to see joints flying around the seats of a stadium during a music festival. It's part of the experience. I certainly had no plans to smoke dope on the air, and if you're looking for a reason to fire me, I'm sure you'll find one. But I didn't intend to sound like Dan Rather reporting from a rock concert. Our listeners expect something special. They expect me to be me."

Of course, I didn't know who the hell I was. I glanced to the left and noticed an open bottle of Dewar's clearly visible on that bar of hers next to the desk, with fresh ice in the bucket. "And how many pops have *you* had this morning?"

Steam was rising from her bouffant, and her eyes narrowed to slits. "Don't think I don't have an arsenal of shit I can throw at you, Ed."

Whoa! The Arsenal of Shit! I tried in vain to mask that visual as I continued to stare at the bar—a passive-aggressive exclamation point.

She blinked first. "I think we're finished here," she said with awesome finality, and she stood up behind her desk, her eyes dark as pitch.

As I left her office, all eyes followed me back to the studio, anticipating that I'd exit carrying mementos, headphones, dirty carts—my professional life from the last four years stuffed into a brown box. I crossed the hall to the men's room and splashed a gallon of water on my face to calm down, took the elevator to the garage, and drove home. I was scheduled to be on the air the next day, and figured it might be my last shift. I won the battle, but . . .

"THE BIG Z FM, this is Ed Mann, the Mann with the plan and no idea how to make it work, so let's ask these guys, Men at Work." I pulled off my cans and stared at the dials, perhaps for the last time. The DJ fame trip was flaming out—the end of that long, gleaming road seemed near. A song request call buzzed me out of my thoughts.

"BIG Z, yes," I answered.

"Eddie, it's Julie."

"How've you been, Jules? Everything all right?"

"Oh, I'm fine. Are you on the market?" I was instantly suspicious.

"You know me, Jules. I'm always for sale. What's up? Does Cindy Crawford need a date?" I had to see this through. Julie had always been seen with the pretty people, and I was still a sucker.

"Close, actually. I know someone that you should meet."

"I'm hoping it's a female."

"Yes, dope. And she's gorgeous."

"All right, I'll bite. Who is it?"

"Her name is Alex. Alex Grossinger. The comedian's daughter." *What*?! She had to be kidding me. Julie was hand-delivering this object of beauty to my door in the midst of a crisis. How could she have known?

"Where can we meet?"

"Geoffrey's Restaurant on PCH in Malibu. 7:30 tonight. Can you make it?"

"See you then."

"So, no 'thank you?'" she asked.

"You have no idea." I hung up, looked upwards, and thanked God for little favors.

I pulled into the parking lot at Geoffrey's, an established beach restaurant that would get rave reviews, if you were on your honeymoon. It was dimly lit, decked with twinkling lights and overlooked the ocean, close to the famous Malibu Colony, where Johnny Carson, Larry Hagman, and other celebs had their second homes. I was early and climbed up the outdoor staircase to the bar overlooking the entrance; I wanted to see her as she arrived, before our introductions.

A piano player was tinkling *The Way You Look Tonight* while waves crashed against the rocks below. Most every table was filled with couples engaged in quiet conversation and dressed to the nines. I was swishing the ice in my vodka tonic with my index finger, and it was quite numb and cold when she entered. She was as stunning as I had remembered, and elegant—with a certain regal bearing—as if she deserved her beauty. Her torso was hidden behind a pink pashmina sweater wrap, but I could make out her figure as she walked: thin, an ample chest, and the prettiest legs that ever moved a human across a restaurant floor. My princess had arrived.

I saw Julie following right behind and waved her down, my chest beating like a snare drum. Julie poked Alex, they looked up, and I pointed back with my frozen finger.

"Alex, this is Ed." We smiled and shook hands. I had wiped the mild sweat off of my palms and warmed my finger on the inside of my pants pockets. I got a sensation that she'd recognized me. Impossible.

"Hi. I heard so much about you. Oh, and this is my boyfriend, Mike." She motioned to this hulking presence, shorter than me but definitely a gym rat.

He shook my hand, his eyes were blank, and his head tilted slightly as if regarding a crooked painting at a gallery. I kissed Julie on the cheek and whispered in her ear.

"What the hell are you doing?"

She patted me on the behind. "It's fine. Let's talk later."

"Damn right."

We were led to our table and were tucked into a booth; too cozy for my taste. I wasn't pleased, but took my seat next to Julie, sitting across from Alex. I looked at Alex, Julie looked at Alex, and Mike stared across the room at an empty table.

"So," I began. "I understand your folks have a beach house nearby." The corners of her smiling face dropped to neutral, matching her boyfriend's detached demeanor.

"Yeah," she replied, flatly. "It's actually right down PCH." She appeared disillusioned to be kicking off the evening speaking about her parents' place. Julie was shifting around in her seat, feeling the building tension, before she finally thought of something to say.

"So, Alex. Ed was on *The Young and the Restless*," she exclaimed in an over-the-top falsetto and then slugged me in the arm like Ali. I almost fell out of the booth.

"Wow. Mr. Show Business," replied Alex, exhibiting zero emotion on the subject.

"I've gotta run to the restroom," I said, and Julie followed me out of the booth. We both walked toward the bathrooms off to the right of the bar and out of sight of our table—where I cornered her.

"What in howling hell are you doing?" I spoke in a loud whisper. "Her boyfriend? What am I doing at dinner with a girl's boyfriend?" I was furious, literally spitting while I spoke.

"What are you asking about her parents' beach house for? What does that have to do with shit? You could see she was really put off by that question. She's a celebrity's daughter, you know."

Julie stood there with her hands on her hips. I was ready to slap her.

"It was a perfectly legitimate question! She is who she is. And how did you know?" My volume was escalating, so Julie shushed me.

"Know what?" she asked innocently.

"Know that I wanted, uh, thought that I'd like to meet her?"

"You fucking announced it on the radio. You don't think I've got ears?"

"In Eureka you've got ears?" I was getting agitated, and the decibels were multiplying. Julie slugged me again in the same damn spot on my shoulder. I grabbed the spot in pain.

"People talk, Ed."

"I don't know how the fuck I'm going to get through this meal, but I'm going to try, and stop slugging me like a frat boy." I turned and stood on my toes to peek over the wall and saw the happy couple—sitting quietly, not touching, not speaking.

"Are those two long for each other?" I whispered to Julie.

"If you'll let me explain, I'll tell you."

I turned back, crossing my arms, still incensed—but listening.

"She was coming on her own tonight, until Mike got time off from his shift . . ."

"What does he do?" I asked in a monotone.

"He's a security cop."

My head almost flew off my neck. "What's a Jewish American Princess doing with a security cop? How does that happen?"

"She was working at a Beverly Hills department store, and he was the in-store cop. They hit it off, and next thing you know, they're an item. Been together for like three years, probably three years too long. They're having their problems, but trying to work it out. He wormed his way into dinner tonight, thinking that's what she wanted; all she wanted was to meet you. We were hanging out at this club, and I told her about your stoned broadcast in Eureka. I left out the part about her dad, of course. And the weed. She was interested, and that was that. By the way, how did you know who she was?"

"Never mind. One day I'll fill you in." A small curl of a smile was returning to my face, and I thought that I'd better shut up and let Alex do some talking. I was gaining back confidence when we both returned to the booth, massaging my shoulder again as I slid in. I opened the menu and tried for a reboot.

"I've never eaten here, have you?" directing the question to Alex.

"Just about to," answered Julie.

I gave her a raised eyebrow that said, *"shut up."* "How about you, Alex?"

"Oh, all the time. It's my parents' favorite, and we can just roll right in like we're family."

"Well, this isn't exactly a family style menu, is it?"

"You want a stack of pancakes? I'm sure they can whip some up for you."

I laughed out loud and noticed that Mike was silent, staring at the salad at the next table.

"So, how do you go from being Julie's favorite cousin to becoming a radio star?" Alex asked, her smile returning.

"So, you've heard me?"

Her face contorted a bit. Then a shy grin. She was a listener. I was sure of it! But Security Sam was next to her, and she couldn't tell all. I instantly imagined her driving around town, hearing my show, hearing my voice, visualizing what I looked like. Did I meet with her expectations? But here she was, putting up a little wall I could knock down with a breath. I figured I'd let her be coy and do likewise.

"Well, first," I continued, "you announce diving meets in high school, then you get a job with an evangelist who hires Jews to host Christian programs, who then fires you, so you can end up drunk in a bar with an alcoholic Irish DJ with connections at BIG Z."

She revealed the most dazzlingly white teeth I'd ever seen—finally, a smile. "That may have been more than I need to know."

I was charmed—but uncomfortable nonetheless—sitting a few inches from Lou Ferrigno, Junior.

As we drank and ate, any tension evaporated. We laughed through the night, except for Mike, who jolted to life only when the conversation turned to sports. When I mentioned the Lakers, his head spun on a spindle and he said, "Heard that Bird might come join the team. Wouldn't that be awesome?" That was his total output—from cocktails to dessert.

I got the check, and Mike shoved a credit card in my face without a word, so I split it with him. I walked them to the curb, where we awaited our cars in valet. Theirs came before mine.

"Very nice to meet you, Alex." I went to shake hands, but she kissed me sweetly on the cheek. I stiffened in the presence of Mike, but I was smitten.

"I hope to see you soon," she said, her eyes lingering on me for a moment.

Mike gave me his trademark vacant gaze as they pulled away. What the hell was he doing there? My car arrived, and I drove off—happy.

# CHAPTER 17

"Stu, I'm seriously considering the offer, but this is no easy decision. How much time can you give me?"

He sighed over the phone; I was putting him off. "Oh, I don't know. It's a good idea, Eddie. And Jesus, look at your situation. You can't fuck around with these THE BIG Z guys forever."

He was right, but I'd just won a skirmish with the Big Girl and was feeling my oats. I might have called Tom about it, but he was already soaking in Stu's juices. What the hell was I waiting for?

"Hell, let's do it," I said. "Ya gotta take a chance some time."

"Good move, Edwardo! *Now I'm Edwardo?* We can get started right away. And you can keep your gig at THE BIG Z, too, you know. Let's see how that plays out."

My Y&R episode finally aired, playing to an audience of millions. THE BIG Z refused to promote it; Lindi had a problem telling her audience to watch television. And she clearly didn't want to elevate my career.

Stu, Tom, and I began gearing up to start the new company. There was office space to rent, chairs to buy, phones to hook up, studios to build. I was getting enthusiastic about working for myself, but very concerned about money. There was no piggy bank brimming with leftovers; I was never the star morning man, never the prime attraction. Being on the radio was a labor of love, but it brought me no closer to wealth, marriage, divorce, remarriage, Dodger games with my boys, kissing my grandkids.

I was 30 while living the life of a 20-year-old idiot—body surfing on the weekends and pulling errant gray hairs out of my chest for sport. I was growing disgusted at the turn of events that stemmed from this "let the river carry me" lifestyle I had embraced like a religion. I could form my own sect, the prophet of Semi-Famous Nobodies everywhere.

Before me, though, was an opportunity to pull myself out of this chaos, to find prosperity and material gain. It was ironic that I went to a synagogue for counsel.

Less than a week after accepting the position to co-found RossiRadio, I drove to the Wilshire Blvd. Temple, near downtown Los Angeles, one of the oldest in Southern California. Although I'd never joined, I felt that the timing was right to reconnect spiritually with my religion. Maybe I'd find God in a whimsical mood, happy to hook up and discuss my trivial situation. I arrived on a weekday and found the temple nearly empty.

I was flashing back on my childhood as I took it all in. I'd done the Bar Mitzvah thing, the Confirmation thing, but hadn't really bonded with Adonai until high school when I found myself in temple before a High Holy Day service. I had arrived before my parents, really before anyone, and ventured into the empty synagogue, standing before the bima, staring up at the eternal light above the ark.

Without warning, I felt I was pushed down on one knee, and a sudden warmth came over me, a feeling of bliss that I never quite pinned down. In that cavernous temple with no one in sight, I was hardly alone, and quite unexpectedly happy. I hadn't experienced anything like that since—a sense of companionship, of membership, of total joy. Live Aid was close, but here I was, alone in a room.

"May I help you?" asked a member. He was elderly but stood erect as the palm trees outside the temple entrance on Wilshire Blvd. at Hobart Avenue.

"Thank you, no. I'm just looking for a quiet place to pray, uh, think things over."

"Follow me." The old man led me to a corner of the sanctuary, where I could have a moment alone, undisturbed. It was a small anteroom behind the bima; the choir sang there during Friday night Shabbat services. Above me was the eternal light, attached to heavy support beams. I fixated on the light, trying to recall my lessons on what that represents. Of course, I couldn't—they were in Hebrew. I didn't remember a word of it. Then it flickered, making me giggle— some eternal light; I could blow it out from 40 feet below.

I put on a yarmulke, sat in a pew, and closed my eyes, looking for divine guidance in the darkness of shut eyelids. I was so damn conflicted, wanting to be on my own; a business could offer me that, but then there was that screaming hyena, Stu. And what of my on-air career? My old dreams? The noose tightened as I sat.

Upon entering earlier, I didn't know what I might experience. Maybe I'd find a page in the Union Prayer Book or the Torah regarding my insignificant problems. *"Let's see, it must be in Leviticus, 'and the shepherd boy wandered in the wilderness, only to be sacrificed by Esther to please God, and then they feasted.'"* I picked up no book, checked no verse. There was no strike of lightning, no voice of reason, I just sat there in my own darkness. Quite suddenly, I felt a warm wave work over me. It surprised me at first. I could feel this warmth radiate through me, like a sunny day on the beach. And like so many years ago, the furrow in my brow flattened, I sensed my sweat glands retracting, resting. Then, a rush of happiness. An enormous smile overcame my anxiety.

This joy was complete and overwhelming, flushing every fiber of anxiety and distress from my being, filling me with an eternal, soulful satisfaction—as if I were slipping through and past thousands of years of history—and lifting my perspective away from the quotidian and into the whole of life.

Now, I had perspective on what had happened to me in that synagogue long ago and could see that all of my nonsense over the recent years was just filler; silly things to do while Adonai sat up there, looking down, cheering. He beamed at my bizarre nervousness, my tendency to land on my face when I was most down. He applauded when I learned a lesson from these antics that had given me absolute consternation and frustration. He was there for it all, laughing, loving, caring. God was in me and loved me. It was crystal clear, as if writ boldface on a blackboard. There could be no better guidance. He was there and wasn't going anywhere, no matter what. I felt a tear form at the corner of my left eye and didn't wipe it away, just let it fill up and drop onto my lap.

I got to my feet on wobbly legs, began to walk out, and the old man smiled at me.

"Did you find what you were looking for?" he asked, knowing the answer.

"Very clearly, sir. Very clearly." I felt an honest humility in that moment and never forgot the experience or the look of peace on the old man's face. He had known where to lead me and what I might experience in that room, and he wished nothing more in exchange than a blessing.

"God keep you and bless you, my son," he said, as if God had said it himself.

I thought of Cumpepper and his false sincerity as he delivered his sanctimonious, members-only sermons to his minions on the mount—the mount of manure. I left the building to find brilliant sunshine and, on my car, a parking ticket under the windshield wiper.

# CHAPTER 18

I COLLAPSED ON MY COACH IN THE apartment and thought, *"That was the best meeting I've ever had!"* Who better to get direction from than the big guy himself? I was motivated to move life along, get a firm bearing, put a plan into action, and see results. I'd stumbled through enough obstacles; gotta brush that shit away. My personal apocalypse could wait.

Life at THE BIG Z was going along as if no confrontations with the Big Girl had taken place. My on-air world settled into a foggy sameness. The helicopter deal was a thing of the past, but I was hosting late night Saturday and Sunday shifts on the air, playing the hits and being silly, all while kicking off this new syndication thing that conceivably could change my life. And I had this dream girl, this goddess ripe for the taking, if it weren't for Beefcake Boyle standing in my way, staring at salads.

Actually, nothing much in the world had changed either: Reagan had been President for the duration, the Cold War was raging silently, the stock market kept rising and rising, but something called AIDS was appearing in headlines more often, and fear found its way into the behavior of our fans, who suddenly had shown less interest in sleeping with us. And likewise, I was more reticent to jump from mattress to mattress with anyone willing to stare at my private parts.

As my 31st birthday approached, I gave up marijuana for good; I'd been hacking up all sorts of lovely chunks in the morning and getting colds in the summer, a sure sign that my defenses were down, and I didn't need some AIDS virus creeping into my system as I slept; for all I knew, it was carried by mosquitoes and toilet seats. It was much later that it became clearer how this horrible disease was transmitted and incubated in humans, healthy or otherwise.

After a BIG Z show I hosted at the old Hollywood Palace on Vine Street, one young lady was adamant about getting me into bed. I went through a door, she was on the other side. I walked down the stairs, she was at the bottom. I got to my car, she jumped into the passenger seat. Nameless Lady sat there silently, looking straight ahead, no word where to take her. *Sooooo*, I took her to my place down at the beach and parked the car. Before I could say, "and you are . . ." she jumped me, and off we ran to the sack. I pulled out the now-obligatory condom, slipped it on, and her eyes bulged in abject horror.

"We don't need that," she said. "I'm on the pill."

"You think I'm worried about babies?" Well I was, but that wasn't the point. "Haven't you read about AIDS?"

"The candies?" She looked puzzled, so I ran to the kitchen and found the latest copy of *Time*; the cover story was all about this horror. I shoved it in her face.

"What are you, a hydro-chondriac or something?" she said, throwing it aside.

"That's *hypo*chondriac, moron."

"Yeah. That's it. Hypochondriac. You're a hypochondriac!"

I rolled my eyes, pulled up my pants, and showed her the door. "Read the article," I said and tossed the magazine to her as she turned to go down the steps.

I shook my fist at God that night for allowing myself to float down yet another dark tributary. It's not like I didn't know what I was doing, but this was a sad, familiar road. Enough.

Late that night, I had another radio dream and woke up with a start at 4 a.m. in a cold sweat. I felt that was an exclamation point on my on-air career. I fell back to sleep and dreamed again. Now, I was older. I had a house full of kids. Two boys, actually, and they were laughing. They were happy.

# CHAPTER 19

A STU THAT I NEVER KNEW DECLARED himself president of our nascent operation; he was the bull, and we all took turns working the cape. Well, most days we had no cape. We just ran around trying to avoid getting gored. His work ethic was unmatched: in at 6:30 a.m., out at 8 p.m., and within a few weeks of starting the company, I barely recognized him.

He screamed at everyone, he scheduled impromptu board meetings to brag about how well he was doing, he spoke in short, clipped, declarative sentences, he got a haircut every two weeks from a barber with a buzz saw, who transformed his curly, floppy locks into a crew cut so sharp and straight it could slice drywall, he laughed only at *his* jokes, his shirts were starched *"what DJ wears starched shirts?"*, his ties matched his shoes, he had his assistant stamp that day's date on his meeting notes after he left the conference room (he couldn't be bothered to write it himself), and he quit his on-air gig at THE BIG Z to devote 100 percent of his time to his brand of screaming leadership at the company.

His flip in demeanor was more than disquieting, it was frightening. In short, he was the boss. And he never wavered; sick or well, he was there. This was his dream, and we happened to be in it. I shrugged every day, realizing I never knew this guy.

Our offices were in the same building as THE BIG Z, and the station became a client. We produced countdown shows, comedy bits, talk shows . . . all manner of programming that local radio stations wanted but couldn't do on their own. And I signed up stations from all over around the country at a pretty fast clip.

Like any business, though, we got it going in fits and starts. Early one morning, he brought me into his office and—in rare, hushed tones—said, "I've got good news and bad news. The good news is we've got $10,000 dollars in the bank. The bad news, payroll is due and we're short $20,000. Think about what you want to do." What *I* want? Either we pony up, or we head to Vegas and put it all on "00."

Later that afternoon, the advertising checks arrived in the mail, and Stu steamrolled out of his office in front of our low-paid staff, his eyes on fire, arms flailing, mouth roaring.

"We got a check for $120,000! We got a *big fucking check*!"

I ran up to him and whispered, "Jesus, shut up Stu! These guys are making minimum wage." He skulked back to his office, slammed the door and screamed, "*YYYAAAAHHHOOOOOOO!!!!!*"

I once designed a mailer to promote one of our programs—like a magazine insert you'd see in *Vanity Fair*. I spent days assembling it and got one small detail wrong—the zip code. It was one numeral off. Stu spotted the error but only after the piece was printed. He called me into his office and tore my head off.

"Are you trying to fuck my shit up, or do you want to? These pieces could be going to the wrong post office! Didn't you consider that? What kind of idiot makes that mistake!?"

Actually, every piece arrived at the correct destination anyway. But no one, to this day, has ever shrieked at my general direction like Stu, and he'd do it several times a week. He harbored a burning desire to demonstrate to us who was king. What a contrast to Lucky Sinclair, who had the innate ability to drive us to perform at our best while never, ever raising his voice above a hush. Even the Big Girl slapped us around in style without once mussing her scarf or hairdo. These were talents lost on Stu.

I despaired at losing my funny friend. The Stu I had known was gone. The silly, loud DJ, who hosted dirty-dating games and did the Laurel and Hardy routine with me at movie screenings, was replaced by the coarse, gravelly Mr. Spacely character from *The Jetsons*. That he could transform himself into personality so different alarmed me, and the segue was swift. Lightening quick. He was now the Great and Powerful Oz, formerly known as the sweet man behind the curtain.

I stayed the course, getting solace from my new friend, God, and others who commiserated around the water cooler to relieve their stress. RossiRadio soon found a sense of humor and a sharp touch for comedy. Our comedy bits, short sketches performed by local LA comics, were designed for morning radio shows, which had to provide four hours of funny stuff for their listeners every single day. We shipped them around the country every week, and the stations ate 'em up.

Stu couldn't help himself, though. Instead of relying on our stable of uber-talented comedic geniuses, he ran into the studio every week to recreate his former on-air self and voiced one he called *Little Bobby, the Annoying Intern*. He taped it with an insane falsetto, sounding a lot like Mr. Bill from the first years of *Saturday Night Live*. One segment had "Little Bobby" offering the morning show a fresh pot of coffee, andin his haste to please them—he'd spill it on the host.

"*Ohhh, I'm sooooo sorry, Mister Morning Host, sir. OHHH NOOO.*" In another he plugged in an appliance and electrocuted himself. I actually thought that many of them were pretty funny. It was the old Stu.

We sent out buckets of hilarious stuff to the stations, but it was difficult for us to know if the morning shows truly dug our comedy, so I included survey forms with the tapes, and they rated them from 1 to 10. With no live audience laughing, and no phones ringing like they did when I was on the radio, we needed a barometer. One day, Stu came charging out of his office, waving one of the returned forms as if he'd just won the lottery.

In that silly Mr. Bill falsetto, he screamed, "Little Bobby got a 10! They love Little Bobby in Milwaukee!"

As he approached my office with his ranting, I grabbed the card to see for myself—and doubled over with laughter. "Stu, there's a minus sign in front of the 10. You got a *minus* 10, dude!" He strode away like a dog sprayed by a skunk.

The notion that I'd be stuck with this guy for the duration of my working life was a depressing thought, but his demeanor never affected my performance, and the company was doing fine after the first year of floating checks and shit salaries. My side job at THE BIG Z was secure for the moment; I still was on the air—in spite of myself. I was leading a double life, behind a desk and behind a mic. I felt like Dick Clark—without the money.

My Monday through Friday life was changed forever. I had sought refuge in radio from the day I left UCLA and had avoided a standard-issue nine-to-five existence for years. I had grown accustomed to my ways, and now the glamour of the DJ life floated away by the day. Those days now were mostly occupied calling other radio stations, frantically pitching Stu's annoying Little Bobby bits.

And I found I could barely talk to Tom; he had transformed. In a clumsy attempt to look corporate, he wore white shirts and red ties but forgot to cut his hair and get respectable shoes. It was as if he tried to plug himself into an electric corporate socket—but it didn't fit.

My gig was a burner. I made around 80 calls a day to program directors around the country, working my ass off to interest them in our stuff. Most never picked up the receiver. I envisioned my name on hundreds of message slips at the end of every week, stacked on the edges of desks around the country, hovering desperately close to the trash can. There were always more shows, always more calls. My RossiRadio hours climbed to more than 50 a week, then 60, and I took no pride in that. This exercise was boring through me, draining my energy.

I fell into a dull, lethargic pattern. After work, I'd trudge home, pop open a bottle of Becks and crank on the Playboy channel. More often, I strolled downstairs right there in my building for a bite of sushi at the bar of the new Chaya Venice restaurant, hoping to talk to someone about something other than radio, but usually, it was me, my fresh-water eel, and the bartender. I was a salesman all day long, and when it was time for an airshift, an ostensibly creative outlet at THE BIG Z, my attitude was no better.

With the station's lack of commitment to me (I never made it to full-time), I now was only working the late shift. Frankly, I didn't care if anyone tuned in for my antics or was bored to tears by the same songs over and over again. During these shifts, the lights in the offices were darkened, and there was no one in the building but me and the security guard downstairs. It was depressing, but they consistently paid cash money, which was more than I could say about RossiRadio's irregular pay.

One night on the air, my nerves were shot, and I was getting fed up playing *Oh, oh, It's Magic* by the Cars, or the Ace of Base, or whoever the fuck it was, every hour on the hour. During those late shows, commercials were scarce, and I often ran out of songs that were on the playlist. We had very particular songs to play and were obligated to mention the station promotions, concerts, and events; these dry, dull announcements superseded any entertainment value I could muster. Sell, sell, sell all day; sell, sell, sell all night.

The musical repetition was mind-numbing, and it was all a creation of management. Our program director, the Big Girl, and a short guy with floppy ears had weekly music meetings that consisted of munching corn nuts and listening to new songs. If the song was an obvious hit, they put it in the music rotation, but if they decided otherwise, the record company rep responsible for getting spins on the radio barged in bearing a "gift" for someone in charge. A week later, the song magically appeared on the playlist. If there wasn't a quid pro quo, it sure appeared that way.

Staring out on Vine Street, I could see the clouds thickening through the moonlight, and it began to drizzle; my little world below all but vanished. It was like a scene from *Play Misty for Me*, with Clint Eastwood as the solitary DJ in foggy Monterey—just my mic and me. My little brain got to thinking . . . what would it hurt if all of this modern, brand-new music we played, like *Walk Like an Egyptian* by The Bangles and *I Wanna Dance With Somebody* by Whitney Houston, were interspersed with—perhaps—The Beatles?!

I debated the topic with myself as the time fast approached to find an extra song to fill the hour. I knew that Oldies stations still played them; all the kiddies who listened to us were asleep by that hour, I reasoned—even though most of them, who were younger than the age of my shoes, had heard of The Beatles. We got requests for The Fab Four from time to time, but to play an old song on a current-based, hit-music station was a form of radio blasphemy—it simply was not done.

I took a deep breath and swiveled my chair to face the back wall, which was filled with carts dating from the Pleistocene era. The short, floppy-eared guy, whose job it was to update the music on the wall, hadn't. Up and down I searched until I found it; smudged, dusty, but cued up and ready: *Revolution* by the Beatles. I popped the cart into the machine and, as the previous Gap Band record was winding down on the air, here came the roar of John Lennon's lead guitar and vocal.

"*Ruh, na, nan, na, na, rah, na, na, na,* Ya say you want a revoluuuution, well, ya know, we all want to change the world . . ."

The speakers were cranked so loud I thought I might break a window. I was dancing like a geek, thrusting from one side of the studio to the other, reveling in my power to totally control this monster radio station that I had no right to totally control. I was actually enjoying myself, for the first time in months. About 30 seconds into my fun, *the hot line rang*—a blinding red light that blinked right in my face. Either some dummy was dialing the wrong number—or my boss was on the line.

"What the fuck are you doing?" It was the Big Girl . She was up. At 4 a.m. "Since when are you the goddamn music director?"

"*Well, this must not be a song she got paid to play.*"

"Take that thing off the air and plug in *Tears for Fears*, NOW!"

I SPENT THE NEXT FEW HOURS STARING at the box where my paycheck was delivered, thinking that I might never see one in there again. She was pissed. I had little right to choose the music of a $150 million-dollar radio station, even at four in the morning. The shift ended about an hour later, and I passed the mic to Ron Dixey, who greeted me in one of his usual cartoon-character voices. He raised his voice to a high, Porky Pig pitch and pointed his fingers up and down while bouncing on his toes. He was his own vaudeville show.

"Hey Eddie. Did you hear about the one about the Jew who eats pork?"

"I missed that one, Ron. What happened?" I replied, barely whispering.

"He got a trayf-i-otomy!"

I was in no mood to laugh.

"Hey," he continued, as if he was killing it down at the Comedy Store, "I didn't know we were an Oldies station. Great to hear that old Beatles song. I'll let you know later if you still work here."

I stared at him, stunned by his gleeful, apocalyptic prediction while smiling to reveal teeth brighter than fluorescent lighting. But there it was—from the biggest radio star in the city. My car was parked in my usual space, four or five speed bumps from Ron's. "*Fitting.*" I drove home with my mouth dry as a sock.

Later that morning, I was awakened by a call from the Big Girl's assistant.

"Ed, I'm calling from Lindi's office. She wants you in here today. Does that work for you?" He spoke to me as if he were ordering a sandwich, with no concern that it was Monday and that I had a full-time position as a monkey making phone calls for a maniac.

I rubbed the sleep out of my eyes, cleared my throat, and said, "I'll be in this afternoon." I hung up, sure that I'd reached the end of the line at THE BIG Z. I didn't call a soul, washed up, and headed to the beach to get some sun—and think.

When I entered THE BIG Z offices, the receptionist went wide-eyed like I was a ghost, her eyes focused a few yards behind me.

Christ, they told everyone. "*I'm a dead man.*" The girl at the sales desk looked petrified. The hallway was clear of people. It seemed like a Sunday. As I approached the Big Girl's office, there was a sudden burst of activity. Two men wearing off-the-rack-jackets, white shirts, and matching narrow ties exited her office, then turned to guide two cops, guns in holsters with Lindi sandwiched between them. Her hands were cuffed behind her back and they were escorting her from the premises. She eyed me as she walked by, but I couldn't figure the emotion; she appeared disembodied. Her assistant stood, with hands on hips watching from the opposite side of the hallway.

"What the hell is going on?" I asked.

"She's being taken downtown. They want to question her."

"Looks to me like she's being arrested."

"Well, you'd know the difference," he snarled.

"Can we get past me for one minute? Who were the guys in front?"

He took a deep breath, as if this all was just *sooooooo* boring. "The FBI. If you want to know more, you'll have to ask someone else." He marched back to his desk, arms swaying, with his head cocked back as if it were just another sunny day in LA.

What kind of chicanery was going on here? The assistant rifled through a stack of papers, and he returned to hand me an envelope that I opened right there. It was my severance check. So that was it. I was going down, after five crazy years.

"By the way, honcho," he intoned, "you're not alone."

Before I could ask him what that meant, he darted down the hallway toward the sales office. I lost all energy to continue my inquiry and headed back to the beach. There were three messages on my phone machine when I arrived.

"Hi Ed, it's Tom. We're all gone. Call me."

"Eddie, Stu. We're on our own! Let's make it happen!"

"Ed, Big Sam. Do you know any other program directors that would be interested in me?"

The staff was being liquidated. I dialed Tom immediately.

"Yeah, we're all shelved and the station's just playing music. No jocks except for Dixey. He stays. After all, he's the station's big star."

"Well, I guess that happens, but what's up with . . . ?"

"Apparently she's been taking checks, selling tapes of BIG Z radio shows overseas, and pocketing it."

"Overseas? Our programs aired overseas?" I asked.

"Yep. Korea mostly."

"And no one knew?"

"Well, the Koreans knew." Tom could always find the humor. "The Big Girl kept the deals confidential and didn't tell the owners. From what I was told, she was getting these big checks every week and popping them into her account, not realizing that the bank might report it. The FBI came in and busted her. We had a little corporate fraud happening right here in our happy home. Makes you want to move to Eureka, doesn't it?"

"Hardly." I took a long pause to digest this. It was so far out, so nuts. "I suppose this ends a chapter?"

"A long, sordid chapter, my friend. Let's get together and turn a pint around."

I agreed and met my old friend at Reuben's, where it all began, and drank 'til we closed the place. I drove home that night and, aside from discovering how big a star I was in Seoul, I wondered how honest my dealings with those I worked with could be.

TUESDAY RAMPED UP AND I SAT there in my office, wondering where the fuck I should turn. No news from Julie, which could only mean that Alex was still with Jack Friday. And I was practically living at the bar downstairs, eating sushi for dinner with total strangers and drinking more than I had in years.

I was getting busier and busier at RossiRadio, and we finally began getting payroll checks. Just in time, but it wasn't enough to put me on Easy Street. I dialed and dialed, buzzing through the days with all the excitement of a TV test pattern, waiting for something, anything to happen.

I didn't have to wait long.

"Want to go to New York?" Stu asked.

"Why would I want to do that?"

He gave me a quick glare; my preferences were of zero concern to him. He stood and began pacing the room, hatching the grand plan as he was speaking.

"Most of the U.S. radio audience lives on the East Coast, about 70 percent actually. If I could get you out there for a chunk of time, you'd be closer to the stations that reach the most people."

He was right. My mind reeled for a minute. I could segue well into a part-time life there. My LA scene was dull as hell.

"We have a trade deal in New York with the Essex House. I figure you could stay a few weeks, come back, go back. Maybe stay longer."

"Well, now we're talkin'! This sounded like fun. I could use a change in venue, and last I heard, there were ladies in New York. I would be a businessman with a briefcase. My luggage would be my friend; my cab driver would be my chauffeur, and to hell with LA.

"Sure, what the hell. It gets me away from you from time to time, too." I grinned at my candor, but Stu stopped pacing; he didn't see the humor—his lips flat and straight. This was no longer my old pal, my funny partner, my Oliver Hardy. He was living his dream of megalomania, and I could not have contemplated how ultimately grandiose he saw things.

# CHAPTER 20

ARRIVED AT JFK AND GRABBED THE stinkiest, rankest taxi in town—
a cross between body odor and dog shit. Wilting in a cab in New
York City during the summer, with an Eastern European driver lack-
ing rudimentary hygiene, was no place to hang for the dog days. I
wanted to address him by name, but every letter on his taxi badge
was a symbol from the periodic table. I dug into my pocket for tip
money. I was advised to carry a wad of singles wherever I went—and
as counseled—there was the driver (to whom I should have tossed
a bar of Dial), the doorman, the bellman, some other guy standing
around my luggage, another bellman who brought the bags up, the
housekeeper who brought up pillows without asking, the engineer for
the clogged toilet (he was an engineer?). I was out 18 bucks and hadn't
even unpacked.

The phone rang only moments after I arrived to the room. It was
Shelly Fishkin, our New York ad-sales guy.

"Ed Head. Shelly Deli. Big Ad party tonight. Want you there!" I
had met Shelly on the phone. Nice guy, but he often forgot to start his
sentences properly, dropping pronouns like loose change, and he had

acquired Stu's annoying habit of nicknaming everyone he wished to endear, including himself.

"Where do we meet up?" I asked.

"Loft in SoHo. Prince Street. You'll see it near West Broadway. See you in 30, Edly!" I washed up and changed, grabbed my wads of singles, and headed downtown.

I poked my head out of the cab as it drew close to Broadway and saw a party spewing out of a large apartment and onto the street below, like it was leaking people. Everyone was dressed in business clothes, so different from LA, where the nice shoes stay in the closet and emerge only for weddings and funerals. The smell of weed wafted by. It was remarkable that the cops didn't bust this up—everyone was stoned on the street—but I figured these were business people who paid serious taxes. The cops were busy in Harlem and apparently didn't care much about marijuana in Lower Manhattan. I found Shelly in a sea of people, puffing away on a joint.

"Hey, Eddie. How was the trip? Shel-Del wants you to have a hit."

*"Jesus, third person . . ."* "No thanks. Where's the beer?"

"Up in the loft, but you'll never get there. Here."

He passed me his flask filled with Stoli. I took a long swig and immediately felt the rush of alcohol and jet lag mixing in my system. Shelly motioned me over to meet a young lady. At first I didn't see her; she was a foot shorter than I, dark hair, and black puppy-dog eyes gazing up at me like a lost beagle.

"I'd like you to meet Monique. Monique, Ed. He's from LA." I shook her nervous hand.

"Nice to meet you, Ed." Her accent was right off the Left Bank. She began to giggle.

"What's so funny," I asked, smiling at her warm greeting.

"Nice. Whenever I say zat, I laugh. That's a city in France, you know. Nice," which she pronounced, "Neece." Another giggle.

I wondered what she would've done if I'd said, "Nice 'Cannes.'" I motioned Shelly over. "How old is she?" I whispered, leaning over casually.

"Nineteen. Isn't she adorable?"

*"Isn't every 19 year old?"* She had a beautiful figure, ample, perky boobs parked under a loose fitting t-shirt that made her middle look large at first glance. As the spotlight moved over the crowd and a light breeze drew her t-shirt closer to her waist, her shadow cast a stunning portrait across the asphalt on Prince Street, and I could see that she was deceptively thin, with tiny features, like a music-box figurine. I figured I'd better control myself. This was Shelly's territory. I looked around, distracting myself, giving this petite croissant scant attention. When I moved to the left a few feet, she moved. When I moved back, so did she. I had my own little doggie. Giving up, I thought of a few innocuous questions.

"So you're French?"

"Oui. From Paris."

I'd never been there and had no thoughts about it one way or the other. She was female, and that was fine.

"How long have you been in the U.S.?"

"Oh, about seven monss. I am working with C&T."

"Captain and Tennille?" I asked.

"No silly. Carlson and Towne, zee advertising agency." Her laugh was infectious and I joined in. Shelly eyed me, nodding his head at our apparent harmony, not hearing a word thanks to the loudspeakers blaring Bruce Springsteen and the E-Street Band.

"Ever been to Los Angeles?" I asked, thinking in a corner of my mind that she might have heard me on the air. I had to get over myself.

"No, but I'd like to try iiit. Um, you know, go and see iiit." She was embarrassed. Very cute, and I was growing enamored. Shelly motioned us over.

"Eddie, meet Phyllis. She's with DDB Needham."

I shook hands, very businesslike, and moved on to the next person. Monique stayed by my side as I sauntered through the crowd. I even introduced her to her own boss, drawing serious laughter.

"You're a hit, my boy," said Shelly, clapping me on the back.

"I didn't know I was here to impress anyone."

"Are you kidding? This is for you! I wanted you to meet the people who buy our ads, who support the company. You're the man of honor!" I was dumbstruck. Shelly had arranged everything; a way to get the East Coast money people married to the West Coast partners. Quite a little scheme, and I got a cute poodle in the exchange.

"I must say, I'm incredulous. Everyone is so friendly. This is a quite the happy group."

"Everyone, I mean *everyone* likes to party in this industry. We have stuff like this a lot." I got to thinking how dreary things were for me in LA, but this is the impact we were having in a place 3,000 miles from home. It was gratifying.

A couple of hours passed and Shelly took off, his job accomplished. It was after 1 a.m., so Monique and I retired to a bar on Broadway for a nightcap.

"So, you're a media planner?" I asked.

"Oui. I decide, or plan where the clients spend zer money. For example, if Mars Candy wants to spend $200 million on radio, or split iiit between zat and print . . ."

Holy Fuck! This lithe, frog-leg-eating neophyte is in control of millions. "So, um, how do you go about planning this?"

She took a sip of her beer, looked me in the eye and said, "I can justify just about any zing," then gave me the slyest grin this side of Butch Cassidy. "I've got to get home, iiit's late. Do you want to share a taxiii?" she purred.

I paid the bill and we left to wave down a cab. She sat closer to me than I figured she had to, and the driver dropped her off first.

"Zank you for a nice evening, Ed. I hope to see you soon." We shook hands cordially but lingered for a moment, both of us smiling.

She walked up to the brownstone, and another young lady opened the door for her. The girl's in control of an empire and she needs a roommate? Something was wrong with the math, but I didn't care. I was captivated.

RossiRadio's New York office was easily more austere than what we had going in Los Angeles; there were three threadbare, two-window offices with used desks and noisy air conditioning on the 25th floor of an old building on Madison Avenue, close to all the ad agencies. Shelly's game was to sell the commercial time to planners like Monique, who guided the money directly to our company. We then placed their clients' ads on our radio programs. We were generating all kinds of buzz as the new kids on the block, and the media planners ate us up. We were growing very fast, and they wanted part of that steam.

Everywhere I needed to be—the office, the agencies, New York's radio stations—was within walking distance of the hotel, in the hub of the action. The Essex House on Central Park South afforded me a pit stop, where I could rest my bones at the bar and be content with my own company, but I didn't expect to see who I saw my second night there. I entered from the lobby and parked my ass in a chair nearest the door.

The Essex House bar was strictly old school, with a polished cherry-wood counter, gleaming even in the near darkness, behind which stood an elegant bartender fronting the largest selection of liquor I'd ever seen. The wait staff wore tuxes, and the patrons all looked about 90. One old couple in the booth behind me was eating buffalo wings and getting the sauce all over their mouths. Classy group. When I turned back to order, I looked to my right and pulled a muscle doing a double take. It was Billy Joel—Billy fucking Joel—sitting right next to me.

I was a huge, *huge* fan of the Piano Man since my days at UCLA, and there he was. He was an unqualified musical genius, and I admired him deeply. I always had marveled at how he could sprinkle his strong lyrics with elegant contradictions and ironies while keeping the melody fluid, almost classical. Even the most uncomplicated of songs, like *Just the Way You Are*, bared his soul, like an index to his heart. And he was sitting two feet away!

I debated with myself for what seemed like an hour. Should I speak to him? Say, *"Hey, Billy, big fan,"* and leave it at that? I rarely had an opportunity to work up a conversation with someone whom I admired, *and* was truly famous, someone who could relate to my petty issues with semi-fame. I was conflicted and considered one or two opening lines—when I heard a familiar voice.

"Hey man, what's up?"

I turned to my right. It was *him*. Billy was speaking. To *me*!

*"Well, fuck me."* "Just hanging. Tough day," I replied, staring down, cold as a carp. I was overplaying my casualness. My sweat glands were close to ignition.

"Can I buy you a beer?" Billy Joel was offering to buy me a drink, but it didn't register.

"Excuse me?" I gave him my weary, workingman face while I jumped up and down inside.

"A beer. Can I get you a beer? Or perhaps something else?" he asked.

"Uh, sure. Sorry. A beer's fine. Anything on tap."

"Hey, Sol. One Heineken for the young man." He took a sip of his after ordering and gave me his patented eyes-half-closed look that betrayed little. I thought the contradiction fascinating; his songs were so open and honest.

"So, what's so tough?" he continued.

"I'm just in from LA and we're working on some radio deals. You'll have to excuse me but you're Billy Joel, aren't you?"

"Yep."

"Ed Mann. I'm in from LA."

"Uh, yes, we've confirmed your point of origin."

I was losing whatever cool I brought to the bar, but he smiled, certainly aware of his awkward effect on others. "What kind of radio, young man?"

"We do syndication." I explained.

"Oh really? I love radio, you know. Made me what I am, aside from my piano teacher. Actually I'm working on a new album, and I'm just all twisted up about it, wondering how it'll play to you guys."

Jesus, he was confiding in me. The irony of it made me snort as I laughed. "I got a feeling radio will love it. I don't ever recall a song of yours that didn't hit."

"Ingratiating dishonesty always works with me." We both laughed at my attempt to kiss his ass. Then, a bold move.

"While we're baring our souls, I'd like to ask your take on this. I've got this girl back in California. She's a knockout. A gem." I could see I had his attention, our gazes locked.

"Yeah, go on."

"Well, she's been with this cop for—like years, at least I think she is, and I'm out here for longer than I may know. I met a young French girl here in New York, and she seems totally into me but, oh hell, what do you care?" I gulped down a large slug of beer while Billy swirled his in his glass, like it was wine.

"Hey, I'm about people, my man. That's what I write about. Sounds like you got a problem with choices." I turned to face him and nodded.

"See? See? I was right. You can't choose. That's *their* gig."

I squinted at the implication. "What about free will? You went and found your Uptown Girl, even though you came from, shall we say, not uptown. Isn't that what it's about, choosing well?" I asked.

"Man, they choose *you*. Period. End of sentence."

"So, you're saying you've had your problems?" I asked.

"You name it. Just when I've got her, *bang*, she's gone. Just like that." He snapped his fingers.

*"Shit, he's no different than me, just on a more elevated, supermodel level . . . OK, wwaaaayy different."*

The bartender approached and whispered something to him. Billy looked at me, stood, and shook hands. "Gotta run, Ed. Good luck to you." He dropped a twenty on the bar.

"You too, Bill." *"Bill? Who was I, his mother?"*

The bartender cleared his mug and then glared at me with a *"The Piano Man is always right, so drink the fucking Kool-Aid"* glare.

I finished my beer and retired to my room, thinking how far I'd come from announcing diving meets in high school to hanging with Billy Joel at a bar in New York City, to find he's just a guy—with a wisdom totally counter to Tom's.

# CHAPTER 21

MONIQUE AND ENJOYED DINNERS ON THE Upper East Side, went to jazz clubs in the Village, barged in on art gallery openings in SoHo, and took considerable advantage of New York City. We kept our hands off of each other, a relief from my earlier life of no-named-girl sex fests, and then the no-girl, no-sex fests. I was looking at two full weeks in the city, and she was a constant companion. Shelly was very pleased to see me hook up with a big-time media planner while RossiRadio raked in bigger and bigger dollars from her ad agency. I was the company prostitute, but I wasn't getting laid. I was as happy as I had been for sometime.

Late in the week, I took a call from Monique.

"Ed, do you know much about visas?" she asked, her voice tight.

"Not a thing. Is there a problem?" She paused for a long moment.

"Well, I zink I might have messed something up wiss zee French consulate. I didn't renew my work visa, and I may, um," her voiced caught for a moment and I thought she might cry. "I may have to return to Paris."

I rolled my eyes. This was typical for me; it fit right in with my personal History of the World with Fucked Up Women. "Well, what are your options? Is there a lawyer you could see?"

"I don't know. I'm very confused. I zink I could go to Canada and get a stamp, come back, and be fine. Once I reenter zee U.S., I start fresh."

I really didn't know what to think about this problem of hers, and it really wasn't my place. "You could try it," I said. "What could happen? Canada has a very open relationship with the United States, and surely there would be little problem getting back here from there."

"But what if customs in Canada stop me? Putain de merde! Je suis *ras-le-bol!*"

I had no idea what she was saying, but she clearly was frustrated— and I loved how romantic her French sounded, even while spewing apparent invective.

"Look. Calm down. I'll meet you in Central Park, near the entrance at 59th and Fifth Avenue. How about seven?"

"Okay." She hung up.

After my meetings at the office, I hurried back to the Essex and let my mind wander in the shower. Through the fog of condensation on the shower door, I could almost make out Alex, sitting alone in her apartment in Los Angeles, wondering when I might make a move. *Fuck. She's* supposed to choose. And how's that supposed to happen? She's over there. And I've got my own little money-spewing poodle right here, right now.

She was on time and looking wonderful, irrespective of her mental state—fresh and dewy as if scrubbed and polished with a damp chamois. I escorted her to a bar near the hotel and she immediately unloaded.

"I zink zat I have more at stake zan just my job or my apartment. I might lose *you* if I leave."

I was surprised and pleased—but worried. "I think the Canada plan is good, but why can't you just go back to France to get a new visa?"

"If I go back, I have to reapply and wait for weeks, I could lose my job, and you, and New York." She began to shake mildly, and I took her hand to give her assurance. I took a deep breath.

"I'll go with you to Canada," I blurted, before I could hear myself. She looked up at me with wet, red eyes and grabbed my other hand.

"You will do zat? Wiss me? For me?" I hesitated, but didn't mean to.

"Yes. Why not? Let's take a road trip. It's Thursday, and I could take off early from work."

We kissed, at last, and for about a minute, her mouth affectionate and ready. I embraced her and felt her warm breasts push into my body, almost like a clay mold that joined me to her. I escorted her down the street to a taxi.

"Pack up and I'll call you in the morning. I'll take care of the car." She squeezed my hand hard and entered the cab. I passed a ten to the driver, and she smiled at me from the rear window as the taxi departed.

Back in the room, after staring at my stupid face in the mirror—the star of my own movie, *The Guy Who Gets in His Own Way*—I called an attorney friend in Los Angeles. He confirmed that many people crossed the border, got stamped, and headed back to the U.S. with few problems—but as a foreigner of both the U.S. and Canada—she could be detained. Hell, how long could she be detained in a country that speaks French? He assured me it was worth a shot while reminding me that he was only a contract lawyer.

I shrugged it off; it was all I needed to feel comfortable. That night, I called for a car and a map from the concierge and packed a day bag for the trip. It was a good bet we could reach the border in about half a day, deal with customs, and turn around—but I planned for a night in Canada nevertheless.

At around 8 the next morning, I bolted out the revolving door of the hotel to find the car I rented—a small, douchey looking Toyota Celica—double-parked, with the attendant waiting by the opened car door, hand outstretched, anticipating his gratuity. I tore down

Central Park South toward Monique's apartment. She was out front, nervously shifting her weight from one foot to the other. I couldn't take my eyes off of her. Mademoiselle climbed in, and we headed north out of Manhattan, up the Thruway, and on through the Hudson Valley toward Canada. I'd heard all the reports of the pollution in the New York waterways and how the Hudson River coursed through one smelly Superfund site after another, but that was invisible from our vantage point; it was the loveliest drive I could remember.

We didn't speak four words to each other as we passed Peekskill, drove on past Albany, and pulled in for a late lunch at a café a couple hours short of the border.

"I can't believe you would do ziss, Ed. Ziis is a wonderful gift."

"Here's to a new life, or a 'renew' life," I toasted her with my lemonade, and we hastily devoured our chicken sandwiches. We were anxious to see what fate awaited us at the border. I was wondering if she was just a poodle or a full grown human, capable of choice, of making a decision to see this through, to see *me* through.

We got to Champlain on the 87, and Canadian Customs was waving cars through the border checkpoint with alacrity, scrutinizing them only periodically and stamping passports in a daze. We were heartened by the pace of events as we pulled up to the Customs post.

"Passports please," he asked in a daydream. We handed them to him with a smile. He cocked his head sideways, like a dog hearing a whistle.

"Mademoiselle, que-ce que votre affaire aux Etats Unis?" I sort of got that. He was inquiring about her business in the States.

"Publicité, monsieur."

He regarded her papers again and checked out the pages of stamps. "Attendez, si'l vous plait." He turned to scan through a book, presumably of regulations, then back at her passport. He narrowed his eyes. He saw her U.S. work visa.

"I plan to return to France from Montreal, where we're going for zee weekend," she explained. "My friend is spending zee weekend with me."

He seemed relieved, stamped our papers, and we crossed. We were in Canada!

"I made it," Monique said, as if having won the Tour de France.

"Not yet," I reminded her. "We've got to run the gauntlet right back here in the opposite direction. Once you get a fresh stamp going back across, you should have no problems with your work visa. But you have to get that U.S. entry stamp."

"Pas de probleme," she replied, waving her hand dismissively. She felt confident of my attorney friend's comments and my determination. She was relying on me and wrapped her arm around mine as we forged down the highway. It was near the summer solstice, and the evening sun hardly budged from its spot above the horizon, shining right in my eyes. I squinted to the northwest, the sky turning slightly amber. We pulled into a fast-food place for dinner, grinning at each other over croissant sandwiches and fries. We hadn't discussed our evening arrangements, but we both knew where this was leading.

I spotted a roadside motel about an hour from the border, and we checked in as Mr. and Mrs. Mann of Los Angeles, CA. Our room was a cozy affair, with a view of nothing but streaks of sunshine through the paper-thin drapes. After the door closed, Monique drew close to me.

"I love you for ziis."

"I'm only driving you. I'm your chauffeur." I knew, though, that I was more than that. *Did she just say the L word?*

"Vien à moi, toi." I was puzzled. "Come to me, you," she repeated and kissed me sweetly, like a leaf landing on grass. Her tongue entered my mouth, sweeping around mine softly, with a caress so slight I felt like it might not be happening. I opened my eyes to see hers closed.

We picked up the pace and landed on the bed, her body on top, yet her kiss never overpowering me, staying light and easy. I could get used to this, maybe forever.

I was lost in time and had no idea where I was or when it was. With the late-evening daylight streaming into the room through the window, it had to be near 10 or 11 at night. If we were much farther north, we'd be in the land of the midnight sun, I imagined. I stripped off my shirt and unfastened her bra. She gently pulled off my pants and unbuttoned her jeans to reveal her little French panties, with adorable feathery lace around the top. Women, for all the trouble they'd been to me, always had a pretty surprise under their clothes.

We rubbed against each other, warming our bodies to a boiling point as my mind wrapped around the idea of late-night lovemaking while never seeing darkness. She reached for every inch of my body, and I responded to her gestures, easing into her with a sense of open warmth. I never felt pressured or rushed, and she flowed with my energy, reading me, looking into my eyes for clues. I was transported to a place I hadn't imagined, bouncing slowly from the edges of orgasm in a light that departed the skies achingly slow; it was a match for our rhythm. We finally climaxed and fell back on the rumpled bed, smiling and giggling like children playing doctor. From our bedroom window, I could see the sun dipping below the horizon in a purple glow as we dozed off, melting into the sheets.

I'D BEEN AWAKE FOR AN HOUR, sitting cross-legged on the bed thumbing through the hotel phone directory for the number of the French consulate while Monique slept away.

"Shit," I exclaimed, louder than I wanted to say it, with Monique snoring only a few feet from me.

She awoke slowly, as if a soft breeze had awakened her—not a loud Jew. *"Qu'est-ce qui se passe?"* she muttered, meaning "what's happening?" That much French I knew. She gave me a sweet smile and yawned, rubbing the sleep out of her eyes.

"I've been looking through these numbers of consulates and Customs contacts and just realized that it's Saturday. These are government offices, and I'm sure they'll be closed today. So, I thought we could just go back today, get stamped, and there you'd be. Back at work Monday, and in my sights." She stopped smiling.

"What about last night? Wasn't it wonderful?" She felt slighted by my clumsy lead line.

I turned to face her. "Sweetie, it was wonderful. Just amazing. You're an exquisite creature, and I just want to get you back to the States." She warmed up and kissed me. I remarked to myself that her breath was fresh, even upon waking. She was a goddess from another planet.

There was little choice but to return as soon as possible; a drive-through border crossing back to the U.S. as my unqualified contract attorney had recommended. I was praying that this would work. We dressed quickly, checked out, grabbed donuts in the lobby, and loaded ourselves into the rental car under cloudy, threatening skies.

"We'll get back to New York." I said, reassuringly. "I'll talk to Stu and Tom and see what I can do about getting longer stays on the East Coast. I should be able to see you much more . . ."

"You're way ahead of yourself, monsieur," she interrupted. She gripped my hand hard, frightened of the outcome. I was more afraid than she. We didn't let go of each other from that moment until maybe 50 feet from the border crossing, where she released her hand from mine and grabbed her passport from her purse. I found mine in the glove compartment. She was shaking. I was perspiring. Darkening

clouds loomed behind the guard's booth, giving him a matte, black-
and-white background, against which his crisply ironed, khaki uni-
form stood stiffly, as if hung on a wire coat hanger. He was a Customs
mannequin, barely moving as he passed the passports back to the
drivers. We were one car from the front of the line.

"Good luck," we both said in unison, and laughed for the first time
that day.

"Passports, please," said the U.S. Customs agent, looking far more
stern than he appeared only three cars back. He thumbed through mine
quickly, stamped it, and put it aside. He regarded Monique's far more
carefully, looking at every page. His eyes froze on the work visa. *"Shit."*

"Ma'am, you have an expired work visa. Why did you come to
Canada?" She leaned over me to speak with him directly, nervous
as hell.

"We were here for an evening at a motel across ze border to get
a taste of Canadian cuisine." Hell, we ate donuts and chicken sandwiches at Jack in the Box, and the wrappers were clearly visible from
his window.

"Ma'am, I can't let you through now. Please pull the car to the side
please."

*"Fuck!"* Now it was off to the border Customs office for a long
harangue from the security experts that keep us safe from French
advertising executives. I was limp. This could not be happening. We
pulled over to the office on the Canadian side and hung our heads as
we entered like condemned prisoners.

The office stood apart from the guard station on the right shoulder, the interior barren of any festive accoutrement, not even a travel
poster—just bare walls and the smell of fresh paint—a sterile, austere
environment. I thought it a fitting metaphor for keeping our country
uncontaminated. We were waved over to two chairs in front of a small,
gleaming metal desk. Then another grim mannequin appeared and

took his seat. That desk was spotless. Dust feared his desk. I thought I smelled lemon Pledge.

"Passport, ma'am," he demanded, unsmiling. She passed it over, he inspected it, and within seconds declared, "I'm afraid that you'll have to stay in Canada until we can work this out with the French Consulate."

"But she was only two days late renewing her work visa," I declared. Stupid move. I gave away the motive for the trip—with no provocation.

He shot back a look that turned me to jelly and continued addressing Monique.

"You cannot enter the United States without proper papers, young lady, and your work visa has expired. Furthermore, you exited the United States of your own free will and cannot reenter until this is cleared up. I'm sorry," and with that, he passed her passport back to her. We both stared at each other, disbelieving. Where could we go? How long could this last?

"You go ahead, Ed. I'll be fine."

"What?" I screamed. The officer gave me the look again, and I calmed down. "What are you thinking?"

"I have a credit card and saw a rental-car agency up zee road. I can't have you wait an eternity to work ziss out. It's my problem. You've been wonderful, but you're not my husband, you know."

She blindsided me with that one. I really had extended myself to offer companionship and support, but her comment reminded me that this indeed was her deal. I felt helpless, but the intransigent U.S. Government and this stubborn French girl were making it clear that I was unwelcome.

"I'll visit zee consulate on Monday and call you, my love," softening her touch slightly. "Please don't worry. Go back to New York. I'll call you." She reached over to clutch my hand in a quick goodbye, her eyes dry as flour.

I walked toward the door and looked back over my shoulder. She blew me a kiss, and I climbed in the car for the drive back to New York—my loneliest, dreariest day in memory. Just past Albany, the rain that had been accumulating in the gloomy, low-slung clouds all day finally found its way toward my windshield. I cranked up the wipers, but they just pushed the water in globs around the glass. Perfect. I squinted my way through percussive rain splats all the way to Manhattan. I turned on the radio, and out poured *A New York State of Mind*—by my prophetic pal, Billy Joel. It was a fitting ending for my blurry weekend.

# CHAPTER 22

I WAS IN THE NEW YORK OFFICE, slogging through my early Monday morning and wondering who'd miss me if I leapt from the building and splatted all over Madison Avenue. Who'd call the coroner? Would they gingerly pick up my squished body or scrape it off the pavement like roadkill? The receptionist buzzed me with a phone call.

"What in holy fuck were you thinking?" It was Stu, fuming at full fume from Los Angeles. It was 8 a.m. in New York, but 5 a.m. for him.

"I was trying to help her, Stu. She was in trouble and . . ."

"Let me get this straight," he interrupted. "You drove our most important media planner to another country, slept with her *I'm sure*, came back to New York, left her there for deportation—and *it was all your idea*?!" His breathing got fast and shallow; he sounded on the brink of cardiac arrest. I had to admit, if someone had told me that story I would have put their IQ at around 40. It was pretty fucking bad.

"Stu, she was desperate. She came to me for help, I called my attorney and he suggested . . ."

"You knew her for a week! Did you ever consider that maybe her company could help her? She could have phoned her Paris office, she could have called anyone—but *you*. She panicked, you panicked, and now we have this goddamn mess." I heard a shuffling and stood to see Shelly in the office next door; he was searching frantically, digging through his desk drawer for his pills.

"I'll see you in LA, and we'll talk more about it then," I declared to Stu, as I felt the color drain from my face. I hung up and faced a concerned Shelly.

"You're more of a mess than I am," I began. Shelly had just swallowed four multi-colored pills. "What were those?"

"Ginseng, St. John's Wort, Vitamin C and Valium." He looked up at me across the desk, eyes as wide as searchlights. Shelly hadn't jumped on me for this—that was Stu's province—but I hadn't accounted for what Stu might have said to Shelly, who introduced Monique to me in the first place.

"She's my client, and it's my ass. If we don't get those buys in from her company, I'm in deep shit. You're a partner, Ed. You don't have to sweat this like I do. This is my j-o-b. And there aren't a whole lot of those around these days." He abruptly grabbed his side as if struck by a cramp.

"What the hell is that?" I asked, alarmed.

"My lumbago's acting up."

"Lumbago? Who are you, Myrna Loy?"

He laughed at that one. *I still had it.* "Hell," he groaned, "I've got more maladies than a Bangkok whore."

"Take it easy. You know, she very well may be on her way here right now."

"A whore?"

"No dope. Monique!"

"Ed, she's way more likely in a boulangerie on the Champs Elysee, munching on a fresh croissant and laughing about the fun time she had in New York fucking with us."

"By the way, Shelly. Explain to me how a young girl bunking with another young girl just to make ends meet controls so much money."

Shelly narrowed his eyes; he hated to explain his end of the business—the money end—to an ex-DJ clown who'd just fucked with his end.

He took a deep sigh. "Suffice it say that she's an employee. Her job is to find the right place for the money. She doesn't *have* the money. She just moves it around. Now, if you were sitting at a table and shoving someone else's hundred-dollar bills around, would you expect to be paid a lot for that?"

I didn't appreciate the demeaning analogy and the belittling tone, but evidently, Shelly and Stu had no other key connection to this agency money. Losing Monique meant losing the money. I gave Shelly a reassuring clap on the back and stalked out to the hotel. I had a lot to sort out.

Later that evening in my room, I picked up the ringing phone. It was Tom.

"Where are you?" I asked.

"In the bar."

"Of course you're in the bar. Where else would you be?"

"I'm downstairs, you moron. Join me for a pint."

I headed down the elevator and was pleasantly surprised to find my old pal in New York City at Billy Joel's spot in front of the bar, with a dark, fizzy, diabolical beverage waiting for me. He'd just checked in—his black, brand spanking new executive-monogrammed luggage leaning against the leg of his stool.

"Your timing is magnificent. I can use a familiar face right now. You didn't tell me you were coming." I was smiling broadly and was truly happy to see Tom, sans uncomfortable necktie and Little Lord Fauntleroy blue blazer. He was wearing the same Lacoste pullover he wore when we first met. I reeled in the years, half forgetting where we'd been and what we'd done since he'd taken me in. We were fucking famous for a minute. Just a memory.

"Mate, I'm always just around the corner." He slugged down half a pint in one gulp and left a sizable moustache above his lips, then wiped it off with his tiny cocktail napkin, pinkies raised. Humorous, but only one of us was smiling.

"Don't tell me you're just here for me," I asked.

"All right, I won't tell you."

"Why in hell is everyone so bent out of shape about this girl? She let her visa expire. Happens all the time. For all I know, she'll be back in a week."

Tom drank while I talked as if in perfectly synchronized rhythm, like a well-timed clock. Then I talked when he drank, and when he talked, I listened, and he drank when I talked again—never once missing a beat. It was like he still was on the radio and wanted to avoid dead air. I hadn't taken a sip.

"Well, turns out that your little French treat was key to that agency. No one else there deals with us directly, and she was in control of more money than you know."

"Oh, please. She was a kid. How much could they have let her handle?"

"How about one and a half million," said Tom, with a casualness that reminded me of Jack Benny. "And that's just our slice of the pie. She was working media plans for tens of millions."

So there it was, but to get the corroboration from Tom was mind-bending.

"Please tell me that you're kidding," I said. "That's absurd. She was a young media planner. A kid!"

"Interesting how we're using the past tense," Tom said. "Regardless, she's *our* kid media planner, and that's what we stand to lose if you don't get her back."

I almost fell off my stool. "*Me?*"

"Yes, you. You dropped her off in Canada, and you're going to have to fucking find her. If she's in Paris, you'll go there. I don't care if she's in Bangladesh. You'll get her and anchor her back at her desk at

C&T. You did this, and you'd better fix it." Tom's voice was escalating with each sentence. We all stood to lose a boatload of money, and all fingers were pointing at me. I felt like a sixth grader who talked out of turn.

"Let's just calm down a second," I replied. "I'll call her office in New York first thing and see what they know. Perhaps she left word of her dilemma and they could lead us in the right direction."

"Lead *you*, buddy," Tom reminded me. "It's not my ass on the line here."

I didn't appreciate the stern tone from my friend, my partner, but I did care for her. I had additional incentive. "So, what does this mean for me?" I asked.

"You'll get time off with pay while you're gone. We'll cover for you. Your number-one priority is to get her back. Period. And Ed, don't take this wrong. We're friends, pals, but you're going to have to find a way to fix this."

So, now our friendship is in the balance? Rockefeller's words were ringing in my brain. Tom obviously was sent to New York to lecture me, maybe against his wishes. This smelled like Stu. I began to think that Stu sent me to New York in the first place to keep Monique in line. Jesus. Tom pushed back from the bar, offered me a hug that I returned without much vigor, and I escorted him to the lobby.

"I'm going up," he said. "Have a good night, and let's work on this more tomorrow." He vanished behind the elevator door. I was somewhere between pissed, frightened, and excited—and it looked like I was going to see the world.

I arose Tuesday morning, having slept only four hours. It took two cups of coffee for me to dress myself. Worse, there was a steady drizzle outside my window overlooking Central Park. I never was prepared for the rain in New York; it always took me by surprise, after spending so much time in LA, where the sun blasts every damn day. I exited the hotel, lumbered toward the office, and suddenly realized I had no cash for as much as a donut, so I stopped at an ATM, facing a monstrous line. Banks had just begun installing these automated machines around town, and they were an instant hit, so the lines, especially in Manhattan, were unforgiving. This one was a good 10 deep, but I hung in there, bouncing from foot to foot.

A homeless man was working his way down the line, asking for money. I thought that odd—we had no money yet. He should be going after everyone *leaving* the machine. It sounded like he might be singing, but I had trouble hearing—this part of town was noisy with traffic, plus the weather had turned nastier. The umbrellas in front of me were muffling his voice, but as he got closer to my position in line, I could tell that he was attempting opera and playing a ukulele. He possessed the most miserable voice I'd ever heard: way off key, mumbling half the words—an awful performance.

Meanwhile, I hadn't moved more than an inch in that line for more than five minutes, so I swayed to the left and raised my heels to get a view of what was happening at the front. A young lady was rifling through her purse, looking for her PIN number or her card. We were prisoners and were in for a serenade. I braced as Pavarotti approached.

"How 'bout a song for a dollar?" he garbled. I reached into my pocket and replied, "Here's a dollar. Don't sing." The guys in front of me began howling. The poor guy was shattered, but regrettably began singing anyway. Only in New York, I thought.

Shelly was in the office to greet me, happy as a clam, and sure enough, asked me for a five to get bagels for the crew. He darted out only to return five minutes later with the bagels, touting his good deed to all: "Bagels, on me! Bagels are hot and ready!" On my dime. What a schmuck. He followed me into my office like a dog.

"Have you called C&T yet?" he begged. I guessed that Tom had spoken to him.

"I'm just about to. I'll let you know what happens. By the way, how's your Lumbago?" He glared as I dialed my fugitive's office.

"C&T."

"Yes, is Monique Bertrand available?"

"Uh, no, she's not in this week. Can someone else help you?" At least they didn't say she was no longer in their employ.

"No, thank you. Oh wait," I exclaimed. "Do you have a forwarding number for her?"

"She still works here, sir. You can leave a message."

I'm an idiot. "Yeah, of course," I laughed, unsmiling, "but it's very important that I reach her as soon as possible."

"We can't give out personal information."

"But I'm her boyfriend and . . ."

"I'm very sorry. That's company policy. I'm sure you understand."

I did, but didn't want to. "Miss, she may be in some kind of trouble. Could you please make an exception?" There was a long pause, then a deep exhale.

"Try 555-5698." Damn. Her home number in New York. Of course I had that.

"Thank you. But, uh, you don't happen to have her family's number in France, do you?" I implored.

"Are you joking?" And with that she hung up.

I dialed the number and got her home machine, where I left a concerned message. I sat with my head propped up by my arms thinking I really might have to go to Paris to work this out, which I had carte blanche to do. This could be intriguing, but risky. It didn't escape me that I could be fired from my own company for this shitstorm.

I checked my travel docs—I had a prearranged flight back to LA that evening, one of those non-refundable deals. I worked through the day, met with Tom and Shelly about other company crap, headed back to the hotel to pack, and took the last flight out to Los Angeles—form-fitted into an economy seat in the back of the plane. I could smell the cookies baking in the first-class galley and was pissed that I couldn't get an upgrade.

I found my car at LAX, drove the short distance down Vista del Mar toward Manhattan Beach, and parked. My place was as I had left it—a lonely hole. It was late, but before I tucked myself in between my low-thread-count sheets, I sat at the kitchen table, put pen to paper, and wrote my to-do list for the following day—as I normally did. I realized that it had shortened considerably: Find Monique.

I set it aside and was getting ready for bed when the phone rang. It was after 11.

"Yes," I answered.

"Ed, it's your dad." I sorely needed someone on my side, but he simply hadn't been there. I collapsed onto the rattan chair next to my bed.

"Yes, Dad. I just got in from New York and I'm beat. What's up?"

"Is everything all right? You haven't phoned your mom or me in quite some time."

"Sorry. Really, I'm sorry, but things have gotten crazy. I met a girl and she flew the coop, and I have to find her, and frankly I don't where to turn."

"Not so famous anymore, are you?"

"Funny. Million laughs." My tone was distraught.

"What kind of mess are you in? How bad?" He was feeling me. Hit it right on. I was getting a little wet in the eyes as the events of the past week caught up with me, and although my dad was tough on me, he was still my dad.

"Well, I kind of lost her. In Canada."

"Huh?"

"It's a long story, but she's rather important to both the company and to me. I may have to go to Europe for a while. She's French." We both paused for a moment.

"*A* wing and a prayer," he said, as if there was only one wing. I couldn't stop laughing.

"You're right, Dad," I chuckled. "One wing and a prayer. That's exactly what I'll need."

"Do what you have to do, Ed. We're proud of you."

"Thanks, Dad." I hung up and stared at the wall for an hour. He filled some of the emptiness and doubt in me, but my mind was on tomorrow. I shifted in my seat like I had lice in my pants. It was getting late, but I dialed Julie anyway.

"Jules. It's your cuz. I'm on my way outta town soon. I think I'm going to Paris, of all places."

"You *think* you're going? Sounds romantic. You got someone there?"

"It's not what it seems. It's business, really. But that's not why I called. Julie, ya gotta get straight with me on this, babe." I took a long, strained breath. "Do I have a shot with Alex?"

The pause that followed was longer than a Super Bowl Pre-Game show. "She's gone. I think."

"You *think*? What do you mean? Is she here or . . ."

"Pretty sure, Eddie. And I hate to tell you. The last time I saw her was Vegas."

"When were you in Las Vegas?" I asked, sweating.

"Well, Alex invited a group of girls there for, well, uh, there was kind of a, like, bachelorette party."

"Don't tell me. For Alex." Another outrageously long pause. This time I thought she might have put me on hold.

"Yes. She's planning on marrying Mike. I mean, they're engaged."

"Did they set a date?"

"No. I mean, I don't know. It was a little while ago, and, well, I just don't know."

"Thanks, Jules. Love you."

This didn't match up right—Alex and Mike—but there it was, and a celebration in her dad's old stomping ground. I wanted to go back to the synagogue and throw myself on the alter. I hung up, pulled my dusty afghan over my chest, and fell asleep right there on the chair, the chill of the ocean air filling the apartment from the open bedroom window.

# CHAPTER 23

In the LA office the next morning, Stu and I avoided each other entirely. He knew what I had to do: call C&T in Paris, call a private investigator, call the U.S. Consulate in Paris, put out an APB, hire a K-9 unit, quit my job . . . now *that* might be an option—if I had anywhere to go. My last on-air gig was overseen by a woman out on bail for grand theft—some reference she'd be. My mind flashed to several nightmares of what RossiRadio could do to me: Hold me responsible for some loss of revenue? The loss of a person? Maybe they take my shares away? Would I be a pariah in my own company, my industry? I marked down one more to-do: call a lawyer.

After a solitary lunch in a food court using splintered chopsticks to sort through a smelly order of Kung Pao chicken, Stu paged me, and I entered his office—a more palatial affair by the week. He had knocked down the office next to his and doubled the square footage, and there were framed pictures of him with Reagan and Bush—and even Casey Kasem. I had one in my office with Weird Al.

"Eddie, how goes it? Are you closer to finding her?" He was twisting a piece of Scotch tape in his hand, sticking it to his fingers and unsticking it, over and over. He peeled a fresh piece off and gestured toward me, the tape hanging off his finger for me to play with. I demurred and grabbed a paper clip from his desk and began bending it around in different angles. The two of us must have looked like kindergarteners.

"Well, I've put together a project list of what I need to do to find her. I'm working on executing it. *"Executing. Bad choice of word."*"

Stu leaned into me, only a foot from my face. His breath smelled like floor polish. "I don't need "working." I need "results-ing." A wordsmith he wasn't. "Get your shit together and let's get you to Paris." I knew it. Where else could she go with no work visa but home?

"Funny you should mention it. I was on the phone with my cousin last night and . . ."

"Tom and Shelly are in New York," he interrupted, "and they've got a couple of good leads in Europe. She's in Paris, we're almost sure. You're going. Book your flight. Tom will be in first thing to brief you." He swiveled his chair to face away from me, leaving me to molt, fingering his tape. Tom and Shelly had done my investigating for me.

"So, no "bon voyage?" I asked plaintively.

He didn't bother turning back and mumbled, "You've got to be kidding."

Back in my office, I checked my schedule for the next two weeks: pretty dry. I could leave in a matter of days. I booked a flight for that Friday and drove home.


TOM HAD ARRIVED BACK FROM NEW York the following day and slid into my office guest chair sometime before lunch, munching a banana.

"Hey, Manndelsteinawitz," he declared and took a seat, slouching like he was on a chaise lounge. At least he was attempting niceties.

"Charming."

"Okay, so here're the leads that we found." He flipped through a small, handwritten notepad. "Her family lives in the 6th District, her mother is a small film producer, her dad's an accountant. She's never lived away from home, except for her stint in New York and summer trips with whomever her boyfriend was at the time, and there were a few. She applied for a position in Belgium, so you may have to bop around. If I were you, and *I'm not*, I'd start at her house. Here's the number." He ripped off the first sheet of paper on the pad and passed me all the info. I was stupefied at the detail of his research.

"How did you get all this, and who were the boyfriends?"

"It took major leg work," he said, avoiding the latter part of my question. "There's more. This is going to be tricky, Ed."

"Oh, you figure? I'm supposed to find a girl who hasn't contacted me since she fled the scene, convince her that she's the one for me, and haul her ass back to work. And who knows if she can with that old visa." I let out a deep sigh. "By the way, how do you know that C&T wants her back?"

"Well, we found out a thing or two about that. Turns out that she was very well-liked and left behind more than just you. Evidently, she was, um, sleeping with the boss."

"Oh, that's fine." I stood up and began pacing. Tom sat with his legs posted on my desk, munching on his banana as if it were his last meal, closing his eyes in gastro-ecstasy.

"So I'm going to charm her into my pants and his, too? This is insane."

Tom threw the peel in the trash. "That's about the size of it. Are you ready to go."

"What about her replacement? I asked.

"Ed, grow up. There's no guarantee that another girl will do for us what Monique did. None. Monique's not dead. Let's get her!" He stormed out of the office like a man I never met.

I plopped back in my chair, resigned to this Mission Impossible.

# CHAPTER 24

FRIDAY FOUND ME MAKING FINAL PREPARATIONS for the 10 p.m. flight on American from LAX to Charles de Gaulle in Paris. As I predicted, Monique hadn't called me the entire week. I packed a big black duffle bag with most of my worldly goods for the stay—about two to three weeks I figured—and then I'll have mademoiselle winging her way to New York, making us enough money to fill a swimming pool. How to accomplish that was a mystery to me; and I had to do this on the fly. All I had was a French-English dictionary that I'd devoured over the past few days.

I was passing Terminal 3 at LAX with Achmed, my pleasant driver from Iraq, when he caught my eye. It was Mike. Alex's Mike. Unmistakable. He was pacing back and forth along the walkway in front of the Tom Bradley Terminal, head jutted forward, then side to side, looking for someone. We were stopped at the light and out of his view. I told the driver to stay put while I observed, but the light turned green, and he took off. Asshole!

Mike's head craned and seemed to focus across the street toward the parking structure. As we pulled away, I swiveled my head and saw a young lady, a tall brunette, carrying a fancy Louis Vuitton duffle bag, waving as she waited for the Do Not Walk sign to change, but I couldn't make her out—thanks to the scum on Achmed's back window. She crossed the street and jumped into his waiting arms, receiving a squeeze so tight I thought her head might pop off. I watched slack-jawed as they entered the terminal. Was it Alex? I guess Julie was right. We arrived at the American Airlines terminal; I clambered out of the taxi and ducked into the building. Man, that hurt like hell.

It was a short walk to the gate. I took a seat in the lounge, thumbing through the dozen or so magazines I brought for the flight and only *seeing* the words on the page; my mind was focused on two women, both out of reach.

Then the announcement came: "All passengers for American Airlines, Flight 10 to Paris-Charles de Gaulle, please have your passports ready and boarding passes available." Then something in French. I was half-hoping he was telling us that France was closed for the season and to go home. I could feel my pulse rising. I had to calm down. As long as I didn't think of the task, I was just a kid taking a plane to an exotic place. Yeah, like a fantasy land, but where everything I said would be misunderstood and I'd stare blankly at strangers as they addressed me with the simplest of statements, like "who do you think you are taking one of our citizens back to another country, you fucking ugly American." Ugh, how could this possibly work?

I boarded, found my seat on the aisle, and settled in. Others stumbled to their seats, lugging their bulky carry-ons. One enormous lady dragged hers across my lap and then sat right next to me. She might as well have sat right on me. I felt bad for her, stuck in a middle seat, but now I had half a seat left. This could be an achingly long flight. The plane pulled away from the gate, on time, and left the ground slower than any plane I'd ever flown; it must have been loaded for bear with jet fuel for the 10-hour flight. That didn't concern me in the least; within 20 minutes, I let the seat back fall and I drifted off to sleep.

Nine hours later, I was awakened by an announcement—first in French and then in English. "Please prepare for our descent into Paris-Charles de Gaulle." I jerked my head off of the large lady's shoulder and checked my watch. Jesus, I'd slept for seven hours. I didn't get seven at home. I missed the meal, the movie, the whole trip. I thought of the old saying, *"It's not the destination, it's the journey!"* Bullshit. I readjusted my watch, moving the hands nine hours ahead. It was around 4:30 p.m. local time, and I had the entire evening to myself in the City of Light.

We landed precisely on time, only to wait forever in an enormous line at Customs. I lifted myself onto my toes to see up front and noticed that they were pulling all people of color aside for further questioning. I gave the French *douanne* agents a hard gaze while the rest of us moved through the turnstiles as if on a river raft. The black media community gave me my first job in LA, at KUTE, and this bullshit made me realize how little had changed in the world. It was the dawn of the '90s for Christ's sake!

I was quizzed by an agent and headed toward baggage claim, where I collected my giant duffle. I passed additional Customs agents, smoking cigarettes and amusing each other as thick, unfiltered smoke curled above them, then lugged the bag out to the curb and grabbed a waiting taxi.

It whisked me away at a frightening clip toward a Paris I couldn't recognize in the least. One after the other, unappealing, neon-flooded, cement-block office buildings lined the A-1 roadway, barring my vision of the *banlieues*; it was not what I expected. This could be Cincinnati. Strings of aging apartment buildings and convenience shops serving stationary bystanders were sprinkled among them. After 20 unfortunate minutes on the ghastly *autoroute*, a spire appeared above the low skyline—the Eiffel Tower. My eyes widened. It was staggering, and I had an immediate, palpable awareness of where I was and how monumentally different from California my environment would be for the coming days.

We pulled onto the *Périphérique* highway and into Paris proper. What a contrast from only moments earlier—stunning from every angle, from every corner. There were no harsh lines or distracting skyscrapers; everything fit together like copper-topped Legos. The signature Haussman-esque roofs I'd seen only in photographs and films topped every building. The structural similarity reminded me of San Francisco, with its contiguous line of Victorian townhouses, minus the colorful paint and the smelly Tenderloin. And there was little deviation in that breathtakingly beautiful architecture, until we made the right turn past Concorde and burrowed through a short tunnel that delivered me to the Quai, the highway that parallels the Seine along the Right Bank, near Châtelet. We rolled under *pont* after ancient *pont* as the hazy, late-afternoon sunlight reflected off the river, illuminating the structures on the Left Bank in a glowing sepia tone.

The taxi approached the 4th District and, without warning, we were back in medieval times—side streets narrowed to the width of a wheelbarrow. I pictured young maidens cavorting with their men in armor as they prepared for battle during the Crusades. The oldest-looking buildings I'd ever seen hedged streets named Rue du Petit-Musc and Rue des Rosiers. Many had gargoyles posted on the eaves, guarding against intruders. This area couldn't have changed much in the 600 years since it was laid out and paved. I was mesmerized by the unassuming beauty and enduring continuity of Paris, its settled confines stretching out for a centuries-long ride astride the Seine. I thought, *"Thank God the Nazis left this alone."*

"C'est terminé, monsieur," said the driver, his brakes squeaking as we came to a stop in front of my small hotel, the Hôtel des Vosges, adjacent to the Place des Vosges in the Marais District. I collected my things with no help from the driver, paid him, and checked in. The lobby was small and quiet, and luckily the clerk spoke decent English.

"Oui, monsieur, your room izz ready," he began with a frown shaped like a croissant.

"Merci, monsieur," I replied in a shitty accent. I was prepared for the famous rude Parisians, but attempting to speak a little French turned his frown around. He collected my passport and kept it in an open key slot behind the front desk. At first, I was alarmed but then noticed that he had a hefty collection of about 20 passports, many of them American.

He must have seen my concern when he blurted, "Zat izz zee law, monsieur." He said I could pick it up whenever I left the hotel, but I'd have to offer up my key. I shrugged and dragged my duffle without elevator assistance, to my room on the third floor.

I plopped my things on the parquet floor, bounced on the bed, and could feel the springs on my ass. I fluffed the pillows; they were thinner than the pillow covers. Nevertheless, I was charmed out of my pants and pulled them off, along with the rest of my clothes, for a hot shower in a tub with no curtain and no shower head—only a hand-held device that I had to carefully negotiate without a manual to avoid soaking the floor. I dried off with the non-absorbent towels, changed, and headed out for dinner.

It didn't matter much which direction I headed. Food was available every few feet, and the aroma was overwhelming. I popped into a small bistro at Rue St. Paul, near an old church. The chalkboard menu bore a mysterious combination of letters that I recognized individually, but I had no idea what they meant when strung together or how they were pronounced. As I fumbled through my dictionary, the waitress—a hurried, handsome woman in her forties—approached me as I fretted about how I'd address her.

"May I help you?" she asked in accented English. I relaxed immediately,

"How did you know I was English speaking?"

"You are American, no?" she grinned, pleased at having her prediction come true.

"Well, yes."

"It izz your shoes, monsieur. Zay are large."

I looked down at my footwear and saw that I was wearing Nike basketball shoes, then checked the feet of the customers. No one was wearing anything like them. There were loafers, a few beat-up leather tie-ups, one pair looked like giant clown shoes, but no tennies, and certainly no high-tops.

"Well, you found me out," I exclaimed in mock exasperation. "What do you recommend? I've never been to a Parisian café."

"Pleeease try zee Croque Monsieur."

"Crock?" I mispronounced.

"No, monsieur. Croque. Croque Monsieur. Wiz a hard O."

"What's in it?" I asked.

"It'z a ham sandwich wiz a *delicieux* cheese that I am sure you will have never tasted."

"Sounds wonderful," I decided.

"So, it'z zee Croque Monsieur?"

"Yes please, but you don't have to keep addressing me as 'monsieur.'" She threw her head back in delight at my remark, laughing hysterically.

"Zee sandwich, it'z called 'monsieur,' and so are you." Tears came to her eyes she was laughing so giddily. I checked the chalkboard again, and sure enough: "Croque Monsieur." I began blushing, and she giggled her way back to the kitchen. One hour into my French adventure and a waitress and I were Abbott and Costello.

She returned only a few minutes later with a beautiful plate arranged with a lightly pan-toasted sandwich, slices of prosciutto peeking over the edges, and a melted cheese more aromatic than anything I'd smelled before, all placed symmetrically over a salad with a light, oily dressing that clung to the fresh leaves of lettuce like dew. I tried the salad first, and my taste buds exploded. I closed my eyes in ecstasy and chewed slowly, savoring every moment. I couldn't wait to taste that "croque." With the first bite, I almost fell out of my chair. The ham must have been carved off the bone as I arrived—it was that fresh. The cheese was indescribable, like a cross between Swiss and some sort of fine Brie, creamy but not thick and chewy like Brie can be. And there was a Dijon mustard at the table that tasted beyond perfection—gritty and fresh—I couldn't imagine slathering it on anything but the finest food in a first-rate restaurant, but there it was on a cheap sandwich at a corner bistro. I looked back at the chalkboard to check the price: 18 francs, about $3.50. I thought, "*incroyable.*"

"Do you like?" she asked, seeing my gesticulations while I chewed every bite as if I'd never eaten before.

"If I may tell you, this is the finest meal I've ever had."

She laughed out loud. "We eat like zis every day, monsieur. Every, every day." That seemed like a plan to me. She suggested a coffee to finish me off and turned to scream, "Un express!!!" A guy in the back hustled to the stainless-steel coffee machine as if Mitterrand was calling. Man, they took their coffee seriously.

I finished my meal, radiating a joyful tingling from my stomach to the tips of my fingers and taunted my tongue with the espresso, a burst of bitter pleasure. I paid the bill and took a stroll around the neighborhood. In clear view to my right was the Bastille tower, where the old Bastille prison once stood. It wasn't very accessible, stuck in the middle of a round circular drive where several broad and busy avenues filled with tiny, speeding Renaults converged into incomprehensible traffic jams. I walked the circumference of the drive to L'*Opéra* Bastille, a new opera house that didn't mesh with the surrounding architecture—very modern and hardly "*Parisien*." Farther around the circle, I found a bar on one of the smaller streets surrounding the Bastille. The bartender happily took my order in English, and I sipped a beer while the sun set slowly, around the same hour of the evening that Monique and I collapsed in Canada. The beer had the odd effect of washing that "tingling" down my throat.

Hunched over the bar, watching the yellow headlights circling the Bastille, I felt a slower passing of time, the Parisian modus operandi, and couldn't help but consider how I came to be there. Everything in my life led to this moment, in this bar. I felt dragged here by forces completely beyond my control. I had begun tasting fame behind a mic, then stuck behind a *desk* of all things—and now, a sudden segue to the scene from *Chinatown*, where John Huston's character says to Jack Nicholson, "Just find the girl, Mr. Gittes."

God, if I hadn't followed Tom around like a dog, I might have chosen a more sensible tributary. And fucking Stu had sold me a bill of goods that was barely relevant to me. But the Jewish lemming followed him. I had wanted to be creative and funny and maybe just a *little* famous. I was once pre-funny. Semi-famous! Now I was post-traumatic—the river that delivered me here was pulling me from my dreams.

And if I did find Monique—what of it? What good comes of that? She clearly wanted away from me, or New York City, or her boss, or perhaps she just wanted to go back to France, motivated by her own primal forces of home. Hell, now *I* wanted to go home.

If my existence had any meaning, I had better look a little deeper than the notion of some current powering me downstream. I had faced down my own personal demons—my father, my employers, my partners, and landed in Frogland, watching the sun set over a city I'd never considered more than a tourist stop, and now I was hoping for a lightening bolt to end my odyssey? Insane!

As I brought the last of the beer to my lips, the contents sloshing toward my mouth like a tide, I considered the ebb and flow of my life, looking for what? Shelly and Stu's meal ticket? Personal salvation? The glass was about empty. Time to get enlightened. Fuck Sartre, bring on Voltaire!

I headed back to the hotel. Sleep soon found me under the paper-mâché sheets, dreaming of a swim upstream in the smelly Seine, chasing a boat, the captain pointing at me, laughing.

I WOKE UP WITH NO PLAN, BUT at least I wanted one. Meanwhile, I had to see Paris. I popped on light clothes to address the French summer, and went to slip on my shoes. I stopped mid-stream, double-thinking my choice of high-top basketball Nike Air Jordans, deciding instead on a pair of Mephistos; at least my shoes were French. I turned right on Rue Saint Antoine, a major thoroughfare bifurcating the 4th Arrondissement. There was a café on virtually every corner, and I had to investigate another after my surreal sandwich experience. I was a tourist, still on Pacific Time and hungry for an evening meal in the morning; it was 9 a.m. locally but midnight in LA, presenting a unique problem—I could find no food to suit my taste. The cafés served only *tartines*, just a slice of French bread and butter, and croissants. I figured I'd better acclimate to the time zone; I picked the *tartine*. Delightful, of course.

As I exited the café, I felt a certain freedom 7,000 miles from home—like a vacation. Although I did have a purpose here, I felt no rush. The French laissez-faire frame of mind was infecting my being; I had a sense that everything will happen in due course—rush the gig, fuck it up. I took it easy and let the city come to me.

The walk was a revelation in beauty. Every street, every building, every storefront materialized as if from a Monet or a Renoir. I was charmed and falling in love with Paris, letting every angle of the city stab me with pleasure. I was smitten. Then a most remarkable thing happened. A blind man was making his way up the sidewalk toward me, tapping his cane for the edges of the curb. He was elderly and dressed in an old, drab coat. I gave him a wide berth as he approached, but he appeared to sense my presence and veered into my path, halting my progress. Just a few feet ahead of me, he stopped cold—and stared at me.

"You will find what you're looking for, monsieur," he said clearly, in plain English.

"How did you know, that is, how do you know I speak English?" I was astonished and looked down to remind myself that I was wearing something other than Nikes. As I responded, I heard a tinge of fear creeping into my voice.

"Don't worry, my son, but don't waste your time."

"What the hell are you talking about, sir? And what . . ."

"Don't ask what," he interrupted calmly, "Ask why."

Great. A new mentor. And with that, he moved on, shuffling along the narrow sidewalk and straight for the dog shit that now stuck out the sides of his soles. Was there a simple method to get answers? I felt as if my clothes had been ripped off in public by a blind psychic.

Drifting around Paris was getting me nowhere. I headed back toward the hotel and grabbed a crêpe from a street vendor. It was filled with the tastiest cheese I could imagine. I salivated all the way back to the Place des Vosges, a large, square courtyard near my hotel, surrounded by ancient buildings, housing antique stores and the like. As I sat on the bench, with the noonday sun hitting me squarely on the forehead, I reached into my coat pocket to find the leads that Tom had worked to get me. Laissez-faire my ass. The distance from the problem was one phone call away. I stared at the notes, knowing what I had to do.

# CHAPTER 25

HAD A DESIRE FOR SOMETHING SWEET and devoured a lemon tarte from a pâtisserie on the corner, near the hotel. This was now the best food I'd ever tasted. How long could this last? I traipsed upstairs to my room, picked up the phone, and dialed the number on the sheet—my mouth going dry as the phone rang.

"Allô?"

"Oui, est Monique là?"

"Oui, c'est moi."

"Monique, it's Ed. I'm in Paris."

"Ah yes, Ed." She responded as if expecting the call.

"I've thought a lot about you and wanted to see you."

"Did your company send you, or are you on your own?" So, she knew the stakes.

"I'm on my own, Monique. This always has been about you and me."

She offered up a long pause, perhaps not buying my manufactured sincerity. It sounded good to me.

"Meet me at vingt et une heure, 9 p.m. at ze gates of ze Jardin du Luxembourg in ze 6ᵗʰ."

"See you then, Monique," I finished sweetly. If I could charm her for the evening, I had a chance. I didn't know what she was doing now, but I had a hunch. In my brain, a chance and a hunch equals Monique funneling millions to us once again. I would chain her to her desk in the states, and she could screw me and her boss, and her boss' boss— any boss she wanted. I didn't give a shit. I was a cynic. I was *Cynico* D'Bergerac! My afternoon was spent browsing antique stores and sipping espressos in cafés 'til my head exploded.

Back at the hotel, I dressed for the evening, shirt with no tie and a greenish sports coat—I was looking more Parisian every hour. A taxi was waiting for me as I exited the hotel. I scrambled into the backseat and handed him the address.

"Non, monsieur," he exclaimed, waving his right hand dismissively. "L'adresse est trop proche d'ici."

"Je ne comprends pas. Je suis americain,"

"Iiiitzz too close. No taxi!" he yelled, and he motioned me out of the cab. I was flabbergasted; this was unheard of in New York. I pulled out my pocket map and—sure enough—the Gardens were just across the Seine River, but it was hardly a short walk. The evening was pleasant enough, although clouds were gathering to the north, and I felt the breeze pick up as I crossed the river. I marveled at the view of Notre Dame to my right and the tourist boats below Pont Sully, the bridge I was taking to the Left Bank.

I felt if I was treading on the same soil as Louis IV, or perhaps his horse did the treading. My mind drifted, daydreaming of my return here one day in triumph, with a wife and kids trailing me. I dreamed of water-skiing on the Seine, slaloming around the bridge supports, spraying tourists along the banks. I dreamed of painting with oils, of cooking with Julia Child, of bottling wine, of wearing a beret, of walking from work with a fragrant baguette under each arm, of humid afternoons at the Rodin Museum—watching statues think—of hiking up the hills of Montmartre from Square Louis Michel to Sacré-Coeur, of kissing Monique in the streets in front of the frowning Frogs—or was it Alex? I daydreamed all the way to the gates of the Gardens, stunning in a gothic sort of way as darkness set in, made gloomier by the thick, sinister clouds now moving directly over me, unfurling like a dark-grey carpet.

And there she was, standing against the garden gate, closed due to the late hour. I was brimming with anticipation. She was dressed casually, her hair pinned back, her shapely hips hugged by tight blue jeans, her breasts holding up her loose-fitting blouse that danced in the breeze with a life of its own. I saw that fresh, dewy face and went back in time to our night in Canada. But her reaction was indifferent now, her face parked in neutral.

"It's gooood to see you, Ed." She gave the more traditional kiss on each cheek, as opposed to the kiss I forecasted: a big wet slobbering one, with tongues lashing about.

"I'm glad we could meet. We should find a taxi. The weather looks like it could turn. Are you hungry?" I asked.

"Not really." She seemed stiff, nearly petrified.

"Is everything all right?"

"Well, iit was a surprise to hear from you. So much has happened, and I don't know how . . ."

Just then I heard a rustling in the bushes behind the gate. Out of the corner of my eye, I caught a sudden motion in the shadows. Before I could get the gist of it, the gate swung open. Monique stumbled and fell to the ground. A man came rushing toward me. It was quite dark, and I squinted to see his face. A fist found my jaw, and I heard my neck crack as it jerked to one side. I instinctively put my arms up to protect myself—but from what? Where? Another punch, this one to the stomach, and I doubled over. I tasted blood from the first punch. Then a knee to the forehead and I was flat on the ground.

I hadn't been in a knockdown fight since I was a kid and had forgotten the viciousness, the helplessness of a sucker punch. A tall man was standing over me and breathing as if he had been running for miles. I was in abject fear. He could crush my skull with his boot, its metal tip coming into view when a passing car lit the scene in a brassy, yellow glow. I was frozen, prepared to die.

"If you come after my wife again, I'll kill you." He spit at me, grabbed Monique, and rambled on in French while I lay bleeding on the ground. All I could think was, *"What the hell did I do? Kill HER!"*

I LAY THERE, STARING AT SODDEN, SLATE-GREY clouds, rain pouring in puddles around me. I'd passed out for an hour, maybe more. A woman walked her dog right around me as if I was a post in the road. I had blood dripping from the fresh cuts on my face, my shirt splayed around me; she must have thought me homeless. *"Did he say, 'wife?'"*

Oddly, the whole episode created little physical pain—until I tried to stand. That took every ounce of strength I had. I felt my jaw; it seemed to be in place, but there was blood on my cheek and my shirt, dripping. I tried to get my bearings but had no clue how to get back to the hotel without walking, which I truly wanted to avoid. My pocket Metro map was now a rain-soaked, fuzzy, foreign mystery, and the taxis only stop for pick-ups at taxi stands and hotels. I buttoned my tainted shirt and gathered myself, heading for the traffic sounds some distance from the quiet neighborhood of the Luxembourg Gardens. The Paris sidewalks were rolled up for the evening, and there was no place to clean up. Given my appearance and lack of communication skills, I figured I'd better keep walking.

Busy Boulevard Montparnasse loomed ahead, bordering the 6th and 14th Districts. Off to the right was a Metro stop, still open. I negotiated the stairs carefully while searching for a restroom. I'd heard that certain stations had them—but not this one. And I had no clue if this train would drop me anywhere near my hotel. No. I'd be much better off in a taxi. Back on the street, I found one of those pay-as-you-go potties. It resembled the orgasmatrons in the Woody Allen movie, *Bananas*. I dug into my pants pocket and found a few francs, popped them into the slot, and opened the door. I scrubbed the blood off of my face and was somewhat successful in combing my hair. If the guys in LA heard this tale, I was sure to be drummed out of there with a Louisville slugger. The now-prescient comment Monique made to me when we were at Customs in Canada blew into my head: *"You're not my husband, you know."* Evidently someone was.

I exited the toilet and spotted a hotel a few hundred yards to the north. From there, I grabbed a taxi and gave the driver the address of my hotel. He spoke passable English.

"You looook like you neeed a drink. I know a superb place. You try?"

"Yeah, why not. Take me to your leader."

The driver tooled around while rain splattered on the windshield. With every bump in the road, I felt my frayed nerve endings in my swollen jaw. He stopped at a dark, unmarked doorway. I figured that this wasn't unusual in Paris. I read that there were many cool, chic bars with no marquee, so I went with it. The driver motioned for me to stay put while he exited the taxi and knocked on the door. There was a peephole about the size of my fist; it opened around eye level. The driver exchanged words with the greeter, the "fist" closed, and he waved me over.

We walked together into an entryway area no bigger than a small closet, where a well-appointed man wearing a seersucker suit below an ear-to-ear smile offered me a spot in the downstairs bar. I could smell his hair tonic; it reminded me of the Brylcream that my dad used when I was a young guy. It made his hair look like Jerry

Lewis'—whom the greeter resembled. As I made my way to the stairs, I looked over my shoulder to notice the driver and the greasy greeter sharing a friendly word and a very long handshake. That was strange for Frenchmen. Most of them perform the ritual in a very casual, up-and-down motion, almost limp-wristed and over in a second, as opposed to the English, who like to take your hand off and keep it as a souvenir.

The crowd downstairs was sparse and mixed evenly by gender. The scene resembled a Toulouse-Lautrec painting from the turn-of-the-century, complete with brushed-brass décor, crushed-velvet couches on opposite sides of an old zinc bar, and at the end of the bartender's service area, an antique German cappuccino machine that might have survived the Kaiser. As I descended, the Gauloise cigarette smoke thickened. Fucking Gauloise, the foulest-smelling cigarettes of all time. The New York Euro crowd at Au Bar on the Upper East Side smoked them by the hundreds. You could pick up the stench from the Lower East Side. They smell like a dog's ass. I grabbed a seat at the bar, tears straining to cleanse my red eyes of the smoke.

Oddly, some of the women were offering shoulder massages to the men. Before long, a young woman dressed like a Vegas showgirl came down the stairs and prepared to perform a dance routine. Brilliant. A floorshow! I could use the diversion after an evening of blood and gore. She began by stretching to an old disco song. And she stretched forward farther, then farther still—as her hands worked their way around her tush and down to her thingy—her head hanging between legs perched on six-inch heels, her knees unbent. She prodded her head between her legs, closer to her ass, and then turned to smile at me. I had to admit it; this was entertaining as hell.

"*Une bière, s'il vous plaît,*" and in a second, the bartender brought me a Heineken as a hefty young lady sidled up and asked my name. Her English was good, but heavily accented. She was dressed in dowdy, blousy clothes to hide her extra kilos and smelled musty, like an old couch.

"You'll buy a drink for the lady?" asked the bartender. I raised my eyebrows, and *goddammit* they fucking hurt! I was a long way from well.

"What are you having?" I asked her in a total monotone.

"Well, a kir from zee Americain," she replied to the bartender like the demure young woman she wasn't.

While the floorshow continued to a silent but rapt crowd, I was getting grilled.

"Where are you from, monsieur . . . Oh, you don't look so old . . . What izz your sign of zee Zodiac?" and on and on. Finally, she offered me something I could use.

"Would you like a massage, monsieur? I'm verrry good."

I guess I wasn't too quick on the uptake that night, but it finally hit me that I was in a brothel, and she was a whore. "Thank you, but no merci."

She pouted, and I motioned to the bartender for the check. I thought I'd better get out of there before I got rolled or got lung cancer. He returned with a piece of handwritten paper that read 750 francs. Even in my condition, I could do the math—it was around $150 for two drinks, and that didn't include the tip or the floorshow. I put down 50 francs, the usual fare for two drinks at any legitimate bar in Paris and got up to leave. He grabbed me by the back of my shirt and turned me around.

"What kind of sheet is theeeese? Cinquante francs!?"

I shot back with a mild roar, "I'm not paying 150 bucks for two drinks, pal. I'm an American." I shook him off and headed upstairs, where the well-dressed man with the slick-backed hair was prepared for an encounter, having heard it all from his stool perch.

"What's the meaning of this?" he asked in perfect English.

"I'm not paying a king's ransom for a drink, and you can accept my 50 francs or take it up with the American Consulate. I'm a diplomat from Washington." What a performance!

He took one look at the bruises on my face and the dirt on my shirt and shook his head. "Perhaps we take this outside."

"Take this where you like, you churlish frog. I'll have you shut down in 30 minutes."

He opened the door, shoved me outside, and shouted, "Go ahead. Go tell your mommy. *Va te faire enculer!*" And with that, he slammed the door and closed the fist-sized peephole.

After regaining my balance, I realized a few things: it was cold, it was raining, and I was no diplomat. That fucking cab driver got a payoff for finding a poor dupe to enter a brothel and pay hundreds of francs for a kir and a beer. I should have known better. I should have seen it coming, but I was so disoriented.

It was midnight, and all the Metro stations were closing. Cabs would be very difficult to find, and I had no idea where I was. I was getting soaked to the bone and walked on, hoping to find a hotel or a restaurant that had a cab line. There wasn't a soul on the streets, and I wasn't sure if the raindrops dripping down my face weren't tears. *"What was I doing so fucking far from home?!"*

After 30 wet minutes, I came upon a hotel and grabbed the first cab in the queue, gave him the address of my hotel, and told him I did *not* want a drink. He glanced at me in the rearview mirror and gave me a knowing grin. These motherfuckers did this shit as a matter of course. I climbed out and trudged upstairs to my room, where I found my shower/bathtub waiting; this time, a bath, filling it to the brim with near-boiling water. This was the best idea I had all day.

At that moment, I couldn't have cared less if I ever saw Paris again and was no closer to getting my girl back to her desk at C&T in New York—clearly farther than ever. I thought of a thousand reasons for me to leave and had only one to stay. I approached this chore with a flimsy plan, resulting in an appalling outcome in a country I didn't know that harbored a woman with sociopathic tendencies. A woman I thought I needed. I felt the hot water seep into my pores, toward my aching my bones, and I slowly, finally relaxed.

I lay there in a meditative state for the better part of an hour—disturbing visions of the old blind man swirling around in my brain—as I flitted in and out of consciousness. My pains of the day were drifting away, when it hit me like a shot of adrenaline. Yes, that's it! This could work! I sat up in a start, the bathwater sloshing onto the floor. I wiped the soap from my eyes, and the clarity of my new plan took hold. There was only one way to mop up this mess—and it wasn't with the bath towel.

I climbed out of the tub and dried off, with a thousand thoughts careening around my little brain of how I might frame this plan and pull it off. I checked the clock. Two in the morning. With all the shit floating around in my head I figured I'd be lucky to get three hours of sleep. I got two.

# CHAPTER 26

GUESS IT'S MY NATURE, BUT A new day consistently brings me supreme confidence in the face of any mission. A jumble of thoughts the night before becomes a concrete plan of action, including accommodations for Monique, my radio partners, myself, and a solution to save me some face. Like the captain of the Titanic, I charged full speed ahead.

With the early hour in Paris, I had to wait until four in the afternoon until I could call Stu in LA and get the party rolling. But by 1 p.m. my time, Shelly would arrive in the New York office.

Basically, my plan was bribery; get Monique a tidy pile of money that might incentivize her to relocate back to New York and restart the dough-flow back in our direction. It had to be enough for her but not too much for us to part with—maybe a few grand. She was barely 20, so that would be a hearty sum for her. I stayed close to our financial guys in LA. As far as I knew, they kept our books legit, and I'd have to account for the withdrawal properly—perhaps a one-time service fee. I laughed aloud at that thought. She was my Irma La Douce. I was scribbling illegible notes on the cheap hotel letterhead when there was a knock on the door. I looked up in alarm; I hadn't ordered room service and there was a "Ne Pas Deranger" sign hanging on the outside doorknob.

"Qui est-ce?" I inquired in full voice.

"Iiit's Monique."

Well, the culprit arrives for her mea culpa. I opened the door, half-expecting that there would be a fist leaping to meet my face, but it was my dewy friend, alone and harmless in a bright sundress, cut so low it exposed both her cleavage and her belly button. "You've got some nerve, lady."

"May I come in?" she asked with a whimper.

"Why should I let you in? You almost had me killed."

"I can explain. Please let me explain." She seemed contrite.

I was agitated but gave her the benefit of my doubt—against any sane account of recent history. I motioned for her to have a seat on the edge of the bed while I stood over her like a judge. "Monique, I don't know how you can explain this, but I'm very curious to hear how you're going to try."

She gathered herself, took a breath, and looked up at me. Puppy dog eyes. "Your arrival in Paris took me by surprise."

"So did your departure from North America."

"Please, let me finish." She regrouped. "Let's begin backwards, from ze crazy meeting at ze Jardin du Luxembourg. I had no idea zat he would follow me. He never knew about you, but he always suspected that I was, let's say, busy."

"So, you're married?" I interrupted in a staccato clip.

"Please, Ed." She took a long, strained breath. "Zat evening, he decided to follow me, and he found you and went berserk. He and I are not long for each ozzer, as you can imagine. I can't live wis a man wis so much violence in him. And no, he's not my husband, but we've had a relationship for a few years now."

"*Like since you were 17?*" I didn't believe a word. "Forget about him," I said flatly. "Why didn't you tell me of your fate after our trip to Canada? I got zero phone calls."

Her eyes darted around; the truth was probably not forthcoming. "You do know that ze trip was your idea and zat I was forced to return to France."

What a slap in the face. I turned my head and crossed my arms. I was furious. "I got the best legal advice I could find to help you," I screamed. "You came to me with your problem, and I went the extra mile—actually the extra *five-hundred miles*—to help you. You let your fucking visa expire."

"Yes, but I didn't know what else zay may find."

"What else? What *else* would that be?" I demanded.

"I did a little, um, money wiring." Her eyes now fixed straight at me.

"Care to explain?"

"Well, Shelly and Stu were intent on keeping me at zee agency and were willing to do whatever zat might take, so I spoke to zem in terms zay could understand. Ed, zay were sending me money for monss, tens of thousands of dollars, and I was wiring it to offshore accounts to avoid taxes. The FBI and the French police were on my trail, and getting out of ze country to Canada was just about ze best idea I had heard. So when you presented zat to me, I leapt on it. Unfortunately, ze Canadians were alerted, found me out, and deported me back to France, where my beau posted bail. I have a hearing in a few days, and I'm terribly scared."

I scrunched my eyes, which still hurt a great deal. "Shelly and Stu were doing this? Sending you money after you sent them money? I don't quite get it?" "*Well, I DID get it. That's what I was planning.*"

"Shelly was my main contact at RossiRadio, but ze checks came from Stu. I was never to discuss zis with Shelly."

"Why not? I thought he was your guy." I said.

"Yes, yes, but Stu made me sign a contract. A *tais toi* deal, as we say, to keep quiet."

What a story. Evidently Stu had a jump on my idea, and I was an in-bed insurance policy. With her in my arms, my guys must have figured she'd stay with us. Quite a risk, but better to have me in New York than not. They kept her in line, I kept her busy, and she continued to feed us millions of dollars, that is, until the bottom dropped out and she left the continent. And I had grossly underestimated her asking price.

"Monique, you're basically accusing my partner of fraud, or tax evasion, or bribery. Pick any of the above federal crimes."

My mind cursed through all sorts of nasty questions. Was he pulling the money out of the company? Where was that on the books? She said the money was from Stu. Why keep Shelly out of it? Maybe he couldn't keep her in line, so enter Ed. Fresh-faced, sex-crazed Ed.

"So, you diidn't know?"

I creased my brow. "I didn't know shit, Monique. I was with you, for you. I had no clue that my company was doing this." I was growing concerned that these large sums of money sent to Monique were connected to profits, *my* profits. It was one thing to send along petty cash, quite another to unleash the wheel of fortune.

She dropped her head in disgust. She was ashamed, and the tears began flowing.

"I've made a very biiig mistake and have nowhere to go," she sobbed. "My parents have practically disowned me, my boyfriend and I are finished, I have no job and I may end up in prison." She pulled a tissue from her handbag and wiped her eyes.

I made no move toward her while my mind swirled. Were my partners setting me up? I was the one closest to her and helped get her out of the country. And now I had a stamp on my passport putting me in Paris, her hometown. Her fingerprints were all over my hotel room. I pictured myself in the Bastille prison being flogged. Meanwhile, I had this sorry soul before me. I posted up an emotional doorman to blunt her attempts to play my heartstrings; I didn't find it too difficult and reached for her hand.

"I think you'd better leave."

She got up slowly, her cleavage covered in tears, and I escorted her to the door. I did not want to continue being a company whore, and it looked like her goose was *été cuit*. Helping her get back to New York was off the table.

"I don't really know what to say, Monique. And I think you know that I had nothing to do with your problem. I've got some of my own and have to make plans to find my way back home."

For a sweet instant, I felt like taking her in my arms, packing her in my luggage, and keeping her, but she was like a broken toy—suddenly unlovable and too damn hard to fix.

She left me alone with my thoughts. I became convinced that Shelly, Stu, and maybe Tom had found their fall guy if things didn't work out—easy to blame the guy who was sleeping with the lady in chains. I phoned Air France—fuck American and their shitty seats—and reserved a flight to Los Angeles the next morning. The remainder of my time was spent plotting—and eating.

# CHAPTER 27

IT WAS A WHITE-KNUCKLE, TURBULENT FLIGHT home. I really should have taken a sedative. The plane hit LAX in the late afternoon, same day as I left Paris, and I thought how long this fucking day was. I arrived at the beach pad and saw the message light flashing—three times.

The first was from my dad. He must be a mind-melding Vulcan; I had wanted to call him to get a feel for the amended plan I chicken-scratched on napkins during the flight, but deep down I knew that he wouldn't approve. I winced hearing his gravelly voice asking me to call him. The message was three days old, and he was likely concerned that I hadn't called my mother.

"Beep." "Hey, Ed. It's Tom. You better call me. Something's up." Fuck me, the feds were on to them! Or he's just pissed about my media blackout of the Parisian adventure; Tom would often announce on the interoffice intercom, "Ed, come see me," which got on my nerves—he'd only want to show me how well he did on computer solitaire. He'd have to wait for me to finish with my dad, Spock.

"Beep." "Eddie, it's Shelly. I haven't heard anything, and I'm getting worried. Call me." Thank God Shelly took meds. Otherwise, he'd be wandering through Grand Central Station, calling for his mommy.

It was curious that Stu hadn't called, but he was always such a confident fucker, convinced that guys like me could solve his problems. He was *always* correct and his plan would *always* work. "*Later, Stu.*"

I got busy making my first and most important call.

"Dad, it's Ed."

"Jesus, there you are. We've been worried about you. Well, your mother was worried. I was, you know, a little worried." Wow, some rare emotion.

"I'm fine, just fine, Dad. I've got a plan that I want to run by you. It may involve leaving my company." There was a silence that could have filled a canyon.

"Ed, whatever it is, you've always come through, and I know that I haven't always been as supportive as I could have been, but you know, that's me. That's just me."

I felt my eyes water a little, but didn't let it affect my voice. "Thanks, Dad. That means a lot. A whole lot. You know I'm in my 30s now. I'm no kid and . . ."

"So, when are you getting married already? Are you done being made a fool of, chasing these girls around the world?" As usual, he hit me on the head, but I loved the abuse and laughed.

"I'll get to that, Dad. One tragedy at a time."

"Hey," he yelled. *"Uh, oh. "Hey" is always followed by a joke"* "Did you hear the one about the difference between being senile and having Alzheimer's?"

"OK. I'll bite. What's the difference?" I asked in a monotone.

"If you ask a senile person what that white box in the kitchen is, he'll pause, look quizzical and say, 'It's a fridge.' If you ask an Alzheimer's patient what it is, he'll say, 'It's a fridge, and I put a turkey in there an hour ago, but it's still not done.'" I laughed for about a minute straight.

"So what are you saying?" I asked, tears of laughter coming from my eyes.

"I don't know. I guess things aren't always what they seem." On the head.

"Dad, I've got a plan that you may find shocking, so I want you to take a seat and listen." I never ordered my father around like that, even to sit down.

"I'm sitting, Ed. And whatever it is, I'm sure you can pull it off."

"Thanks, Dad. I love you."

"Love you, too, Ed." I detailed the plan for him. He paused and said, "Good luck. And don't get hurt, my son."

# CHAPTER 28

I'D DISCOVERED MORE ON MY VOYAGE than Stu and Shelley had hoped, or wanted. I awoke to a brilliant day, sun streaming through every window, every crevice. I splashed water on my face and stared at my reflection in the mirror. Here was a take-charge guy! Just look at that stubble, those rough-hewn features. I sauntered over to the john and saw that same reflection in the toilet water. I spit in it, and my image vanished into a pool of ripples and distortions.

After washing, I stared at the phone. Tom was either in on their plan or was clueless, only a tool to get me to Paris to solve Stu's problem. I had to know before spouting off in Stu's general direction and dialed him up.

"St. John residence," intoned a housekeeper. I cocked an eyebrow. Such a big shot.

"Yes, is Tom in please?"

"One minute. I'll see if Mr. Tom is in." "*Mr. Tom?*" He picked up the receiver and then promptly dropped it.

"Yes?" he said, as if he were at the office, unflappable.

"It's me. I'm back from France. So, you and the housekeeper are playing catch with the phone?" I could hear his face scowl.

"So? What happened? Did you find her? Is she ready to come back? Any problems?" He was an anxious 16-year-old pining for information about the hot girl in homeroom.

"Yep. Found her, and I have one question for you, Tom. Did you know?"

"Know what?"

"About the money."

"What money? What are you talking about? You mean the ad dollars she brought in? You know I know that. What money, man?" He was prattling along at full speed.

"Tom, I mean *her* money."

"What do I know about her money? What the hell are you talking about?" He was agitated and probing and, if I knew Tom, he was telling me the truth. He did not know about the wires.

"It seems, my dear friend, that Stu had been arranging to have money sent to Monique, regular wires sent overseas to France in order to keep the money flowing to the company from C&T. Then she attempted to launder the funds through overseas accounts. While I was up in Canada fucking her—I mean, doing my job—the Canadians, who were onto her shenanigans, had designs to have her shipped back to Paris for prosecution. How 'bout them apples?" I felt like Deep Throat. *"Just follow the money, Mr. Woodward."*

"So, that explains it," Tom said.

"Explains what?"

"The phone calls. The feds were calling Stu."

I froze. "How did you know?" I was nearly yelling.

"It happened in his office, in front of me. His face turned white, and then he waved it off as something technical about his Foundation."

"What Foundation? What did he tell you?" I pressed.

"He said they were asking questions about charitable trusts and whether he had one."

I was lost on that count. "Anyway, looks like we got a real crime saga brewing."

Tom took a long breath and asked, "Do you have any verification of this? These transfers to France?"

"*Oh Christ! I never saw any paperwork.*" "I can get that," I said, wondering how the fuck I could. "It's not like she handed me papers, but I can get that."

Tom fell silent again. "Ed, I can guarantee you—absolutely and without reservation—that I had *nothing* to do with this. If you want to march up to the office and accuse our lead partner of racketeering or some such crime, go right ahead, but you'd better have something better than her word."

He was right. I needed to dig. If Stu had done this through the company, he could be thrown out, jailed, then molested by a guy named Jake. But if he hadn't, I was back at Square None. I headed to the sand to think for a couple of hours; I needed to plot and plan with an ocean in my face.

LATER THAT AFTERNOON, I DROVE TO the office while working over my speech to Stu in the car, mouthing it to myself. It drew attention from neighboring drivers as I gestured and contorted for emphasis, getting just the right tone, impressing myself. I should've done this on the way to CBS; would've nailed those lines on Y&R. I parked, left my car/rehearsal studio and rode the elevator solo. I got to my office and shuffled papers around on my desk, gathering my nerve. I checked my watch as if the exact time had anything to do with anything, and walked into Stu's office. My heart was racing.

"Eddie! You're back. Have a seat, my man. How'd it go, huh? How'd it go?" The anxiety was thick, but I could see he was nervous as a crab soaking in Quell.

"I think we got her back," I replied. I had to lead Stu to the well and give him hope, slacken the reins.

"Great! When does she get back to New York? What's the deal?" said the kid with a new lollipop, ready to lick.

"Won't take long. I'll need to coordinate with Shelly. Since this is his account, I'll need to work . . ."

"What are you talking about?" interrupted Stu. "Shelly's my man. He'll do as I ask, and you won't need to worry about him."

I needed time, an excuse to get my confirmation. "Stu, it's his account, and I was involved, deep. Let me make the first move to Shel and get him back in the loop. She was my girl, after all." Neither he nor Stu would be able to reach her. I was in charge, for the moment.

"Of course, Ed. Get to Shelly and have him work with Monique to get us back online. We'll talk after." He stood up and pounded his fist on the desk so deliberately it jolted my head back nearly a foot.

"You cool?" I asked, as I rose to shake his hand, glancing at the file cabinet on his office wall.

"Yes! Totally wired." *"No shit."*

I sat in my office for the day, doing my best impression of a hardworking executive while I sweated over what files I had to pilfer and what to do with what I might find. I called Shelly and lied about the new deal with Monique, telling him it's on hold until she arrives back in New York. Then, I headed home to refine the plan.

Tonight would be the night.

LATE THAT EVENING, I DRESSED IN dark clothes, as if I were Cary Grant in *It Takes a Thief,* drove to the office, taking deep breaths the whole way, and arrived at about 11 to find our security guard at the front of the elevators in the lobby. I avoided direct eye contact.

"Hey, Charlie. Got a little extra work upstairs." He never raised his head from the desk as I signed the nighttime security log as Robin Leach. He didn't know my name, just the face, and Charlie never checked the directory; I had to leave as little evidence as possible. I took the elevator to the 20th floor. It opened to the spacious RossiRadio lobby in near-total darkness, and I walked by rote memory to Stu's office, pulled out my master key, and wiggled it. Crap. He must have changed the locks. He was wont to do that from time to time. Now I knew why.

I grabbed my Swiss knife, fiddled with one of the smaller steel inserts, and worked that into the lock mechanism. Then, I pulled a credit card from my wallet to slide between the door and the door-jamb—one hand with my knife's insert jammed into the key hole and the other sliding the card back and forth—as if prodding a cash machine. Click. The door popped open.

To the left were Stu's precious personal files. Those were the ones I wanted. Again, I reached for the thin insert and plunged it into the keyhole of the top drawer. Voila. Thank God for shitty filing-cabinet locks. I pulled the drawer open and clicked on the flashlight that had been hanging from my belt.

Everything was in alphabetical order, so I went straight to the "Bs." Saw it in three seconds. Bertrand. I pulled the folder and thumbed through the papers. On the lead sheet, a wire transfer order to Monique Bertrand, numéro de compte: 2308835, Crédit Lyonnais SA, Boulevard des Italiens 19, 75002 Paris. What followed was astonishing: receipt after receipt of $30-thousand dollar wire transfers, eight from an account that I didn't recognize. And there it was on the front page. "**Rossi Foundation**."

Jesus H! He was wiring this money to her from his own family Foundation. So *that's* what the feds were sniffing at. A foreign national was receiving funds from his charitable Foundation to benefit his company, *my* company. I stood there agape, unable to move. Just behind it, stapled to the back was the *"Tais Toi"* keep-your-mouth-shut agreement.

Stu and Monique had agreed to keep their confidences, a non-disclosure as I read it. I supposed he wanted a shot at her if she blabbed around her office, giving away details. I perused more files until I came upon the "Rs," and I saw it—"Rossi Foundation." Page One was all I needed to see. "The Rossi Foundation, a charitable trust organized to the benefit of the below benefactors:" What followed was a list of charities a foot long, one of them with the same damn French bank account number and the initials MB. Some charity. I had to get copies.

I collated the receipts and paperwork by date, placed them on the copy machine glass, folded them lengthwise into my pants pocket, ran back to Stu's office, and replaced the originals, as I'd found them. I closed the file drawer, went for the door, and—like a florescent sunburst—the lights cranked on in the hallways. Shit! Someone had come in.

I couldn't have one of my people see me darting around in dark clothing with papers stuffed in my pants. I ducked and saw a pull for a fire alarm to the left of Stu's door; I supposed he must have had one installed within easy reach, in case he simultaneously combusted. The footsteps got closer to the office door. I gulped and crawled toward the switch. With sweaty fingers, I pulled the lever. Sirens clanged from every angle. I saw a shadow stop only inches from Stu's door and then turn for the elevator. *"Dummy. You're supposed to take the stairs."* I scooted to the stairwell leading out of the building to the street below and ran for my car.

Once there, I reviewed what I had in my pants: notes totaling $240,000, wired to my girl and sent with a kiss from a non-profit organization under the Rossi name. No wonder Tom had no knowledge of this. A missing piece was how Stu got the money from the company to the foundation, or did he?

I flipped through more of the paperwork—and there it was. Once Monique got her money, C&T cut a check to our company for radio ads and another to the Foundation as a "charitable contribution." That new Foundation money, less a substantial amount, was then funneled back to Monique, and the cycle began all over again. Money left in the

Foundation's coffers collected interest that was wired directly to one Stu Rossi. One payment alone came to $200,000.

I closed the folder and considered how ingenious and greedy this all was. Fire-engine sirens were wailing in the background as they approached the office building, and I figured I'd better put my foot on the gas.

When I arrived back home, I organized a timeline that clearly showed it was Stu's charitable trust that got the ball rolling by paying Monique to plan these huge buys for RossiRadio—they were timed to the day with the wire sends: seemed like wire fraud to me. I'm sure there were another slew of felonious activities that the feds had in the book they used to slap around guys like Stu. She was his bitch, and without her in the loop, the money flow ceased. When she left New York, she stopped sleeping with her boss, and the motivation to continue this charade stopped cold. She was integral to the scheme.

Monique had apparently set up an account in Paris and never paid taxes on the money she received, sending it to the Cayman Islands instead, thinking it was safe and protected since it came from a charitable trust. Turns out the "charity" was Stu and Monique, connected by a wire. The plan unraveled when she panicked and ran away—with me—and got deported by the Canadians. Stu and his trust might even be fingered in the tax-evasion case against Monique in France. I had a damn heavy cudgel over my partner. It felt amazing.

I plopped on the bed, wondering why greed had gotten the best of my old DJ buddy. This was a loony, fun-loving character with a flair for business and hard work. Why stoop to crime to make money, more than he would ever need? *"There it is! The 'why' question."*

I did recall one conversation we had early on regarding what I considered to be a shocking escalation of our wages—particularly his—even as we were owners and making plenty from profits.

Stu stated flatly, "It's never enough, Eddie. Never enough."

# CHAPTER 29

No river was funneling me to her door, no winged Icarus flying me to her heart. My wings had already melted, so I used the phone.

"Alex?" I asked. It was early the next morning.

"Yes? Ed?"

"It's me. Remember me?"

"Hah, hah. Were you the Jew with the crazy cousin?"

"One and the same."

"Did everything go well in Paris?" *"What the what?! Did Paris go well? Is that what she said? Julie must have tipped her off that I was overseas. Why? Was the engagement off? God knows what she said to her. Had to stay cool."*

"Um, Good enough. Alex, I'd like to see you. And I was wondering if you had any interest in seeing me, too." I was stunned at my audacity, but I had to know if Mike was out of the picture. That brunette at LAX with the Louis Vuitton bag could easily have been Alex, but I couldn't really see her face out of Achmed's disgusting rear window—maybe Mike liked lots of brunettes with fancy luggage—my gut had been telling me he was not for her. *I* was, damn it!

"Yes, Ed. I do want to see you. A lot's happened since our dinner. I, uh, I hope we can get past it, I mean, I want to see you, of course." Her voice was light and sweet. I felt welcomed.

"All I know is that I want to see you." I had finally stopped rewinding and playing back every word in my head and went with my gut—my nervous, preoccupied gut.

"Okay, Ed. You name the place and time."

I pressed on, barely believing that it was me speaking. "Alex, I don't know if I believe in destiny. I've been going back and forth on that one over the past few days, but I actually met you years ago. And I'm going back years, even before our Geoffrey's restaurant encounter with Julie. I was in a convenience store, standing right behind you, and you were buying some feminine product when you turned and said . . ."

"Is that Columbian or sensimilla," she finished.

I was floored. She remembered me as I was, a drug-addled goof, weaving around a store, looking for beer. I was embarrassed and began blushing, over the phone.

"And if it weren't for my dad being with me, I might have said hello to you at the Beverly Center. That was you, wasn't it, taping someone for your show?"

Wow. That was our non-encounter years ago when I was the "Millionaire" at THE BIG Z. She had been a listener, perhaps lying in her bed with her headphones on, laughing and enjoying me as I cranked on the next big hit from Depeche Mode. She had been with me all along!

"Unbelievable. And when we met with Julie, you never said a thing."

"I didn't think Mike would appreciate my memory of you. Plus, Julie seemed so pleased to set us up, awkward as it was, I didn't want to embarrass my friend, you know, so I kept kinda quiet. I'll see you at 7:30?" *"Friend? Her fiancé was her friend?"*

"Uh, yeah. That's great. I'll pick you up at your place."

She rattled off her address, her voice full of life and said, "Bye, Ed," sweet as a nectarine.

I DRESSED, SHAKING MY HEAD FROM SIDE to side, regretting the day I followed Tom, and then Stu, into this mess. I could have built a life for myself on the air; charted my own course. Lucky loved me. I could have followed his path, a mentor consistent with my dreams. I would return to that life if I could. I couldn't wipe the smile off my face.

I woke up early the next day and there it was, that same silly smile. I pulled into the office, minus Cary Grant outerwear, with a plan in hand. The place was buzzing, particularly with the news of a late-night fire alarm. I hoped there was no trace of where the alarm had been pulled in the building's fire-alarm system. Everyone had a rumor they were passing. Many were pointing fingers at a young intern who'd wandered into the office during off-hours. She offered up the tepid excuse that she came back to organize her paper clips, insisting she couldn't get to sleep until she had separated the small clips from the large ones, which turns out wasn't an excuse, but the truth. She could've been my patsy, but OCD Paper Clip Freak wasn't going to pull a lever. The subject was dropped and no investigation was forthcoming. *"Whew!"*

I made a few morning calls and double checked notes I'd written to myself the evening before. I was ready for battle when Tom barged in and plopped down on the chair, sitting upright for once.

"Well? What did you find," he whispered. I bolted from my chair to close the door.

"Everything. Way more than I expected. Everything I need. And Tom, separate yourself from me on this. You've always been a close and trusted friend, but it's time I gave *you* advice. You know nothing, and whatever assistance you offered Stu in getting me overseas to find Monique had nothing to do with you."

Tom regarded me with a kind of respect I'd never seen from him before. I was in charge of this; if he stayed clear, he'd be unscathed.

"And you're sure about what you're doing?" he asked.

"No question. But don't expect a bonus from the company this year."

He furrowed his brow. I took a long swig of hot coffee, winked at Tom and marched passed him into Stu's office, a mad house as always, chock full of personnel kissing his ass, dusting his desk, nodding their heads whenever he spoke. His hair was slicked back that day with a gob of greasy kid's stuff. He was Gordon Gekko.

"Eddie! Come in," and he motioned me to an empty seat.

"Stu, can we have a little privacy?" I asked.

He motioned for the entourage to exit, and they trundled out in a line as if pulled by a hook. Stu faced me, ice cold but smiling.

"You know I found Monique," I began.

"Yes, we've established that. Now, when does she get back to . . ."

"She doesn't," I interrupted.

He narrowed his steely blues and focused them at mine. "What do you mean?"

"I mean that she's not coming back. She's in France."

Stu was seething but kept the decibels down. I could see his mind swirling, considering what might have gone wrong. "Your job was simple, Ed. To get her back at work at C&T in New York. We were all counting on you, and I must say, I for one am quite disappointed. Quite disappointed."

He sat back in his thick, smelly, shiny leather chair, rubbed daily with Armor All, and he stared at me, bobbing his head slowly up and down. He was a nervous, greasy, bobble-head doll.

"So, I suppose you'll want to fire me," I inquired.

Stu's head stopped bobbing, sensing I was giving him an easy out. "I just might."

"And from what? RossiRadio or the Rossi Family Foundation?" The words fell out of my mouth and landed with a thud harder than a George Foreman jab.

All color left Stu's face, and he jerked his head in the direction of his filing cabinet—the personal one that I'd just rifled through last night.

"What the hell are you talking about? What Foundation?" He was weak, on the ropes.

"Stu, you know exactly what Foundation. Your charitable trust filled with funds from our advertisers, with the outgoing wires to a certain French girl. Your trust, which landed me in Paris for no other reason than to make you wealthier, to keep your secret. So secret, you couldn't tell me, or anyone what the real game was. Money you wanted off the books, away from actual charities, and in the hands of Monique, only to find more money right back in your hands to keep the flow going. Stu, your silence violated *our* trust. I was on a limb to save *you* and you roped Tom, Shelly, and primarily me into this game *you* profited from—to the exclusion of all of us."

"Hey, that agency was paying us, all of us. And . . ."

"Not even by half, man. You were pocketing interest on charitable funds coming from an agency fronted by a French tart, and I was your insurance policy. Me."

"Fucking Monique, she couldn't keep her mouth shut," he mumbled.

"What are you going do, sue her?"

"You can't prove any of this. I had everything . . ."

"Tucked in a little file. I have that file, Stu, and I know that a federal agent already inquired about it. It'll be in the hands of the feds post haste—unless you can, at last, help *me*."

Stu's back came to rest against his leather chair, and I imagined the shimmering smudge of Armor All left on his shirts every day.

"What do you want?" he asked, sheepish and green.

"Seven-million dollars—wired to an account right here in Los Angeles. Consider it a buyout of my shares of RossiRadio. This was never my company, really. Buy me out, and I shred my copies of your files."

"What about Monique? What's keeping the French police away from her? What about the FBI?"

*"Idiot."* He should have advised her to keep her work visa current. She was a wildcard who might expose him, give the big bad federales someone to hang those wires on.

She was *my* wildcard now.

"Oh, they're after her. And in a big way. She never paid taxes on the money you sent her." I took a deep breath, leaned over the desk to face my partner, our noses separated only by inches. It was more apparent than ever that he was vibrating in fear.

"Stu, you made your bed. You decided to work with a 19 year-old media planner, who had little idea what she was doing, powerful as her planning was. If you want her quiet, I can keep her quiet. She's the one they're after overseas. The wires were from a charitable trust, and she could claim them as advisory fees, or some such thing. That's the story that she'll give on her end, but that's to save her ass—not yours. I can help save yours. You make this wire work for me, the files will be dust."

He stared at a spot on the wall behind my head, and I thought he might be passing out. A cold sweat was covering his forehead as I stood to leave.

"Oh, and Tom knows all about it. I can't stop him from calling his lawyer, so you might think about him, too. I'm packing my things. Make it happen. I'll be in touch about the seven mil—where to send it and how. You'll never see me again." With that, I walked out of his office and into mine, piled my shit into a box, and said goodbye to no one. I was done.

# CHAPTER 30

I SAT BACK IN MY FOLDING CHAIR on the beach in the noonday sun, basking in my success. I had the radio cranked to my old station, KUTE 102, and heard the fun, disco sound from my halcyon days. They had come back to the format that made them big. *Stayin' Alive* by the Bee Gee's was booming as loud as I dared, without attracting glares from the local gentry. I slowly sipped a Pina Colada and thought about where I might go, what I might do, concerned little about the sunburn developing on my bare belly. I certainly knew who I wanted to join me.

That evening, I was preparing to leave for my date with Alex when the phone rang.

"Hello?"

"Ed? It's Tom."

"So, you heard what happened?" I asked.

"Well, not really. But Stu called us in for a vote on buying you out. That's some price you put on your ass. You must have found something big."

"Yep. I had him over my knee, crying for mercy," I bragged. It was hard to be humble, given the circumstances. "You said 'not really.' You mean there was no mention of what I had done, or said?"

"Not at all. Kept it close to the vest. He claimed you wanted out, to strike out on your own. No explanation, but he looked at me like I was Satan. I must say, Ed, it's going to be tough working with this guy from here on out. He's miserable. What did you find exactly?"

Tom knew plenty, but I didn't want Tom to know everything— breaking into Stu's office, plowing through his confidential files, threatening him with felonies. That was for me and Stu to know; maybe the only time I ever kept Stu's confidence over Tom's.

"He broke the law and profited from it, Tom. He was lucky I simply didn't call the FBI. At least the company will continue, albeit with less than before."

Tom sighed, long and strained. He had made his bed with Stu, but he'd be smart to follow my lead.

"So, what are your plans, young man? Do you have one?" he asked.

"For once, yes. I do. I'm afraid you won't hear from me for a while, though. Tom, thank you for everything."

"After all I led you into? You're thanking me?"

"I'm about to become a millionaire, thanks to you, my old friend. And I can only wish the same for you. Hoist a Jack and Lite Beer for me at the bar tonight. I'll do the same for you." I felt a twinge of emotion fill my throat and hung up.

ALEX LIVED IN A CONDOMINIUM COMPLEX on Fountain Avenue in West Hollywood. It was a large, grey, imposing structure. I had to scan through a panoply of names on the electronic security roster until I came to hers. I hit the code for "Grossinger," and the gate popped open. Her place was one floor up from the entry and only feet from the elevator. The door opened, and there stood a vision, straight out of *Vogue*.

"You're right on time, mister," she said smiling, wearing a colorful, low-cut print blouse and black-leather skirt, with matching knee-high boots. She led me in by the hand as soft as a rose petal, and gave me a warm kiss on my cheek, which I returned, noting the full makeup. She was a New York model ready for the runway.

The interior of the place showed off her flair: beautifully decorated, pristinely clean, in perverse contrast to the non-descript exterior of the building, which had all the warmth of a penitentiary. At first glance, her condo seemed enormous, although she had just two modest bedrooms, a small '60s style kitchen—complete with bright orange linoleum prints on the counter tops—and a throwaway dining room that spilled out from a welcoming living room, peppered with recessed lights, giant, fluffy pillows stacked on thickly woven seat cushions, and gold-laced chinoiserie panels adorning the walls. Had to be a $200,000 condo stocked with half-million-bucks worth of decorating. Soft music played in the background that sounded like the soundtrack to *Breakfast at Tiffany's*. And before me was a creature as stunning as Audrey Hepburn.

"Do you like white or red," she asked.

"I'm a cab man, if you got it."

She retired from the kitchen and brought the red out to the living room. I disappeared between two of her ginormous pillows while she poured.

"I'm really sorry. I'm not good with corks, and this one dropped in. There may be cork in your glass."

She seemed frantic, so I made light of her plight, fishing around with my finger, feigning disgust while pulling out millimeter-long pieces of cork from the wine and flicking them onto her coffee table.

She laughed hysterically. *"Jesus, if we could make each other laugh like this, there really might be something there."*

"I don't care about your cork," I said, "I'm just too happy to worry about a thing."

She sat next to me on the sofa and settled in close. "So, Paris went well? You've got a new deal?" she asked while I took a long sip of the cabernet, then pulled a few more pieces of cork from my teeth.

"Yes, you could say that. And I may now have more free time than I know what to do with."

She blinked her lightly-shaded eyelids, clearly curious. "So, do I smell vacation?" she retorted, lowering her voice and raising her glass for a toast. I complied likewise.

"I do believe a vacation is in order. But first things first. Let's eat."

We both gulped down more wine, and I led her out for an evening at Chasen's, only a few blocks away on Beverly Boulevard. After all these years of serving the high and mighty, it was destined to close soon, so I thought we'd get in a last gasp of old-school dining.

Alex was delighted, telling me that her family ate there regularly when she was growing up. I imagined the Grossingers crowded into a red-booth table, with the Sinatras and the Martins, swilling more martinis than a waiter was now allowed to serve while cutting up, laughing, and eating the finest food west of the Mississippi.

The crowd that evening was sparse and hushed, devoid of the convivial crowd noise I enjoyed at most of the hipper restaurants in town. I took her arm and led her to the table. She melted into me.

The food was delicious, and we laughed every minute on the minute. And the vintage 1982 Sterling Reserve Cabernet kept flowing—and flowing—three bottles between the two of us by the time the check arrived. I was in a celebratory mood, and, evidently, she was game.

"We should call a cab," I slurred.

"You already finished three." More drunken laughter. "You OK leaving your car here?" she asked.

"Oh, yeah. These guys look trustworthy." I had treated myself to a late-model Mercedes, but then, so did everyone else in town—LA then was a conveyor belt of Benzs. I passed my keys to the manager, and he called a taxi for our ride back up the hill to her place. She tapped the code into the security pad, missing a couple of numbers and chuckling at herself, before finally getting the buzzer to work.

"You want to come up?" she asked, her eyes lolling about.

"You sure about that? I can take this taxi right home and . . ."

"I'll hear nothing of it," she interrupted. "Come up and relax. You need to relax."

I needed to relax like a turtle needs to relax. She could have pushed me over with a leaf. Upstairs, she opened her door; I followed and spun her around to kiss her. She kissed back, hard and sweet—the warmest mouth in memory. She led me to the sofa, where the passion escalated for a few more minutes, but she was getting tired. And, frankly, I was drunk and didn't want to begin what might be an honest relationship, fired up by three bottles of cab.

"I should go," I demanded.

"No such thing, you hunky Jew."

I laughed and pushed myself up from the couch. "I don't want to impose on you, and this is only our first real, you know, date."

"I'll tell you what," she continued. "You sleep right there. I'll get you some sheets, and then I'll see you for breakfast. Sound good? Is that me being a proper lady?"

"Almost. I prefer sleeping with proper ladies." I was overplaying it, but detected a lingering moment when she seemed to consider the warmth of my body next to hers under a set of *very* high-thread-count sheets. But she turned, fetched a big pile of bedding, and tossed them to me from across the room.

"That's as close as you're getting tonight, Mister Mann." She blew me a kiss and closed her bedroom door. She'd stood her ground. I smiled broadly, tucked the sheets into the big, cushy sofa cushions, threw off my clothes, and hit the pillow—with a glow.

The first words of the morning were abrupt and jarring.

"You into pancakes?" she yelled from the kitchen.

I awoke with a start, my eyelids peeling from my corneas in a painful rip. "Ow!" I screamed.

She came rushing into the living room, where I was sprawled half-naked on the couch, one leg pushing the sheets halfway to the floor. I was gripping my eyes, tears flowing. "What the hell happened?"

My first thought was to laugh as I writhed in pain; she was yelling like a tabloid TV field reporter, and somehow, I found that enormously funny.

"Are you laughing or crying?" It sounded like *she* was almost crying.

I was doing both. She must have thought me schizophrenic while I cursed myself for leaving my eye cream at home. I promised myself to never forget it when sleeping out, and, sure enough, there I was, crying on her couch, scaring her to death.

"I've got a cornea condition; sometimes I can't open my eyes too quickly in the morning, without a ton of pain. The tears will settle it down." I left out the iron-filings description I shared with family as I raised my eyelids for a moment. To this day, I remember the horror in her eyes as she came into view. I blinked the blinding pain away and saw her sitting before me, holding a pancake in a spatula over the couch and began laughing all over again. She lightened up.

"Come in here, drama queen, and eat something," she said.

I pulled on my pants and sat down in the small dining area, bedraggled and groggy. "Where's the coffee? Must have coffee," I groaned.

"Do you like sugar and cream?"

"Sure. Just put the sugar in the cup and the cream in my eyes."

For an instant, she looked at me like I was serious but saw the grin come over me and placed the cream next to the coffee cup.

"So, is this eye thing a big deal?" she asked, as she flipped the other pancakes on the griddle.

"Nah, just a nagging problem. It's only a problem when I wake with a start."

She was leaning, resting her body weight on her hands in front of the blazing hot griddle, her hair dangling dangerously close to the gas flame, in deep thought about it.

"It's no big deal," I insisted. "Really, no harm done."

I plopped the sugar into the cup, left the cream on the side, and took a sip. Perfect. Hot, dark and a little sweet. I was coming to. She brought over the pancakes with a smile, and we dove in, facing each other at the small dining table in the kitchen nook, unfiltered sunlight pouring in from the open window. My eyes soon regained their full optic power, and I gazed at her as she ate. She had no makeup on and was startling pretty without it, even in the harsh morning glare.

"Do you like New York?"

"Huh?" she replied, perplexed.

"You know, the Big Apple, the city that never sleeps?"

She finished chewing another bite of her cakes and cocked her head to one side like a curious dog.

"Very much. My dad's from there. Why do you ask?"

"Well, I had designs on going out there. Maybe for a week." I took a breath and devoured my last bite of pancakes. She just stared at me. A big, blank, but anticipatory stare.

"Want to go with?" I asked, as if it were a trip to the market.

Her eyes doubled in size, her mouth agape. "You're inviting me to New York? She was disbelieving.

"Yep," I replied, confident as a cat.

"That's ridiculous. How could I possibly do that? How could I take that kind of time off? What would my mother think? Is my passport valid? Who would get the mail. Watch my car. Check my watch. I don't even have a bag! Can you tell I haven't traveled in a while?" *"So that WASN'T her at LAX! See ya, Mike."* She was rambling and excitable, her eyes darting from one side of me to the other, half-disbelieving the proposal but visibly happy about it. I tested the waters, and they were fine.

"So, you'll come?"

She jumped across the table to embrace me.

"And you know, you don't need a passport."

"Of course, Ed. Of course, I'll come with you. It sounds wonderful." She kissed me harder then than the night before. I was on a cloud.

I LEFT HER WITH THAT IMAGINATIVE, SCARCELY thought out promise and headed to retrieve my car, then drove to the beach pad. I pushed my front-door key into the keyhole, but the door flung open, and I fell hard on my shoulder, anticipating resistance from a locked door. I stood slowly, wincing as I rubbed my throbbing shoulder, only to see debris on the floor that appeared to be contents from one of my junk drawers. Getting back on my feet, I surveyed a place I didn't recognize. It had been ransacked. Everything was strewn about. Everywhere I turned, destruction. It was like looking at the inside of a totaled car. My couch pillows had been sliced through, my medicine cabinet had been toppled, my kitchen cabinets emptied.

My mouth was agape. I was lost in my own home. I peered into the fridge to find an undisturbed six pack of soda. As I popped one open, I heard a noise; it wasn't the "schvit" sound a soda can makes when it's opened. It was more of a cough, and it was coming from my bedroom. I rushed back there and saw a lump in the sheets the size of a person. The hairs on the back of my neck stood up, goose bumps formed on my arms. With the place such a mess anyway, I poured the soda onto the bed sheets—and out popped a familiar face.

"What the hell is *this* shit?!" I was screaming and gesticulating, with soda flying out of the can and all over the walls. It was Shelly, looking white as the sheets he was in.

"Who the fuck do you think you are, coming in here, trashing my place, and why are you hiding like a fucking ostrich in my bed?"

"I didn't do this."

I jutted my head forward and felt like head-butting him through the wall.

"Then why are you snuggling in my sheets, you fuck?" I pushed him. He was stiff and flimsy, an ironing board collapsing in a heap.

"It was Stu's idea, damn it. He had these guys come in to look around, see if you had something on Monique, shit he could use against her. Or, uh, against you. I came along, and they bolted out the window when they heard you. I figured maybe I could make it, but my leg got caught in the sill. So, I jumped into your bed."

I looked out the bedroom window. Even if Shelly was telling the truth, they were long gone. I was incredulous.

"Shel, she's in France. If you want to call her, I'll give you her goddamn number." I went to my closet, reached into my jacket pocket and shoved the paper into his trembling hand. "She left her miserable boyfriend, and me, and her boss, so now you can jump in. Good fucking luck."

He unfolded the note like a lost hundred-dollar bill and then froze. "So, how do I know that this is her number?"

"You asshole," I mumbled. I reached for an old lava lamp on the dresser and threw it at him. He pulled his head back, and the rough edge along the bottom of the lamp brushed his lower lip, scraping it badly. The lamp crashed onto the wood floor in a blobby, glassy burst. He grabbed his face in pain while I walked slowly to my bathroom.

I cranked on the water in the sink and noticed that the toothpaste had been squeezed so violently that it had exploded on the sink counter, splaying the mirror with a drying, multi-colored goo. What were they expecting to find in tube of Crest? I wet a washcloth and tossed it to Shelly, who lay whimpering on the bed, blood pouring from his lip onto his hands.

"She's under indictment, Shel. Stu knows all about it. She's useless. Stu sent those thugs to cover for his own shit, to somehow pin it on me, to frighten me. This goes deeper than you know, pal. Now, I've got *both* of you under my thumb. How do you feel about breaking and entering?"

"What do you have on, Stu?"

"Enough. I've got enough to keep him busy in court until he drops." I felt the keys in my pocket, one of them a safe-deposit key to a box at the bank, where I kept the files on Stu. I was so pissed I felt smoke must be curling out from my ears. Stu couldn't tell him anything, so he sends him over with his boys to mess up my place while leading Shelly to believe I was the one who lost his C&T account. Meanwhile, Stu gets to muss my hair while he picks his wounds. He wasn't going to send me those millions without a fight.

"Now, get the fuck out of my house."

Shelly picked himself up and tried to hand the bloody washcloth back to me.

Disgusted, I shoved it back in his face, and he scooted out the door he came in, the latch bent inward from the force of his entry. I slammed it behind him, but it popped right open again.

# CHAPTER 31

I SPENT THE GREATER PART OF THE day mopping up the mess my uninvited guests had made of my beach pad, picked up the beach chair, and headed out toward the Pacific for a swim. It was near 90 degrees outside, but the water was cold—as always. After 10 minutes of body surfing and near hypothermia, I laid back on my chair to let the sun placate my shattered nerves while sipping a fresh can of soda.

When I got back to my place, I pulled out my undamaged home computer from the back of my bedroom closet. The idiots were in such a rush that they never bothered to look under a pile of dirty clothes there. I kept everything in that computer, including my notes about Monique and what I might do about it. I fed the printer with a fresh sheet of paper, took a breath, and decided to ignore what Stu had just done to my place. I typed a cordial note to him, thanking him for the "great ride," with instructions to do as he had promised: buy me out at the cost of seven-million dollars wired to my personal account. That was retribution enough.

Then I thought twice—I closed with this little addendum: "I found Shelly in my house today. It was good to see him. I fixed his jaw. Love and kisses, Your ex-partner."

I folded it, addressed it, and walked it over to the post office, sending it registered mail. I even upped the amount of the wire to account for the postage. *"Fuck him."*

I did a search in the computer for the number of my travel agent, and washed up for dinner—alone.

EARLY THE NEXT MORNING, I AWOKE full of wonder. *"Would Stu execute that wire? Would Alex really join me on a trip? Could this really be happening to me, an ex-DJ flunky, who followed the flow long enough to get the current going in his direction?"* I took a walk for a coffee. From my street, I could see Hollywood, where the offices of RossiRadio now took up four glorious floors. For a moment, I thought I saw a puff of smoke rise above the building. Stu must have opened the letter. Back at my place, there was one message.

"Ed, it's Alex. I'm so excited I can barely sleep or eat. Were you serious, or was I dreaming during a hangover? Please call me. I'm ready."

I collapsed onto my couch, feathers flying from the ripped up pillows. *I* was ready. I called the travel agent and made plans for the trip. Our flight was booked for the following evening. Alex was at home when I called back.

"Alex, can you go tomorrow night?"

"I can go now. But I want you to meet my parents first."

I knew this might happen, but so soon? I hadn't even kidnapped her yet. I felt my mouth dry out, a wisp of perspiration forming in the creases of my forehead. "When?" I asked.

"Lunch, at their place, in Malibu." *"Holy shit. The Malibu beach house lunch."* "I'll pick you up. And don't worry about my dad. He's cool."

Oh yeah, the funniest man in the world is "cool." Danny Grossinger was the insult comic of my parents' generation, but he had crossed over, now appealing to a younger crowd as they discovered the genius of the Rat Pack. Danny was part of that coterie, their court jester. And he'd be holding court with me over lunch. I imagined the conversation: *"Oh, hi there, Mr. Grossinger. Yes, I intend to take your daughter to a lonely hotel and fuck the shit out of her for a solid week. And by the way, I don't have a job, but I plan to get money by extorting my ex-partner. Really, I'm a good guy,"*—as I was thrust out of his house on my ass.

Alex picked me up at 11 a.m. Right on time.

"So, what can I expect to come of this?" I asked apprehensively.

"Oh, I don't know. Some heartburn, maybe a rash."

"I'm not laughing," I retorted, flat as one of her pancakes.

"Relax. He's not like you'd think. My mom's more of a wreck than he is. She'll have the table set perfectly, the courses served just right. They're insane about lunch. It's the highlight of their day. You can do no wrong as long as there's food around."

I wasn't placated and picked my cuticles all the way to Malibu.

We pulled into a compound called the Malibu Colony, a collection of homes built right on the ocean. The Grossingers had a modest two-car garage and a small iron entry gate by the street. It didn't seem as ostentatious as I'd expected. Alex pushed the button in a grey box outside the gate, and it swung open. We entered to a wooded walkway, with thick bougainvillea hovering overhead, beige wooden planks underfoot, perfectly aligned and maintained. A perfectly maintained tennis court loomed on our right as we walked the length of it on the walkway toward the front door, again, unimposing and remarkably non-threatening. As we approached, Mrs. Grossinger opened it and waved us in, motioning for us to enter quickly, as if the sky was falling. She was elegant, dressed in a long, flowing housecoat embroidered with colorful chinoiserie. She smelled wonderful, like the bougainvillea.

"Please, Ed, call me Lois," as she extended her hand.

"Thank you for having me, Lois. I've never seen a colony home. This is quite a treat," I gushed, Alex lifting an eyebrow at my Eddie Haskell routine.

The distance from the front door to the living area had to be the length of the tennis court. From the outside, it looked like a well-built tract home but inside, a Rockefeller dream. At the back of the living room to the right, under a stuffed deer head, sat Danny Grossinger in an elegant easy chair, facing the biggest big-screen television I'd ever seen. It was fitted into an aged wooden cabinet, filled with memorabilia and tchotchkes from his long career.

He no longer was the young, crazy guy I remembered from the *Dean Martin Show* and the Catskill circuit. He craned his bald head forward from the chair and pushed himself up with his arms, an older man, older than I had imagined, with the knees to prove it, and he grimaced as he stood to greet me. He was warm and direct—his hand thrust out to meet mine, an honest, recognizable smile plastered across his craggy, but smooth face, a strong, musky smell of cologne accompanying the handshake. And his hands were soft as a baby's bottom.

"Mr. Mann, I presume," he began, forcing his voice down, mocking an announcer voice.

"It's a pleasure to meet you, Mr. Grossinger. I'm, uh, jeez, thrilled." We shook hands for perhaps a moment longer than he wished, his smile turning tired as he motioned for me to sit, and he fell back squarely into his chair, contoured to fit his ass perfectly. He landed like a coin falling into the slot of a vending machine. I was going to share a moment with a legend, perhaps catch up on sports, or look through his photo albums.

"So, Ed, where are you from?" He patted me on the knee.

"Well, from Northern California, but we moved here to LA when I was young. My folks are still up north, in Saratoga, if you know where that is. Moved to LA to go to UCLA," and with that, he promptly fell asleep. Right there as I spoke. I had only a moment to get his attention and bored him dead away.

"Oh, don't worry about him," piped in Alex, who moved in close, holding my hand. "He's on this medication that makes him sleepy during the day."

I felt disappointed, but I was sure, more to come. Lois opened up a set of wooden TV trays, like it was the '50s; I was half-expecting a Swanson's Salisbury steak to be plopped in front me, but a uniformed servant came in and brought the Caesar salads, adorned with little strips of anchovies and croutons. It was simple and faultless, with a touch of lemon in the dressing.

Lois chatted on about the work they were going to do on the house, how things rusted so quickly from the salty air, how the ocean lapped into their pool in the winter months, flooding the deck. *"Rich people problems."*

I nodded back as Danny snored away on the chair, his salad getting soggy.

Next was the meat, fresh slices of London broil. Lois called it entrecôte, pronounced with a perfect Philadelphia accent. "Entrecooooooate." Fingernails on a blackboard. The servant took Danny's salad away without him having touched it and replaced it with the meat. Alex dove in, comfortable in her old beach house surrounded by her parents and clearly proud to show me off. I devoured the steak, loving the dark mushroom sauce, the side of baby potatoes roasted to a moist, delicate perfection.

"Ed is a former DJ, from THE BIG Z." Alex knew what her parents wanted to hear: show business. Some finger-snapping fun. The arcana of the radio-syndication business would wipe expression clean off of their faces. It usually wiped mine off. Sure enough, Lois's eyes were focused lanterns as I prattled on about my days on the radio. Alex listened proudly; her Nancy Reagan eyes gazing at me.

"Did you have many fans?" asked Lois. I immediately thought of the exuberant, auburn-haired girl I danced with at a BIG Z FM Weekend Warmup, who had announced my hard-on to the crowd.

"Oh, a few. Some more eager than others." That generated a slight scowl from Lois. Alex giggled; whatever I hadn't told Alex about my past, Julie had eagerly filled in every detail.

Lois changed the subject. "This is very exciting, you two off to the big city! Why New York, Ed?" She talked a happy talk, but her eyes were boring into me, probing for a nefarious motive. I sensed that Lois didn't suffer fools or posers, and I'm sure she was protective of Alex.

"Frankly, Mrs. Grossinger, uh, Lois, there was no master plan. I always thought it would be wonderful to go there to celebrate, as opposed to just doing business, which is what often brought me to New York."

"Celebrate what? What are you celebrating?" She was shifting in her seat. Danny was slowly coming to, rubbing his eyes like a four-year-old waking from his nap.

"Well, I've just been bought out of my company, and I couldn't think of a better, more exciting place to go, or with a lovelier creature than your daughter."

Danny saw an opening and dove in. "So, you're kidnapping her. When do I get the ransom note? Lois, go up to the safe and bring the money to the coffee table and we'll negotiate."

My eyes bulged, and I was at a loss—the best of the best was throwing curveballs, and I had nothing.

"Oh, Dad. Just give me the ransom. You'll make it up with a week of work in Vegas." Alex came to the rescue. I wasn't ready for this guy.

Danny reached over and pinched Alex's cheek, his famous grin overtaking his weary face. "A chip off the old block, my daughter. She can dish it out with the best of them, Ed." He rose from his chair, again headfirst with his arms pushing him up to his feet. "I'm going out to the pool for a swim. Lois, make sure he doesn't go through the jewelry."

"Oh, Daniel," replied Lois, who began clearing the TV trays of the food. Alex held my hand tightly.

"Want to go for walk on the beach? Look at some of the houses?" she asked.

"Sure. You lead." We rose from the couch, pulled off our shoes, and I grabbed a few chocolate Kisses from an oversized, leaded-crystal bowl, plopped in the middle of a distressed-oak, boardroom-sized coffee table as we headed out.

We walked past a screen door that led to the pool, where Danny was already doing laps in the blinding summer sun, plodding along slower than a snail. The pool was small, but it took him an eternity to finish a lap. He seemed to plummet three feet every stroke, coming up for air at the last second and then descending again for a slow pull of the water, barely advancing. I felt like calling a lifeguard. Alex could see my concern and waved it off.

"He's a submarine," she said, barely reassuringly.

We continued down a short staircase to the beach, and I heard the gentle slap of water on sand. If heaven were on Earth, it would sound like Malibu—the waves were curling tightly and gently that day, receding with a whoosh. Then, an eerie quiet—until the next little wave gathered, repeating the process—energy building and then releasing—with each caress of the shore. The meditative nature of that rhythm is one reason I liked living near the water.

It was the middle of summer, but barely a soul was on the beach. I'd heard how private the colony was—but four people on a stretch of sand from one end of the cove to the other, on day like this! We walked slowly, parallel to the waterline, our feet reaching the cool, damp sand and avoiding the dry, hot stuff closer in to the homes.

"This one is Larry Hagman's. And over there, Pam Anderson's place. She's in such incredible shape. Linda Ronstadt used to live practically next door, but I was little." Alex was proud to show me the environs, her second home for much of her life. We passed house after stunning house, her left arm entwined around mine. I remembered how uncomfortable she was so long ago when I mentioned her parents at the dinner with her cop boyfriend, and how she desperately wanted to change the subject. Now, they were a source of pride she was eager to share with me.

We continued toward a clearing between homes, essentially a vacant lot, and she led me to a corner that appeared quite secluded—unusual, given how the houses were built in such proximity to one another. We stopped between two pristine, parabolic sand dunes, where the sun glistened like starlight as we moved. Every few feet, there were little sun-dried, hourglass-shaped pieces of kelp that I always loved crunching underfoot. The view was nothing but palm trees, ivy, and ocean—alone with Alex on a summer day in Malibu. A light breeze was blowing the smog far inland, leaving us surrounded by a sweet, humid haze—warm and comforting.

Alex turned me around to face her, her arms around my waist, her eyes big and searching, locking their focus on my eyes. The breeze swept strands of Alex's fine hair across her face, and then away. She remained undistracted, her gaze direct and intent. I felt that she was taking in my soul and making it her own, finding an exact match.

Then, a truth.

"I love you, Ed."

Those four words poured out like cool syrup on French toast. It was so soon, but so effortless and sincere. She didn't hesitate a moment and led us to a place perfect for consummation. I kissed her softly, our bodies in sync. I felt her hand move down my chest toward my belt. She began to undo it and press her hand farther south as I became more and more aroused.

I grabbed her, and we both knelt on the sand, my left knee crunching a piece of dried kelp, which made us laugh out loud. I pulled off my shirt and laid it down beneath us as cover, her on the shirt and me on top. She unbuttoned her blouse and undid her bra. More perfect breasts I had never witnessed. I didn't hesitate, and she responded with tender moans, her breathing pacing faster, her chest rising and ebbing rapidly.

I reached for my wallet—I still had an emergency condom in there and pulled it out slowly to tease her. Her expression turned more eager, mine more relieved. I slipped it on as she pulled down her shorts slowly but deliberately. We made love under the sun and over the sand for a good 20 minutes—side by side, on my shirt, our faces and bodies warm and happy.

"I love you, too," I whispered. We embraced and rolled off of my shirt, getting sand stuck in places it would take an hour to rid. There were no two happier people on the planet.

WE SAID OUR GOODBYES TO HER parents, who saw us out to the car. Her father stood at the edge of the gate, waving and smiling as someone other than the guy who regularly appeared to standing Os, the wild man who could turn an audience to jelly. He was someone's dad. I had one of those. I soon could have another.

We arrived back at my place. While Alex showered, I called the bank to check on the wire transfer. Strangely, I felt my heart beating harder than I had expected as I dialed the numbers and listened. It was an automated message.

"*Your balance is . . . seven-million, four-hundred dollars and twenty-seven cents. For deposits and withdrawals, press 1,*" the disembodied voice at the other end was utterly unemotional, without any emphasis or inflection.

What I had hoped to hear was, **"YOU HAVE SEVEN-MILLION FUCKING DOLLARS. YOU'RE RICH, ED!!! JUST LOOK AT YOU. A SCHMUCK DJ WHO MADE GOOD!"** I hung up, walked to the fridge, and popped open a Stella. Somehow, given everything I'd been through, I felt the other shoe still had to drop. And with my little change of plan, it just might. Alex still was showering, and I rifled through her purse. She had a passport.

Her dad was on TV that night, doing the Leno show, and we gathered to watch together, before she left for her place—Alex seemed anticipatory, anxious. We poured a couple of glasses of red wine after a late dinner of Thai take out and curled up in front of the big screen, next to the window with the tiny view of the Pacific.

Leno kicked off his intro: "And now, appearing in Vegas next week, please welcome back, the legend, Daaaaaaaaaany Grossingerrrrrr!"

"Jeez, I hope he doesn't say anything stupid?" worried Alex.

"What could he say?"

"Oh, you don't know. He always gets nervous during these shows."

I reared my head back. It was incredible to me, a guy whose whole life was show business—*"Nervous?"*

"How could that be?" I asked.

"Where do you think he gets the energy from, coffee? He's a wreck."

I watched from this new perspective as Leno started in on him. "So, Danny, I hear you have a daughter, and she's found a guy?" Our eyes bolted from their sockets.

"You know I have a daughter, Jay."

"How would I know that?" Jay giggled.

"You got the invite, didn't you?"

"To what?"

"The wedding," Danny announced.

I fell out of my chair.

"Uh, no, I didn't get a wedding invitation."

"Well, that's because you never send a gift, Jay."

Alex was dumbfounded. "I'm gonna kill him. *Kill him*," she announced.

I began to snicker. She must have discussed me seriously with her parents, and Danny just riffed—found a little comedy wrinkle to bash over Jay's head—and ran with it.

"So, who's the son-in-law?" Jay prodded, like a tabloid reporter.

"He's a DJ from Boston."

Alex began screaming with laughter.

"What the hell was that? I'm from *Boston*?"

Alex barely could speak through her giggles. "He does this all the time. He's going to Boston for a show, right after he finishes with Leno. He just put you and his trip in the same thought."

I thought that was the strangest thing I'd ever heard. His mind worked quite differently from us mortals.

"So, Alex, when's the big event?"

"Ha ha. I don't know how that happened. It was a giant surprise to me, and that's that." She stood to leave and I grabbed her hand to pull her back down. She melted into me and we kissed for minutes.

"Tomorrow will be the beginning. Only the start," I promised. She rose with a dreamy look of pure happiness.

# CHAPTER 32

Alex shot me a look that could kill when I pulled up to the Tom Bradley International Terminal at LAX instead of one of the domestic terminals, but that changed for the better by the time we landed—10 hours later.

Paris never looked so good. Neither did Alex, for that matter, as we walked toward Pont Neuf, after a late dinner on the Right Bank. We were staying at the Intercontinental, and I thought I might be able to liberate the lump in my right pocket somewhere overlooking the Seine as the boats glided below us, their klieg lights blasting directly on apartment windows, the dwellers drawing their blackout drapes to ward themselves of the oppressive beams from the boats. I thought of a quick line. *"They were In-Seine Dwellers."* Ugh, I'd better not repeat that, unless I want groans.

I chuckled as we traversed, mostly to rid myself of nerves. I led Alex to a semi-circular cove that jutted out from the bridge and then farther over the river, like a perch. Standing at the edge, we had a 180-degree view of the Seine as if balanced on a floating concrete precipice. There was a small bench, where we could look out upon the water and see the reflection of the city around us. It was stunning, romantic, perfect.

I dug into my pocket to find the square container, got down on one knee, and professed my love for Alex.

"I've waited a long, long time for this," I said as I exhaled a nervous breath, my heart going crazy. "Alex, will you marry me?"

Before I could open the box to show her the three-carat I figured she couldn't turn down, she exclaimed, "Yes. Oh, yes." When she opened the box and found the solitary princess-cut stone in the platinum ring, her eyes filled with tears. I thought I must have outdone myself. Somewhere above, Sartre and Voltaire finally were shaking hands.

To perform this ritual above a river wasn't without design. A river may have brought me to wherever I had been, but were it not for the choices I made along the way, I might have drowned in it. Our lives course like water, but there are shorelines, coves, shallows, currents, jagged rocks, all of it more significant than the stream itself. And now, I had a gorgeous shipmate to help me navigate the churns and the shoals. I would look back as grateful for my dreams as for the choices I had made.

We strolled back to the hotel, arm-in-arm, got undressed, and didn't let go of each other. Ever.

# FIN

# ACKNOWLEDGEMENTS

THERE'S NO WAY THIS BOOK WOULD have happened without the patience, wit, and counsel of my wife, Mindy. My kids, Ethan and Harrison are a constant inspiration to me, and continue to surprise me in the most wonderful ways. My parents, Gerre and Mort, were there for draft after draft, my mother being an author, and my dad being hilarious. I miss him everyday. My little brother and sister, Scott and Margeaux, and their kids, always there, always supportive. Thank you.

My in-laws, Barbara and Don Rickles, were surprised by my obsession with getting this book done, all while running a full-time business and raising my kids. I was in a friendly competition with Don to get mine done before his, but I had no chance. I thank them for the support, and I miss him everyday, as well.

Among the colleagues and friends to whom I'm indebted for my media career: Manny Pacheco, Pete Demetriou, Rich Watson, Michael Anglado, Al Anthony, Benny Martinez, Scott Lockwood, George Siegel, Pierre Goneau, Hal Jackson, Jan Marie, Tim Kelly, Gerry DeFrancesco, Wally Clark, Gwen Roberts, Big Ron O'Brien, Mike Schaefer, Bruce Vidal, "Brother" Bill McKinney, Paul Freeman,

Ev Kelly, Larry Morgan, Chuck Street, Dave Ervin, Vanessa Thomas, Frankie Ross, Erica Farber, Tom Rounds, Ken Rose, Beth Bacall, Gary Bryan, Greg Mack, Dain and Sharon Blair, Paige Nienaber, Steve Cochran, Joel Denver, Roger Schnur, Kraig Kitchin, Brad Sanders, Steve Lehman, Louise and Amy Palanker, Tanya and Phil Hart, Joe Cipriano, and literally dozens of others along the way, a huge thank you. The inspirational talents of the Real Don Steele, Humble Harve, Harry Nelson, Bill Lee, Charlie Fox, John Landecker, Larry Lujack, Yvonne Daniels, Charlie Tuna, George Carlin, Johnny Carson, Hunter S. Thompson, Casey Kasem, Rick Dees, Bob Newhart, Dan Ingram, Dave "Your Duke" Sholin, Raechel Donahue, Liz Fulton, Bobby Ocean, Howard Stern, Gary Owens, and countless others reside in me forever. Thank you for what you do, and did.

And a thank you to my original agents at Linn Prentis for believing in this story, and Melissa and Larry Coffman for helping get this novel done, and done right.

Ed Mann was born in New York, just as the Cold War was raging at full tilt. He spent most of his elementary school years mapping out the local fallout shelters on Long Island and hiding under his desk. After moving to Northern California at age 10, Ed discovered his lifelong passion, radio, and in the mid-'70s, ventured south to Los Angeles to attend UCLA, where he began his career on the air.

Along with the 19 years Ed spent hosting radio programs in Southern California at KIIS-FM, KBIG and others, he co-founded Premiere Radio Networks, the largest radio syndication company in the country, and currently runs MannGroup Radio, a boutique syndicator of radio programs and services, as well as a podcast company, Mann Web Podcasting. Ed also works as a jazz musician and composer, and heads his own band, the Mann Sextet, which appears all over the Los Angeles area.

His love of writing came from devouring *Time Magazine* every week and early jobs editing the *Daily Bruin* while at UCLA. Ed's written multiple columns for radio trade outlets like *Radio Ink* and *All Access*, and he keeps his headphones warm and ready should a radio station be foolish enough to call him for an airshift.